To The Sangre De Cristo
(Buckskin Chronicles 9)

B. N. Rundell

To The Sangre de Cristo (Buckskin Chronicles 9)

B. N. Rundell

WOLFPACK
PUBLISHING
— EST 2013 —

Wolfpack Publishing
6032 Wheat Penny Avenue
Las Vegas, NV 89122

Copyright © 2017 by B.N. Rundell

Print Edition ISBN 978-1-64119-072-5

Dedication

I can never say enough about the support and encouragement that I've received from my best friend and life-long partner, my wife. She has been by my side through the thick and the thin, always loving and encouraging and faithful. Yet, she would be the first to admit, that it's the many readers that have made this journey as rewarding as it has become. Without so many of you that faithfully buy and read these books, all efforts would be fruitless and wasted. So, it is with great appreciation that we, my wife and I, dedicate this work to you, the readers of this and other books. Our labor of love coupled with your faithful following and reading make a wonderful combination. Thank you, one and all.

Chapter One

Companion

Something stirred in the grey darkness of early morning and Tyrell's eyes opened slowly. Moving nothing but his eyes, he scanned his campsite in the dim light from the coals of the campfire. His horse and mule's heads were raised, ears forward, but they showed no signs of alarm, just curiosity. He listened. Nothing moved, his horse stomped a foot, the mule snorted, but these were common sounds of awakening animals and revealed nothing. But something had stirred his subconscious and brought him from his slumber. He slowly gripped the butt of his Remington pistol and waited.

"Are you gonna sleep all day or are you gonna fix us some coffee?" came a gravelly voice from beyond the small pile of smoldering coals.

Immediately recognizing the voice, Tyrell rolled from his blankets and looked at the dusky face of his childhood friend, Grey Wolf.

"I thought you were headed for the Spring Bear dance with the Yamparika, what're you doin' here?" asked the drowsy Tyrell as he pulled on his high-topped moccasins. The

Bear dance was a long-standing custom of the Ute people that welcomed in the Spring season. Families traveled considerable distances to gather with the rest of the band for this first social gathering of the year. Young couples danced together and often formed bonds that would later lead to marriages, but all the families paid tribute to the Great Spirit by way of the Bear Dance and offered their prayers for the coming year.

"I was going to the dance, but I was warned that Little Squirrel had set her mind on me and was determined to get me to join her family's lodge. So, I thought it would be safer to travel with you."

"Little Squirrel? Ain't she the one that was chasin' after you all last fall?"

"Yup, she's the one."

"Well, she shore ain't no *little* squirrel anymore. But you shouldn't have any trouble gettin' away from her," laughed Tyrell.

"Yeah, but if she ever caught me and sat on me, I'd never be runnin' no more, that's for sure."

Although Grey Wolf was a good-sized young man standing just under six feet tall with broad shoulders and a solid build, Little Squirrel was almost as tall and would out-weigh him by at least twenty pounds.

"The coffee's in the pack yonder, you fetch it an' I'll get us some water for the coffee. Grab the bacon and the pan while you're diggin' in the pack," instructed Tyrell as he reached for the coffee pot beside the coals. He started out of the trees toward the spring-fed creek that was the headwaters of the North Platte River. His campsite was at the edge of a cluster of ponderosa and the thick willows obscured the spring from view. As he pushed his way through the willows, he thought of his long-time friend and smiled at the thought of Grey Wolf joining him on this journey South.

Driven by grief over the loss of his wife and child that both died during childbirth, he wasn't certain where this

2

journey would take him. All he really knew was he couldn't bear the idea of remaining at the Medicine Bow ranch of his parents and where everything would remind him of his Elizabeth. Their entire lives had been spent together growing up on the ranch established by his family and their close-knit circle of friends. Friends like Reuben, the big black stevedore from St. Louis and his wife, Spotted Owl, the parents of Grey Wolf. And Chance Threet and his wife Marylyn, the parents of Elizabeth, that also helped in the building of the earliest ranch in the Medicine Bow mountains of what would later become Wyoming territory. And there were others, but it wasn't just the friends and family, it was everything that held a memory of growing together and lessons learned and the many secret rendezvous. Names carved into the thin bark of Aspen trees, days spent building their home, and nights in each other's arms.

"Hey! You get lost? Hurry up with that water, I'm needin' some coffee!" came the plea from the fire. Grey Wolf had stirred the coals to life and added more wood to start the bacon for their breakfast. He found some biscuits and they were warming on a flat stone beside the fire when Tyrell came into the light with a broad white toothed grin. His dark red wavy hair was tousled and hung across his freckled forehead. The two young men were similar in size and their youthfulness was shown only by their unwrinkled facial features. Grey Wolf resembled his mother, Spotted Owl, a war leader and warrior for the Ute people, but his coloring and build mimicked that of his father. Reuben was a massive man whose stature was of smoothly chiseled coal, rippling muscles that told of his power but with kind eyes that told of his gentle spirit. Grey Wolf had yet to reach his full growth but his leanness gave him speed and agility that served him well in the many contests held among the young warriors of the Ute village that he visited often. Living between the cultures of the Ute, the whites, and the blend of cultures adopted by his father, Grey Wolf had favored that of the Ute and spent much of his life

3

among the people of his mother. But the friendship he had with Tyrell and Talon Thompsett was a bond that was as strong as family and they considered one another as brothers.

Tyrell and Talon Thompsett were twins and the only children of Caleb and Clancy Mae Thompsett, the founders of the Medicine Bow ranch. Caleb and Clancy had been raised by Jeremiah Thompsett and Laughing Waters that lived with Waters people, the Northern Arapaho of the Wind River mountains. With two generations of family that lived among and near the native people of the mountains. Tyrell and Talon had received a wilderness schooling that encompassed the teaching of the Arapaho, the Ute, that of the mountain man and the stevedore of the docks of St. Louis, and more. Their mountain education was the equivalent of a graduate school of survival, yet their youthfulness gave them the eagerness to experience life without the reserve given to maturity. Talon left home a year before and now lived with his wife and baby in the small town of LaPorte on the Eastern slope of the Rockies. This was the first time Tyrell would be without either his twin or his bride and he was glad for the company of Grey Wolf.

He sat the coffee pot as close to the fire as the flat rock allowed and sat back on the nearby grey log as he watched Grey Wolf fork the bacon over. The popping of the bacon grease would occasionally cause the fire to flare up, but the young man would pull the pan back from the burning logs and move the bacon around ensuring that the fat of the bacon was well cooked. He motioned to the warming biscuits and with a nod of his head gave Tyrell the go-ahead. Ty picked up a biscuit, dredged it through the bacon grease and plucked a couple pieces of bacon and sat back to enjoy the meal. Grey Wolf did the same and perched himself on a large boulder across the fire from his friend.

"So, where we goin'?" he inquired.

"Not sure, South I guess. Talon mentioned that General Carson was goin' to be needin' scouts down to Fort

4

Garland and that he'd said I knew a little bit 'bout the Ute people and the General said he could use me. Course, that was before . . ."

"So, you think you know a little about us Ute people, huh?"

Tyrell grinned at his friend and laughed as he responded, "*Us* Ute people? Listen to you, to hear you tell it you were a full-blooded Ute when you ain't but half!"

"Well, that makes me a whole lot more Ute than you are!"

"I never claimed to be Ute, just to know a little about you heathen redskins, or in your case . . . just what color are you anyway?"

Both men laughed at this often-recurring conversation they shared since childhood but Grey Wolf replied as he pushed out his chest, "My momma says I am like the Buffalo of the plains, dark and magnificent!"

"Well come on then, you magnificent buffalo, let's get packed up and get ta' movin'. We got a long way to go, and we ain't gettin' anywhere sittin' here."

Throwing out the dregs of the coffee, they were quickly packed up and hung the panniers on the pack saddle that sat on the big boned and roman nosed bay mule. The sturdy animal normally had a docile spirit and stood waiting for the men to mount. Tyrell swung aboard his strawberry roan gelding that was the four-year-old offspring of his father's Nez Perce Appaloosa and a roan mountain bred mustang mare. Standing fifteen and a half hands, the broad chested big rump well-muscled gelding had soft eyes and a willing spirit.

Grey Wolf mount was a long-legged black stallion with long flowing mane that Tyrell often razzed Grey Wolf about as a brush tanglin' broom-tail. Yet it was anything but, as this stud was the result of careful breeding by Grey Wolf father Reuben, and grandfather, Walkara, the leader of the Ute people. The stallion had proven himself as an exceptional mountain horse that had speed that would rival the fleet antelope and the staying ability of a mustang. While Tyrell called his mount, Roan, Grey Wolf had named his Spirit of the Night.

Chapter Two

Traveling

Tyrell led off with his pack mule following. The dusty game trail wove in and out of the tree line and showed no sign of recent use. The crisp spring air sought access to the collarless tunics of the travelers causing hunched up shoulders that tried to shed the cool breeze. Ty wore a set of buckskins made by his mom and decorated by his wife with blue diamond patterned beadwork nestled among broad bands of porcupine quills. The two bands of decorations draped over his shoulders down to the fringed hem of the tunic. His floppy felt hat gave shade to his eyes from the rising sun off his left shoulder. High topped moccasins with a matching pattern of blue and white beads across the toe were tucked under the buckskin trousers. His beaded belt held a holstered Remington New Model Army pistol with two spare loaded cylinders and a metal blade tomahawk. A possibles bag hung under his right arm and carried extra paper cartridges and caps for his pistol and a handful of cartridges for the Henry now carried in the scabbard beneath his right leg and saddle fender. His bowie knife hung suspended beneath his tunic between his shoulder blades. The twins had identical preferences in weapons with the only difference being Talon's carrying an additional Spencer repeater.

Grey Wolf's attire, though similar to Tyrell's, showed the unique appearance of the Ute. His mother, Spotted Owl, prided herself in her craftsmanship in making the young man's fringed leggings and beaded breechcloth. A thin line of quill and beads ran along the side seam and accented the twisted and lengthy fringe. The tunic had a pattern of blue, red and yellow beadwork accented by quills and elk's teeth that followed the sleeve seam from his wrist over the chest and back and down the opposite seam to his opposing wrist. The bottom of the tunic was an irregular shape with long twisted fringe dangling to mid-thigh that matched the long fringe across the back and chest yoke and sleeves of the tunic. Grey Wolf wore his wavy black hair in braids that were decorated with strips of ochre died leather and two feathers. Armed with a Walker Colt tucked into his beaded belt opposite his tomahawk and another in a saddle holster, a Spencer repeater in the scabbard under his right leg and a sheathed bowie at the small of his back, he presented the picture of a war-like Ute warrior. Both men possessed alder wood bows made by Spotted Owl and secured with their quivers of arrows atop the packs carried by the mule.

The morning sun warmed the travelers as they basked in the beauty of their surroundings. The scattered juniper pointed to the taller ponderosa with their clusters of long needles and the stacked branches of the spruce while the aspen were struggling to give birth to the spring's bouquet of bright green leaves. The valley to their left fell away from the low rising foothills and cradled random clusters of buck brush and scattered sage and all around them the many grasses were showing off their new suits of green. The canopy of blue was unmarked with clouds and the clear spring day gave a sense of wonder to the travelers. The frame for the vista was the far-off snow-capped peaks of the Front range to their left and the quickly rising white tops of the granite peaks of the Gore

8

Range to their right. The fresh scent of pine filtered the mountain air and encouraged them to take in the panorama of God's wondrous creation.

There was no hurry to their travel and the men enjoyed the beautiful day and the magnificent scenery. Anyone that has lived in the mountains always took advantage of any opportunity to appreciate their surroundings. The freedom offered by unhindered views that stretched for miles upon miles in almost every direction gave meaning to daily life and gratefulness for the gift of each new day. But every scene reminded Tyrell of times spent with his Elizabeth for every day they spent together in the mountains afforded the lovers new vistas to enjoy and time to appreciate the beauty of their surroundings and their time together. When his eyes would scan the valley floor for game he would be reminded of the many times they hunted together and how often her keen eyes would spot the animals before he did. A sunrise would touch his spirit as he turned to tell his wife to share the beauty and she was no longer there. Grey Wolf watched his friend knowing the oft-lifted shoulders told of a memory that brought a shrug and a deep breath of grief.

While Tyrell meandered in his mood of melancholy, Grey Wolf kept vigilant for both danger and opportunity for game. They knew the Cheyenne and Arapaho claimed the flat-lands to the East but after the recent conflict many had moved to the North to ally with the Sioux against the encroaching tide of settlers. But there were still some renegade bands that sought retribution against anyone in their claimed territory and they would do well to remain watchful. The mountains to their West and the plains to the South were predominately Ute country, but there were no designated boundaries that prevented any raiding band of warriors from invading another's territory.

The trail led them into the black timber that covered a saddle and sheltered the headwaters of a small creek. They were South bound and following the game trail took them over

9

the saddle and opened above a wide fertile valley. Below them a small lake surrounded on three sides by aspen showed a massive bull moose knee deep in the cat-tails near the inlet. Showing no signs of alarm, he ducked his head into the water and came up with a mouth full of tasty greens taken from the shallow bottom. He was too big for them to take as they would be unable to pack that much meat on an already burdened pack mule. As they cleared the timber they saw a sizable herd of elk grazing in the new grass of the valley. Grey Wolf reined up beside Ty and the two men sat with arms on the pommels of their saddles watching the animals.

"Everything is too big for us to take, we need to find a nice tender doe or maybe an antelope," stated Grey Wolf.

"Ah, we'll find something soon enough. With all this game around, we won't go hungry," replied Tyrell as he stood in his stirrups and waved his arm at the vista before them.

"Well, right now, I'm hungry. How 'bout stoppin' for noon?"

"Sounds good to me, how 'bout over at the edge o' them aspen," agreed Ty as he motioned with his chin to the cluster of bare aspen at the edge of the pines.

As Grey Wolf stepped down from his mount, he motioned to Ty and said, "Look at that rock formation at the top of that hill yonder, don't that look like a big pair of rabbit ears?"

Ty looked in the direction indicated and laughed, "You must be hungrier than I thought if you're seein' animals where there ain't none. Next you'll be talkin' 'bout clouds that look like beef steak!" He reached into his saddle bags and pulled out a handful of jerky, handed some to Grey Wolf and said, "Maybe this'll take your mind offa' fresh meat for a bit."

They loosened the cinches and tethered their animals before finding a shady spot on a patch of grass to stretch out. With hands behind his head and legs crossed, Tyrell watched the camp robber jays build up their bravado to look for some food scraps near the temporary campsite of the men. He remembered how Elizabeth, or Beth as he called her, would coax the birds to eat out of her hand or if there were chipmunks nearby, she would toss food scraps to them and gradually get them to eat out of her hand. She had a gentle nature that was easily read by trusting animals and Ty loved her for it. A tear fought its way free and streamed down his cheek as he looked heavenward and thought of the emptiness he felt. *Will it ever get any easier?* he asked himself. They had been together almost every day since early childhood and they were part of each other's lives in such an integral way that every thought included the other. Without her by his side, his life was not only empty, it seemed void of purpose and reason. But he knew she would want him to go on without her, and it would take special effort each day, each moment, to find reason to live.

Grey Wolf nudged Ty with his elbow and whispered, "Lookee yonder, down there by that juniper. That's that tender doe I was thinkin' 'bout."

Ty leaned forward slowly and looked in the direction his partner had pointed and replied, "So, why don't you get your bow from the pack and fetch us some meat? We don't wanna go shootin' and scarin' all the other animals that're grazin' in peace, do we? Show me just what a good Ute you really are," chuckled Ty as he looked at Grey Wolf.

His friend rose slowly to his feet and walked to the grazing mule, slipped out his bow and quiver and started his stalk through the thick aspen. His chosen line of stalk led over a slight rise covered with oak brush and scattered sage. Moving in a low crouch, he quietly made his way behind a grove of pinion and juniper that shielded him from the grazing doe. Judging himself to be near enough for a shot, he slowly rose with his bow held at arm's length and began to draw back the notched arrow. But just before letting the arrow fly, the doe dropped her head and nosed at a tiny spotted fawn that had been obscured by the nearby sage. Grey Wolf let off on the draw and lowered the bow to watch the fawn nosing for his lunch at his mother's bag. He turned to work his way back to

11

camp, and had taken but a couple of steps when he spotted a long-eared jack rabbit sitting up on his big hind legs and watching the bushes nearby. Grey Wolf quickly lifted his bow and let fly the arrow to impale his lunch.

He retrieved his arrow and placed it on his shoulder with the rabbit hanging behind him as he walked back into the campsite and approached Tyrell with a broad grin on his face. Ty looked at him and said, "I don't see no fresh meat. What happened?"

Grey Wolf brought the rabbit over his shoulder and held it before his friend as he said, "This is our lunch. Any complaints and you have to do the cookin'."

"No complaints! Not a one. I'm sure you can make that rabbit taste just like venison!"

Chapter Three

Confrontation

With appetites satisfied, Ty and Grey Wolf were once again on the trail through the tall timber. Ty noticed that on this side of the saddle crossing, the streams were now running off to the South. On the other side of the crossing, most were running North or East, but without any significant change in the lay of the land, the small mountain creeks were feeding the larger streams that now ran away to the South. The valley below them opened up to a wide park that stretched to the East and South with the distant snow caps bordering the park that showed spring green up and standing water where deep snow had melted away. Even a casual glance showed moose, elk and deer enjoying the bounty of spring.

Ty sucked in a deep breath and savored the redolence of the mountain air. The afternoon sun fed the sprigs that would soon burst forth in blue lupine, clusters of columbine and fields of mouse ears, bear's breeches, and Indian paintbrush. It was a beautiful time of year and the men basked in the beauty. The disinterested horses and mule shuffled along the trail that still showed moisture from snowmelt and revealed deep tracks of earlier passersby.

Ty reined up, stood in his stirrups, and peering through the ponderosa and the standing dead grey snags, surveyed the area below the trail. Shoulder ridges dotted with juniper, cedar, and pinion dropped away to a wide gulley that sheltered a wisp of smoke rising above the ridge. He looked back at Grey Wolf to see his friend nodding recognition of the smoke. Grey Wolf kneed his horse to pull alongside Ty and Ty spoke softly, "Hang back a mite, I'm thinkin' this might be either prospectors or trappers, but I'll move on out and you hang back in the timber 'case there's somebody waitin' up 'head." Grey Wolf nodded and held his mount back as Ty dug heels in his horse's ribs. The big roan moved ahead on the trail with head up and watching the path before him. After less than twenty yards the roan hesitated in his step, head up and ears forward, he heard the sound of metal on rock and paused. Ty listened and recognized the sounds of a prospector at work, but the sounds suddenly stopped with only the giggle of a mountain stream and the breeze through the trees to be heard. The trees shielded the streambed from view and pausing only a short moment, Ty gigged his horse ahead. The clatter of hoof on the rocky trail gave ample warning to whoever waited, but Ty continued.

As the trees gave way to the cascading stream, a voice came from across the water, "Hold it right there!" Ty spotted the source as an unkempt and bearded man with a ruddy complexion that did little to hide the angry stare that came from under the brim of a holey felt hat. Galluses fought their way around a big beer belly that had popped the buttons on a dirty linsey Woolsey shirt. Meaty hands held an imposing Springfield army issue rifle with a big bore staring at Tyrell. Ty dropped the reins across the roan's neck and lifted both hands in the air with a "Hold on there. Don't mean no harm, just passin' through's all."

"This here's muh claim, an' you ain't got no right bein' here!" bellowed the burly prospector as he waved his rifle intimidatingly.

14

"Look mister, I been on this same trail for several days now, an' I ain't interested in any claim of yours. Matter of fact, it looks too much like work to me!" stated Tyrell as he looked over the diggings of the man. A small rocker box sat at stream's edge and an overturned gold pan lay beside it. Evidence of digging in the far bank was revealed with the handle of a shovel protruding from the rocky soil.

"Git down off'n that horse!" demanded the prospector.

Ty dropped his hands and rested his forearms on the saddle horn keeping his hands visible as he replied, "Now just hold on a minute, there's no reason for me to get off my horse. If you'll just step aside, I'll cross on over this little stream and pass you right on by."

The big man hesitated, shifted his step to more secure footing and growled, "You either step off'n that horse or I'll shoot you off!"

Ty looked at the man, waited just a moment without moving and then kicked his right foot free of the stirrup and made as if he would swing his leg over the horse's rump. The metal click of a hammer cocking came from the trees behind the prospector and caused the man's eyes to widen and he started to turn but thought better of it when the voice of Grey Wolf said, "Don't do that! This here Colt will put a hole through you big 'nuff for a squirrel to run through. Now you very carefully lay that rifle on the ground and step back away from it real slow like."

The big prospector bent at the knees and with one hand raised above his head, he leaned to the side and sat the rifle gently on the ground beside his foot. He stepped back toward the sound of the voice and was surprised to hear the voice coming from farther up the stream to his left. Grey Wolf said, "Now lift both hands over your head and walk up to that big ponderosa yonder." The man did as he was told and approached the big tree, having to duck his head below the lowest branch, and neared the trunk. Grey Wolf instructed, "Now, hug that there trunk like it was your momma."

15

"Ain't got no momma," growled the prospector as he looked for the source of the voice. Grey Wolf continued to move among the trees and his voice now came from behind the man as he said, "Then hug it like the momma you wished you had!"

The big man complied and had to turn his face to the side as the wrinkled bark of the tree scratched at his whiskered mug. He no sooner had his hands around the tree, which was too big for even his big arms to encompass, and Grey Wolf slipped a rawhide loop over one wrist and did a figure eight wrap to include the other wrist. With several wraps around both wrists and between the two, he tied off the rawhide and stepped into the clearing to see Tyrell still sitting with forearms resting on his saddle horn. Grey Wolf grinned at him and said, "That's the first time I ever hog-tied a grizzly bear to a tree!"

"He do resemble a grizz, don't he?" replied Tyrell as he egged his mount forward to wade through the shallow stream that chuckled across the rocky bottom. No more than eight feet across and six inches deep, the cold clear water beckoned to the roan that dropped his head for a quick drink of the refreshing mountain dew. The mule pushed his way into the water and with his dark snout in the water, he slurped his share of invigorating snowmelt. Grey Wolf had disappeared into the trees to retrieve his big black and quickly caught up with his friend.

"Ya think he'll have too much trouble gittin' himself free?" asked Ty over his shoulder.

"Nah, he can prob'ly just rub through them binds with the rough bark o' that tree. Course, he's big 'nuff to just pull that tree up by the roots and throw it away, providin' he can get shuck of that pine sap. Long's he don't come after us, I really don't care which way he does it."

Ty chuckled at his friend's caricature of the prospector and continued on the trail. He thought about the influx of prospectors into these mountains and remembered Talon telling him about the numbers of gold-seekers that had invaded

16

the mountains around Pike's Peak ever since '59. With most of the claims petering out around Cherry Creek and nearby areas, the disappointed prospectors had fanned out across the mountains looking for the next big strike. Gold had that effect on men. They forgot their family responsibilities and left good sense behind and went wherever and whenever the siren song of gold beckoned. Most would eventually come to their senses and return to their homes, but many would die in the wilderness as paupers holding nothing but gold-lined dreams. Ty shook his head as his thoughts turned to the memories of his wife and knew that the dreams of riches would never have forced him away from her loving arms. Yet now, grief had driven him from his home and set his feet on the wanderlust path of forgetfulness.

He continued to look through the trees to the park beyond and another tendril of smoke caught his attention. He reined up and scanned the area. It was a ramshackle shack thrown together by someone who cared little for comfort and only desired shelter. Probably another prospector or some dumb pilgrim with unbelievable dreams. He pointed out the cabin to Grey Wolf and said, "There's just too many of 'em. We ain't been on the trail for a full day and already seen two cabins, in what, less'n twenty miles! I remember my Pa tellin' 'bout ridin' in the mountains for more'n a month and never see another livin' soul. There's just too many of 'em." He shook his head in disgust and put heels to his horse and moved away into the trees. It was getting on to dusk and they would need a camp site and maybe enough light to get something for their supper. He thought of a nice tender deer steak sizzlin' over a campfire and licked his lips in anticipation of a filling meal.

To The Sangre de Cristo

Chapter Four

Confederates

The collection of confederates seated at the table in the corner of the Santiago Saloon on Brownsville's main street was not unusual. In the months since the last battle of the Civil War at the Palmito ranch just outside of town, the war had ended and the confederate companies under General James Slaughter and Colonel John "Rip" Ford had been disbanded, many men, with no home to go to, still lingered around Brownville. During the war, Brownsville had been a hub of smuggling of Confederate goods to and from Europe through Mexico to the Mexican port of Bagdad and unknown to most, the depot on Brazos Santiago still held a considerable stash of goods, which were the subject of conversation at the corner table.

The center of attention was Terrel Careington formerly of Mississippi and a Quartermaster under "Rip" Ford in charge of the goods held at Brazos Santiago. Careington, together with Donaphan Donovan, "Dodo", had deserted the 1st Colorado Infantry under Colonel John Chivington after the battle of Glorieta Pass and joined up with the 7th Texas Mounted Rifles under Major Powhatan Jordan on their return to Texas.

Careington rose in ranks until he became the Quartermaster that supplied all the confederate forces throughout Texas.

Around the table were Dodo Donovan, Jasper Wolfton, Jalen Ramsey, and Bull Dominguez. Dodo, Wolfton, "Wolf", and Ramsey, "Mouse", were recently mustered out of the confederacy, but Bull Dominguez was a local with loyalties only to himself.

Careington began, "Fellas, you all know me and you know I'm always lookin' for opportunities to make money. Now, I've got me an idea how all of us can take advantage of all the confusion that's been goin' on since that dust-up out at the Palmito."

"Dust-up he says," blustered Wolf, "Why we done cut them Yankees to pieces. I heerd tell that outta three hunert o' them bluebellies, we done in o'er a hunnert! Best fightin' in the whole consarned war!"

"That's the point, the war's over and if'n you ain't got sumpin' lined up, we gotta make some money somehow. That durned scrip we got fer wages weren't nuthin' and what else we got's plum gone," grumbled Mouse.

"Will you shut up an' listen? That's what I'm talkin' 'bout. Now here's my plan. You see, I've got me a little money, ain't much now, but 'nuff to get us started. I'm plannin' on startin' a freightin' business," he declared as he straightened up from the table and tucked his thumbs under his galluses and sported a broad grin.

The men looked at him askance, waiting for an explanation of their part of this big idea. Careington looked around the circle of men and dropped his elbows back to the table. All leaned in to hear his explanation, "Ya see, I can put in the office with a sign in that ol' storefront yonder an' that'll make it look all legal an' proper. But I ain't got 'nuff for the rest an' that's where you all come in. Now, Bull, you take Mouse and Wolf and you three find us three or four teams of four mules or horses. I'll give you what money I have left, but you need to stretch it somehow, use your imagination, but we need those

20

teams by three days from now." Bull looked to the other two men and nodded his head in understanding, then asked, "What 'bout you two, whatchu gonna be doin'?"

"Me'n Dodo here, we're gonna be down in the Depot gettin' the freighters ready. We'll be paintin' the names on 'em an' such."

"You already bought some freighters?" asked Mouse.

"No, they're left over from the war. They're in the warehouse an' don't nobody know 'bout 'em. We'll paint 'em up with the name of the comp'ny an' ain't nobody gonna know the difference. We got all the harness we need an' oncet you get the teams, we can load up and haul out just like ever'body thinks a freight comp'ny should."

"An' what're we gonna be haulin' an' where to?" asked Bull.

"Rifles! Lots of 'em, and other goods to use for trade. An' we'll be goin' North up to Colorado territory. There's lots o' Injuns that'll pay for guns with gold an' if that ain't good 'nuff, we can sell 'em to the prospectors for gold. Either way, there's money, an' lots of it, to be made. The other goods are in short supply what with the war an' all, an' if we can pull out with three or four wagons full, we can cash in," declared Careington with a broad smile as he looked at his crew.

The men looked from one to another and back at Careington and each one in turn said, "Count me in," and received a nod of agreement from their leader. He responded with, "Alright, then let's get a move on. We gotta get this done cuz I heard tell that ol' Gen'l Grant'll be sendin' some o' his troops down here ta' check ever' thing out an' I wanna be well gone from here 'fore they get here." The two men rose and followed Bull out of the saloon. Dodo turned to Careington and said, "If I'm figgerin' it right, there's more to this little hoorah than you're lettin' on, now what is it? We been together now fer a long time an' I can read you like the weather, so out with it."

21

Careington leaned forward and lowering his voice he started his explanation, "Remember when we was up in Fort Garland an' that French Canadian ol' Beaubien, visited the fort? I found out that the land where the Fort sat was leased from him an' he was the holder of a Spanish Land Grant of over a million acres! Can you imagine, a million acres? It was called the Sangre De Cristo land grant. Well anyway, it was cuz o' him they even built that fort and there's a couple other big pieces of ranch land on further up that San Luis valley that are Spanish Land Grant's too. So, I'm thinkin' that if we get the Injuns armed with them rifles an' get 'em riled up, mebbe they'll run off them folks on the big ranches an' we can step in an' take over. You'n me, big ranchers!"

Dodo grinned and chuckled, "I knew you had sumpin' up your sleeve. Yeah, that'd be sumpin' alright. But the way I figger it is even if we make 'nuff off the guns 'n trade goods, it'll give us a good start. After all, there's been some gold discoveries up thar an if'n we cain't find it, we can shore'nuff steal it," declared the grinning Dodo showing a mouth full of brown teeth. Careington grinned back at his partner and said, "Now, don't you go sayin' nuthin' 'bout this to the rest o' them, y'hear?"

"Course not. I ain't interested in sharin' nuthin with them. Not even their share of the goods!" cackled the grinning man.

Dodo followed Careington from the saloon into the street. They mounted up and headed toward the point of Brazos Santiago that held the two large warehouses that were the subject of their foray. As they approached the solitary structures, Careington said, "See there, ain't no guards or nuthin' like I said. Since the musterin' out, don't nobody care 'bout nuthin' but gettin' home."

"So, how we gonna git in thar?" asked Dodo.

"We'll just get the keys from the quartermaster," grinned Careington.

"Where's he at?"

"Dummy! I'm the quartermaster!" declared Careington with disgust.

"Oh yeah, I forgot!"

The massive lock on the warehouse door was not the usual Confederate style lock, but a large cast iron Polhem lock that required a bronze key that Careington held in his hand. Inserting the key, a quick turn and the lock fell open. The rattle of the hasp and lock caused the men to look around to see if there was anyone nearby that could hear, but they stood alone before the door. Both men pushed back the large door and stepped into the cavernous structure. Careington waved his hand and said, "See what I mean?"

There were stacks of cotton bales, crates, barrels and boxes that lined both side walls. Standing in the middle were four large freight wagons emblazoned with the confederate states large CS emblems. Careington nudged Dodo on the shoulder and motioned for him to follow. They walked to the corner and entered a small office with a tattered desk and chair and shelves of papers and some canned goods. Along the near wall was a covered pail of paint with several different sized brushes. Careington moved to the desk, shuffled some papers and pulled one free from the stack and held it out to his partner. "This is what we need to paint over the Confederate emblem," as he pointed to the drawing. A simple design that read, *T. C. Freight* covered the entire page.

"What's this say?" asked Dodo, revealing his inability to read.

"T.C. Freight. That's the name of the company I started."

"What's the T.C. for?"

"Them's my initials. Terrel Careington."

"T.C. hum? O.K. Mr. T.C., we gonna get started on them wagons?"

"That's what we're here for, but I'll do the paintin' an' you start doin' some loadin'."

"What're we loadin'?"

"First, we'll load the rifles, an' then the rest o' the stuff on top. That way, no one'll see them rifles."

With a nod of his head, Dodo grabbed the handle of a nearby wheeled cart and started for the stack of rifle crates marked, "British Enfield".

Chapter Five

Visitors

Grey Wolf rolled from his blankets, squinted at the line of grey to the East and started to the nearby stream. He knelt on one knee, scooped a palmful of water and sipped at the refreshing ice-cold nectar of the mountains. Dropping on all fours, he splashed water on his face and neck and without rising said in the Ute language, "Are you of the Mouache or Caputa band, my brother?"

The visitors were surprised to hear their own language, but the beadwork on his buckskins told them of Grey Wolf connection to the Ute people. The three men were led by a tall warrior with broad shoulders and long hair that fell below his shoulders who now stepped forward and watched as Grey Wolf rose from the grass and wiped his hands on his leggings. The leader said, "We are of the Mouache, our leader is Katala and I am called War Eagle."

Grey Wolf brought his fist firmly against his chest and said, "I am Grey Wolf of the Yamparika. My mother is Spotted Owl, an honored war leader and the brother of Lame Deer who is now the leader of our band."

Tyrell had heard the conversation and slowly made his way to the small clearing and stayed back at the edge of the trees as he watched the visitors confab with Grey Wolf. Two of the visitors stood at the ready with arrows notched as they watched the two talking. Ty rested his hand on the Remington that hung on his hip, but made no move to intervene.

"Why are you here?" asked War Eagle.

"My brother goes to meet with a leader of his people but I am looking to find a brother of my mother, White Eagle, that took a woman of the Caputa and has joined her people. We were told his people have their village in the mountains of stone where the waters fall far."

One of the men behind War Eagle nodded his head in recognition of the description of the village. He spoke, "I have been to that place. The white eyes call it the mountains of San Juan and the falls are on Wolf Creek."

Grey Wolf grinned at the man's explanation and nodded his head, "I have heard that said of the place. I believe it is where he now lives with the Caputa band. I am told they have many women that are very beautiful and I go to look for a woman of my own."

The three visitors laughed at his confession and readily identified with his mission's purpose. They talked briefly among themselves and Grey Wolf said, "We have coffee and meat if you will join us." Without answer the men stepped across the small stream and joined Grey Wolf as he turned to go back to the camp. When Tyrell heard the invitation, he quickly back-stepped and returned to the camp to get things ready for their visitors. They found Tyrell cutting thin slices of venison from the haunch of the doe taken the evening before and hanging them on willow branches over the fire. The coffee was percolating and he motioned for Grey Wolf to fetch some cups for their visitors from the packs.

Conversation around the morning meal told of the warriors on a meat hunt for their village and a scout for the elk herd movements and looking for any early sign of buffalo.

26

Their village had just completed the Bear Dance and all were now focused on the spring hunts. When they discussed the Bear Dance, Grey Wolf asked if any of the men had made a connection with any of the women but all hung their heads in embarrassment and disappointment as they told of their lack of success. One of the warriors, Stone Calf, suggested they might also visit the Caputa to find a woman for each of them. All the men laughed at his suggestion but their laughter was typical of young men everywhere that search for a life partner.

Ty rose to bring in their animals to prepare for the day's journey and when he was out of earshot, the warrior Yellow Nose, asked, "Who is this white man that you travel with?"

Grey Wolf chuckled and answered, "He is my brother, we have been together since we were born. My father and his father were brothers as well."

"But you are dark and he is white!" stated War Eagle.

"Yes, my father was as dark as the small bear of the mountains, but he is of the whites. His father and mother were raised by the Arapaho."

"Aiiieeee, the Arapaho? But we are enemies with the Arapaho," stated Stone Calf.

"Yes, but my people have made peace with them because of this family."

The three warriors shook their head in wonder as they watched Tyrell lead their animals back into camp. He busied himself with rigging the pack saddle and loading the panniers and parfleche with their supplies. With that done, he started saddling his horse and hollered at Grey Wolf, "Hey partner, unless you're plannin' on ridin' bareback, you might wanna saddle up. We got a ways to go an' we don't wanna waste this fine weather."

Grey Wolf stood and the visitors stood as well when Grey Wolf froze in place peering between the branches of the surrounding pines. The others noticed his reaction and watched to see what had alarmed their new friend. Grey Wolf stepped nearer the edge of trees and slowly pushed aside a low branch for a better view of the valley below. War Eagle stood at his side and whispered, "That is a war party of Cheyenne. We saw their sign earlier and I believe they attacked some wagons at first light. They have some captive horses, but I don't see any captives."

It was a band of fifteen or more warriors that followed a trail through the scattered juniper and pinion at the near edge of the valley. At a distance of almost half a mile, Grey Wolf didn't think they were in danger of discovery. He looked back at the fire and saw the coals were scattered and what little smoke rose was filtered by the overhanging branches of the spruce and ponderosa. Tyrell had joined the observers and said quietly, "Maybe we better be ready to high-tail it soon's they get a bit farther up the valley." Grey Wolf nodded his agreement and looked at their visitors. War Eagle said, "We will avoid them. We are going into the black timber in search of sign of the elk herds. The Cheyenne are many and we are few and I believe they are going back to their villages in the North."

"That suits me," said Tyrell. "Since we are going South, I will not be disappointed if we don't see them again."

"War Eagle said he thought they attacked some wagons South of here. We might want to check on them and see what happened."

Ty looked at War Eagle and the man responded, "We came on the end of the fight. It was at first light and the Cheyenne were still gathering their goods. We saw no sign of life and we stayed in the trees high up on the slopes."

Ty nodded his head in understanding knowing that the Ute had done nothing more than what anyone could have done. In the wilderness, the first consideration must always be for your own safety as all too often there is no one to help and little enough help when there is someone. Grey Wolf was mounted and Ty stepped aboard his roan. With nods, they gigged their mounts away from the camp and back to the previously followed trail.

Smoke still rose from the two wagons that were now nothing more than small piles of debris. The metal rims of the wheels and the few metal parts of the wagons were the only identifiers of what once held the possessions and dreams of the owners. Ty and Grey Wolf cautiously approached and rode beside the smoldering piles of debris and quickly identified the remains of the several settlers. The bodies of one man, two, three, two women and a boy were scattered amongst the smoking planks and bodies of several mules still in harness. The stench of burning flesh came from what was left of the bodies of the woman and boy that hung from the sides of the second wagon. They moved away from the devastation and tied off their horses and mule to a cluster of sagebrush. As they walked back among the ruins, they spotted a shovel and pick and retrieved the prospecting tools to start digging graves.

Ty busied himself with the digging while Grey Wolf, with a bandana over his mouth and nose, drug the bodies to the gravesite. Two hours had passed before they were able to put the remains in the grave and cover it over. They were unable to find any identification and with little wood nearby, they chose to use the nearby rocks for markers for the large grave. Using a piece of charcoal, Grey Wolf marked a large flat stone with *3 men, 1 woman, 1 boy. Unknown. Killed by Cheyenne.* "That won't last long, ya know," stated Ty.

"I know, but not much else we can do."

Both men were suddenly startled when a small voice came from behind them and said, "I know who they are."

The men spun around grabbing for their pistols but were stopped by the sight of a young girl in a tattered dress standing near their horses.

"Who're you?" blurted Ty.

"I'm Abigail. Abigail Pierce. That was my family," she stated solemnly in a voice that was barely heard by the two men.

29

Ty and Grey Wolf straightened up and looked at the girl and Ty began to explain, "If we were to have some boards or something, we might be able to put up a marker. But you can see there's not much to use. 'Sides, if'n we marked it out here, some varmint's liable to dig 'em up just to see if they got anything of value. It's best if we just leave it like it is."

"Can't we say somethin'? You know, like a preacher does?"

"I reckon we can," said Ty as he walked to his horse and retrieved his Bible from his saddlebags. Returning to the grave, he was joined by Abigail and Grey Wolf.

He began, "*I Thessalonians 4:16 "For the Lord himself shall descend from heaven with a shout, with the voice of the archangel, and with the trump of God; and the dead in Christ shall rise first. Then we which are alive and remain shall be caught up together with them in the clouds, to meet the Lord in the air: and so shall we ever be with the Lord."* Then he began to pray, "O Lord, we bring to you these poor souls that met their end here in the middle of nowhere. We didn't know them, but You did and we now commit them to you. We know that if they had accepted your Son as their Savior, they're in heaven with you today. Now we ask that you give special grace to Abigail as she has to go on without her loved ones. Thank you, Lord. In Jesus name, Amen."

He turned to Abigail and said, "Now, what are we gonna do with you, young lady?"

She turned away from Tyrell and walked to a small cluster of sage, bent down and retrieved a small metal box that resembled a cigar box. Returning to Tyrell's side, she said, "All the money my folks had is in that box. My Pa was Homer Pierce and the other two men were his brothers, Daubney and James. My Ma's name was Comfort Pierce and my little brother's name was Zeke. We were headed to the mountains to prospect for gold when the Indians attacked us and Momma made me hide in the bushes yonder. After they left, I fetched that box outta the wagon before the fire got to it. Would you

30

take that money to take care of me?" she asked with wide eyes that showed all the expectancy and hopes of a child.

"Well, kiddo, we'll do our best to make sure you're taken care of properly. But hanging around the likes of us two men just ain't proper. But, we'll take you along with us until we can find a suitable place for a young woman such as yourself. Would that be alright with you?"

"Oh, yessir. I was just afraid you might leave me out here all by my lonesome and I was right scared of being by myself," she replied obviously quite relieved.

Ty looked at Grey Wolf and the dusky man shrugged his shoulders knowing there was nothing else they could do, they were now responsible for a 10-year-old girl and neither one knew anything about taking care of a child, much less a girl child.

To The Sangre de Cristo

Chapter Six

Town

Abigail's enthusiasm and excitement were contagious. The normally staid and stoic partners were smiling and laughing more than they had in a long time. Her curiosity and giggles brought a new-found joy to the duo that had spent their growing-up years always focused on the dangers around them. They were surprised when they realized their responsibility as the adults in the trio was to be circumspect and instructive but instead they were the students and Abigail the instructor in matters of enjoyment and frivolity. With their new perspective on how to enjoy each day to its fullest, Tyrell thought the sun was brighter, the sky bluer, and the beauty of God's creation more enjoyable. He also realized the burden of grief had been lightened and he was remembering how to laugh and smile.

After crossing the Colorado River, the trio had followed the Blue River up the valley, still hanging in the tree-line on the game trails, and were coming in sight of what appeared to be a town. The low-hanging cloud of chimney smoke told of the frosty mornings that were common in the mountains. On their journey of the last three days, there had been a couple of occasions when they had run on placer miners working claims on the Blue and were told of the town that nestled in the valley before them.

"What'd they say the name of this town was?" asked Ty over his shoulder.

"Breckenridge, I think, looks like a powerful lot o' folks there. Ya' think they're all prospectors?" replied Grey Wolf.

"Well, one thing I'm pretty certain of, there's a general store that will have the supplies we need and maybe a few other things too," said Ty thinking of Abigail and her need of clothes and a home.

"Uncle Ty, can't I stay with you and Uncle Wolf?" pleaded the girl, knowing what Ty had been considering.

"Now Abby, we've already explained, we're not gonna just put you off with anybody and until we find a suitable home for you, you'll be stayin' with us. But don't go thinkin' you can stay with us forever. Why, even your Uncle Wolf and I are gonna be goin' in different directions pretty soon."

"I know, but . . . but . . . I'm afraid of what might happen," whined the girl.

"There's nothin' for you to be fearful of Abby. We won't let anything bad happen to you, we promise. Don't we *Uncle Wolf?*" Ty said over his shoulder to his partner with an emphasis on the *Uncle Wolf.* Grey Wolf had been the one to encourage Abby in calling the two men Uncle and the thought of it elicited a chuckle from Ty. Abby was sitting atop the roan behind Ty and holding on to the saddle strings that secured his bedroll behind the cantle.

The usual black timber on the slopes of the rising mountain had been replaced by stumps that stood as mute evidence of the growing town. With the need for both lumber and firewood, the tree-line was retreating farther up the mountain. The trio leaned back in their saddles as the horses picked their way down the hillside toward the town. The roadway that led into the town had been carved by the many wagons carrying the prospectors to their claims with heavy loads of equipment and supplies, and now pointed the way to the cluster of buildings that marked the growing town of Breckenridge.

The sight of the three travelers was unusual for the people of the town. They were accustomed to seeing the typical gold-seeker attired in homespun, Lindsey Woolsey, canvas britches and usually packing prospecting gear. But two men in buckskins with a young girl caused wide eyes and uplifted eyebrows. Paying the passersby no heed, Ty led the way to the hitchrail in front of the largest building on the main street that held the bold sign of the Columbine Hotel and General Store. Another smaller sign that hung swinging and squeaking beneath the first told of Good Food. He gave Abby a hand down and swung his leg over and stepped to the ground beside her. Tying off the roan and the mule, he placed his hands on his hips and arched his back and let out a slow moan that told of the days in the saddle.

Several men walking along the boardwalk gave the visitors a curious glance but quickly realized they were not prospectors and passed on by. Ty pushed open the door and was surprised when a small bell over the door announced their presence but he grinned at the contraption and walked on into the store. There were well-stocked shelves along the back wall that framed the counter which now served as an arm rest for an apron attired woman sitting on a stool and brushing the hair from her face with her other hand. She smiled broadly at the newcomers and caught her breath when she spotted Abigail. With her hand to her mouth she said, "I declare, you have a child and a girl-child at that!"

Ty feigned surprise and looked around as if searching for something and said, "What? Where? Oh, you mean this little lady?" as he drew Abby to his side, "Why, she's no child, she's ever bit a lady, just little is all," declared the proud Uncle of the smiling little girl. "And we need some new clothes for her, can you help us out?"

"Well, I don't know, we don't have much call for little girl clothes," started the clerk and was interrupted by Ty, "lady, if you please."

She looked at Ty and realized he was not trying to be rude but just protective of the girl. "Uh, little lady, yessir. But let me have a look at you. And what might your name be?" inquired the clerk.

Ty said, "I'm sorry, where's my manners? This little lady is Abigail Pierce, and I am Tyrell Thompsett and," pointing to Grey Wolf, "that gentleman is Grey Wolf."

The clerk brought her hand to her mouth and with wide eyes looked at the buckskin attired man with black braids hanging at his shoulders and said, "Are you an Indian?"

"Yes m'am, I am a proud member of the Yamparika Ute nation and my people were here long before you people came and started ruining our land," as he stood with arms folded over his chest and an indignant expression on his face.

"Don't pay him no mind m'am, he's only half Indian and he's better known as Uncle Bear to the little lady here," responded Ty.

The clerk looked from Ty to Grey Wolf and then at the girl and stammered, "You have different names, isn't this gi . . . little lady your daughter?"

"First m'am, I'm accustomed that introductions include the names of all concerned," said Ty as he looked at the clerk with a questioning expression.

"Uh, oh, yes, my name is Marilu Pennington. My husband and I own this business."

"I see, well, pleased to meet you Mrs. Pennington. Now, let me help you understand . . ." While Grey Wolf walked with Abby among the counters and shelves of the store, surveying the many items, Ty told Mrs. Pennington the story of Abby and her family. With several exclamations of "Oh my" and "Oh dear" the very sympathetic woman nodded her head in understanding. When she said, "I understand," Ty responded with, "Do you really?" Mrs. Pennington began her own story about how she and her family traveled by wagon train to this area and about the tragic loss of her two children and her father to the dreadful cholera that struck many wagon trains.

"Now, as to your little lady. I just might have some things upstairs in my trunk that might fit her. You wait right here and I'll be back down in just a moment." Ty nodded his head in agreement and began to browse the merchandise for their needed supplies. While they waited, a man came through the door and looked at the men asking, "Where's my wife?" It was evident by his long apron and garters at his sleeves that this was the other half of the Pennington couple. Ty looked him over at a glance and saw a man with kindly eyes, a full head of curly dark hair, and a gentle manner. He looked from Ty to Grey Wolf, saw the girl and looked back at Ty. "I'm sorry, I didn't mean to be so abrupt, but I expected to find my wife at the counter," he extended his hand to Ty and continued, "I'm Joshua Pennington, may I help you with something?"

"I'm Tyrell Thompsett and this is my partner, Grey Wolf, and the little lady is Abigail Pierce," then looking back at the clerk he said, "and your wife just went upstairs for a moment and she said she'd be right back."

"Upstairs? That's unusual. What on earth for?"

"I think she was looking for some clothes for the little lady," said Ty as he motioned toward Abigail with his chin.

With the heels of her high-top lace up shoes clicking on the stairs, Marilu announced her return. With an armful of clothes, she walked past her husband and with a hand on Abby's shoulder, she steered the girl into the back room. Joshua watched wordlessly as the two disappeared beyond the door. He looked back at Tyrell and Grey Wolf to await an explanation. Ty just shrugged his shoulders and pulled a list of needed goods from his pocket and handed it to the storekeeper.

He looked at the list, up at Ty, and started assembling the goods requested. When the counter was overladen with the supplies, the door to the back room opened and Abby timidly walked out with Marilu following. Abby looked back at the woman and saw her give a motion with her hand to spin around for her admirers and Abby turned a full circle before her admiring audience. When Mr. Pennington saw the girl, he looked at his wife with a puzzled expression and she smiled back at him as she nodded her head. What Ty and Grey Wolf didn't understand was the clothes now modeled by Abby had come from a trunk of memories of the Pennington's lost daughter.

Looking at the pleased expressions on the faces of Tyrell and Grey Wolf, Mrs. Pennington smiled and said, "Mr. Thompsett, Mr. Grey Wolf," and motioning toward the side wall of the store continued, "right through those doors is our restaurant. We'd be pleased if you would join us for lunch."

"Well m'am, thank you kindly, but we've got to settle up for these supplies and get them packed before we can do that. If'n it'd be alright with you, we'll get that done and be pleased to meet you there."

"That would be fine," she replied and turning to her husband said, "and there will be no charge for the clothes, Joshua." Her husband nodded in understanding and busied himself with finalizing the bill for the goods.

As they carried their goods to the pack mule and began securing them, Ty looked at Grey Wolf and said, "I'm thinkin' that woman has designs on our Abigail."

"I noticed her payin' special attention to her. Maybe it's just the motherly instinct I've heard about. You thinkin' these two might be a good family for the girl?" asked Grey Wolf. Ty began to relate the story of the Pennington's losing their two children on the way West and that he thought the clothes had belonged to their daughter.

"They're certainly young enough to take care of her and they've got a good business goin' here. I think they'd be a right nice family for the girl and Abby seems to like the woman," surmised Ty.

"Ummm, maybe. But I shore have grown mighty fond of that girl."

"Yup, me too, but ain't no way we can take her with us, and with a post office right here, she can write to us and we can keep in touch with her. After all, we are her Uncles," declared Ty with a broad smile.

To The Sangre de Cristo

Chapter Seven

Parting

Saying good bye is never easy and even less so when a child is involved. The two men that had previously prided themselves on their strength and tenacity in all circumstances, now found themselves trying to dig out of the hole of sadness. The memories of the previous few days that held happiness and laughter were tempered with the difficulties of telling the little girl good bye, but all agreed her future held promise and possibilities with the Penningtons. Lingering hugs were shared and the men turned in their saddles to get a lasting image of their little sweetheart. She stood beside Marilu with her arm stretched high and waved at the departing men until they were out of sight in the tall timber. Both men daubed at the tears trailing down their cheeks but neither spoke as their mounts zigzagged up the steep mountainside to the crest of the pass between the towering granite peaks.

They had been told of the small settlement of Fairplay on the other side of the pass but were determined to pass it by. They were well supplied and had bought an additional pack mule, pack saddle and panniers in anticipation of the coming separation when the men would each need their own set of supplies. By the time the sun was cradled in the folds of the Western mountains, the two men were making camp in a cluster of juniper on the shoulder of the smaller mountain range. They had an exceptional view of a valley below that harbored the twisting snake of a river that now reflected the disappearing sunlight. Beyond the narrow river bottom rose a long barren flat that was bordered by the beginnings of black timber and scattered aspen groves. It looked to be a fertile valley and even from this distance, there appeared to be at least one herd of grazing elk.

Ty stood with one foot resting on a stone ledge of a larger pile of boulders and surveyed the vast panorama. He admired the distant peaks, still holding considerable snow on their barren tops, and the jagged timberline that told of the great height of the mountains. Grey Wolf stepped to the side of his friend and looked across the distant valley and said, "It looks like good land. Everything seems to be greenin' up and even on the mountains yonder it looks like the aspen are getting' their green on."

"See that line of mountains way down yonder, those that take off toward the Southeast? That's the Sangre De Cristo's. Where I'm headed is way past that last peak. Looks like it's gonna take a while to get there."

"You know what river that is down there?" questioned Grey Wolf motioning with his chin to the valley below.

"Near as I can figger, that's the Arkansas. We're not too far from the headwaters back up there a ways," as he motioned with his chin, "and it turns an' follows the Sangre's for a while."

"That means my route will take me straight on South with that range of mountains yonder," commented Grey Wolf.

"Yup, that's 'bout right. According to what I've been told, you'll follow that range till it peters out, an' then head Southwest toward the San Juan's. But from what I understand, where Fort Garland is, you'll be directly West from there. So, if you can't find you a woman with the Mouache, you can

42

always head on toward Ft. Garland and meet up. Course, I can't promise you no woman, but you could help me out scoutin' for Carson," suggested Ty.

"Well, 'nuff 'bout that. Let's get some vittles goin' cuz I'm powerful hungry."

Two prairie chickens were spitted on the fire and were soon dripping their juices into the low burning flames as the men savored their coffee in anticipation of the meal. Contrary to their usual habit, both men stared into the fire with glassy eyes remembering Abby and missing her constant chatter by the campfire. Ty let loose a heavy shoulder shrugging sigh and said, "Sure do miss that little girl."

Without moving Grey Wolf just answered, "Yup."

The trail dropped them onto the valley floor as the long shadows from the morning sun stretched across the green flats. It promised to be another fine day as the men sought a good crossing of the swift flowing river. The brown water told of the snow-melt runoff and the occasional bit of driftwood that floated past warned of strong currents. The two travelers followed the course of the river and with no hurry to cross, bided their time until they found a suitable location. The wide bend showed long stretches of sand on the inside of the bend and a falling away rocky bottom on their side. Ty led off and with mule in tow, and soon found himself in a strong current that alarmed his mount. He slipped from the saddle on the upstream side to allow his horse to swim without hindrance and with the long lead rope of the mule with one wrap around the horn, he held on to both lead rope and saddle strings. Pumping his legs and pushing for all he was worth, both horse and man soon found footing on the sandy bottom and struggled to shore. Grey Wolf waited on the other side for his friend to reach the shore and now followed. Mimicking his friend's movements, Grey Wolf soon joined Ty on the wide sandy beach and flopped down on the warm sand to gain his breath.

"Woooeee, for a minute there I was thinkin' I shoulda been a fish!" declared Ty.

"For a minute there I thought I was a fish!" answered Grey Wolf.

They chose to continue their journey alongside the river and held to the path just under the bank of the bluff that followed the river bottom. They knew they were in predominately Ute country but believed there would be ample cover near the river if circumstances necessitated. With the easier travel of the flats, they made good time and by the approach of dusk, they neared the obvious site of their separation. Making camp near the bank of a smaller stream that fed into the Arkansas, they tethered their horses and prepared camp for the evening meal. In need of fresh meat, the men separated for a foot hunt and armed with bows and their quiver of arrows, Ty went downstream and Grey Wolf upstream. The willows and cottonwood provided good cover for the hunters and Grey Wolf quickly bagged a thirsty young buck. Sounding off with the agreed upon signal of the call of a dove, Grey Wolf set about the work of dressing the deer.

Ty was soon at the side of his friend and the two men made easy work of the carcass. Back at the campsite, Ty put thin sliced steaks on willow branches suspended over the smoldering coals of the fire. The men busied themselves making willow drying racks for the smoking of the rest of the meat for their continuing journey. While Ty sliced the choice cuts into thin strips, Grey Wolf assembled the rack and began hanging the strips for smoking. With fresh cut and peeled Alder branches lying on the hot coals, the smoke rose to flavor and cure the meat. The men sat back and enjoyed the fresh broiled venison and the sliced and fried cattail root with their dark brewed coffee. They enjoyed the meal and the company as they shared memories of childhood adventures and dreams of their future. Although Ty had already enjoyed the company of a wife, Grey Wolf looked forward to having a mate to share his life and Ty was beginning to think it might be possible to love again.

To The Sangre de Cristo

Chapter Eight

Division

The two friends clasped forearms and looked to one another with memories etched on their faces. There had never been a time in their lives they were farther apart than the opposite ends of the ranch and although Tyrell was a twin to Talon, in the last couple of years with Talon gone, Ty and Grey Wolf had grown even closer. Most always working side by side they understood each other and could almost anticipate what the other would do before the deed was done. It was this closeness that motivated Grey Wolf to accompany his friend on this grief-driven flight from home. But both men knew it was time to step to different paths, Ty to find a renewed purpose to his life without his beloved wife, and Grey Wolf to find the one that would be his life-mate.

"Well, you know where to find me. I'm sure I'll be with Carson at Fort Garland for some time. You'll find the fort where the Spanish Peaks mark the break in the Sangre De Cristo's. They say there's a pass, also called Sangre De Cristo, that goes back over the mountains to the East to what used to be El Pueblo."

"And I'm not sure where I'll be. I figger it'll take a while to find the band that my Mother's brother is with, and then if they have, you know . . ."

"Yeah, I know. Just don't get too anxious about this business of finding a woman. My ma always told me the Lord's timing was not the same as mine and I'm thinkin' that applies to you too."

Grey Wolf dropped his head and chuckled, "That's easy for you, you've already had the company of a good woman, even if it was for too short a time."

"Yeah, well," started Ty but dropped his head and scuffed his moccasins in the dirt. "I better get started, still got a long way to go and you do to." He slapped Grey Wolf on the shoulder and turned to mount up. Grey Wolf handed Ty the lead rope for his pack mule and with a nod of his head, Ty reined his mount around and set his sights on the tall timber on the buffalo hump shaped mountain that marked the beginning of the Sangre De Cristo mountain range. Grey Wolf stood watching his friend leave and waited until he disappeared in the black timber before he swung aboard his tall black and leaning down for the lead rope of his mule, gigged his horse to the trail that followed the small creek through the cut of the hills in the South.

It appeared to be a well-traveled game trail and with the many 'feeder' trails, it soon revealed itself to be the major pathway used by every species of animals in the wilderness. Well up the mountainside, it followed the contours of the high shoulder that fed the many ravines and gullies with snow-melt. With no shortage of water because of the many spring fed streams that originated high up near timber-line, Ty moved easily along the trail. The streams chuckled down the hillsides and were flowing well from both the melting glaciers from the granite peaks, and the subterranean flows from the melting snow. But the trail had been carved by the hooves of migrating elk herds numbering in the hundreds that traveled these mountains for generations and served deer, bear, mountain lion, mountain goats, bighorn sheep, and now man and his domesticated animals.

Sometimes the trail hung tenaciously to the steep granite cliffs and clattered over slide rock, and sometimes the only obstacles were downed trees that fell under the weight of winter snow or succumbed to the high winds that boiled down the mountains or the thick scrub-oak brush that sought to choke the life from all other shrubbery. With few detours, Ty enjoyed the scenery of the valley well below the trail but was revealed from the many parks and meadows that held graze for the woodland creatures and unhindered views of the panorama. Ponderosa, Spruce, Lodgepole and Aspen found footing on the broad shoulders of the mountains and shared their space with kinnikinnick, elderberry, gooseberry, and chokecherry. The sunlit openings and meadows were home to columbine, lupine, bear's breeches, and more. Bushes, plants, flowers, trees in abundance and to Ty, often without names, lent color and character to the hillsides. But he never tired of the beauty and the solitude. With every pleasant sight, whether animal or plant or vista, his mind went to his departed wife thinking of how she always enjoyed and commented on even the common things that held beauty in her eyes. But now his reflections were pleasant ones and he treasured the memories, locking each one away in that special place in his spirit. If someone were to see his expressions that often tugged his lips into a grin or a smile, they would wonder just what was going on in his mind that gave such joy.

Even with the beautiful scenery and the variety of the terrain, Ty's attention had waned. The wide valley below showed off its many shades of green from the scraggly cottonwood that lined the banks of streams to the wide swaths of green Indian grass mixed with the buffalo grass that moved like waves of a lake as the lazy wind moved down the valley. But the weary Ty had succumbed to the hypnotic pleasantries of the trail. With dusk approaching he knew he should be looking for a campsite, but the easy rocking of the big roan's gait and the comfortable saddle, Ty became drowsy and his shoulders slumped and his eyes closed. A cracking of twigs and branches, the rattle of hooves on stone roused the slumbering Ty and he instantly awoke and looked for the source of disturbance. He gazed uphill from the trail and a pair of wide-eyed and scared cow elk were running down the hill towards the trail. Ty reined his horse to a stop and looked to see the cows, mouths open and tongues lolling out with slobbers flying over their shoulders, negotiating the thick aspen. Shoving their way through the smaller saplings with their shoulders, the tops of the trees swayed aside as the parting of the waves on a still lake. Apparently spotting Ty and his animals, the cows veered to a direct downhill path and it was then Ty saw the two frightened spotted calves chasing after their mothers.

Ty pulled back on the reins and the big roan back-stepped, bumped up against the pack mule and continued to push his way back on the trail to separate himself from the commotion coming through the trees. The cows, one pushing against the rear of the other, burst from the trees and vaulted the wider trail not more than five yards in front of Ty. The calves, now staggering with both fear and exhaustion, ignored the man and horse and trotted after their mothers. Then Ty saw the reason for their flight. With head shaking side to side and beady eyes peering from thick fur, a massive Grizzly was in close pursuit of what his red tongue hanging from his gaping mouth could already taste. His lumbering pace, front legs grabbing dirt, hind legs landing beside the front and bringing all his force into a huge mound of thick fur, then stretching out his front legs with massive paws marked by four-inch claws, he dug for another leap. He spotted the horse and mule and slid to a stop, stood on hind legs and let loose a roar that shook the nearby trees and frightened the roan.

Ty's hands grabbed for the horn and pommel as the roan reared and pawed at the clouds to scream his fear and anger to

50

the treetops. The mule jerked the lead-rope free and spun on his hind legs and with his braying echoing across the mountainside, fled back down the trail, bucking and kicking at everything. The bear shook his head side to side and roared at the long-legged roan with the man clinging to his back and the horse dropped to all fours, tucked his head between his front legs and kicked his back legs at the treetops. He tried repeatedly to swap ends and with all fours off the ground, twisted in the middle as he screamed at the frightening figure of fur. The bear dropped to all fours and watched the spectacle of these strange creatures that smelled like nothing he had ever known, then remembering the tasty tidbits of elk calves that he almost had, he trotted across the trail, ignoring the one-man rodeo.

Ty and the roan were almost a half-mile down the trail before the horse seemed to run out of steam and Ty pulled back on the reins with both hands and pulled the horse's head up as he walked and sucked air. His sides heaving, he finally stopped and lowered his head in exhaustion. Ty leaned down and patted the side of his neck and spoke to his horse to help calm both his and the horse's nerves. He reined the horse around and started back on the trail in search of the mule and his supplies. The roan stepped lightly with his head swinging side to side searching for any sign of the bear, but they passed the scene and continued on the trail after the mule. The trail was littered with odds and ends of the supplies, but Ty determined to find the mule and the packs before picking up the goods.

It was well over a mile that the mule traveled before coming to a stop at the edge of a small clearing where he lazily grazed as if nothing happened. Latching onto the lead rope, he pulled the head of the cantankerous mule around and started the task of retrieving the goods. It was just as the sun disappeared over the mountains behind him that Ty chose a clearing beside a stream to make his camp for the night. Too tired for anything more than coffee and jerky, he quickly found his blankets for the night and slept, with hopes of never seeing another Grizzly.

Chapter Nine

Prospectors

The No-Name Saloon in Fairplay stood as mute testimony to the priorities of hard-luck prospectors. With a false front of clapboard that held two windows and the ubiquitous swinging batwing doors, a large canvas tent provided the remainder of the saloon. The interior held a long bar that was nothing but planks on barrels, and several tables with an unmatched assortment of chairs. Even at mid-morning, the clink of glasses and the odor of liquor, smoke, and unwashed bodies told of the social stature of the many patrons. A scarred and dusty player piano sat silent against the side wall and was crowded by the nearby tables. The many conversations were mostly about prospecting, claims, and the many searches for the mother lode.

The largest table, a rough-hewn circular testimony to one man's belief in his carpentry skills, was surrounded by seven men. They were a scruffy looking crew with an assortment of beards and tousled hair, patchwork clothing and muddy boots, but each one bearing the look of disappointment and failure. Two half-empty bottles stood in the middle of the table and each man held a glass before him with different levels of the dark amber liquid that passed for whiskey. Marcus Spann spoke low enough that all the others were hunkered over their drinks giving the appearance of some dark conspiracy.

"Now, let me tell ya' what I heard them fellers talkin' 'bout o'er in Breckenridge. The one fella was goin' down the Sangre De Cristo's and meetin' up with General Carson at Fort Garland. He was gonna be doin' some scoutin' fer him. But th' other'n, I'm thinkin' he was a Nigra but he was dressed an' actin' like a Injun, he was goin' South into the San Juan's. He was talkin' 'bout how them Utes was friendly and had good lookin' wimmen. But here's what I'm thinkin', ain't none of us had much luck neither here nor up ta' Breckenridge. All the good claims done been took, an' I ain't lookin' to be doin' no work fer sumbuddy else. Now, that country down to the San Juan's was where them ol' Spaniards used to get their gold, so I'm thinkin' we oughta head down thataway and try our luck there." He sat back to let the others think about what he said and watched each one as they considered the proposition.

The men knew each other from several contacts in the gold fields. Several had filed claims that didn't prove out, others sought work from the successful claim-holders, and some had simply followed the crowds searching for a big score of any kind. In the West of the times, men kept their past to themselves and revealed little of their history. Some were running from the law, others from family responsibility, while still others were chasing dreams, but the unwritten law was not to ask too many questions about another.

Ira O'Callaghan, the big red-headed Irishman, elbowed his long-time partner, Efe Tuscanny, and nodded his head with a wide grin splitting his face. Alex Romero and Curtis Tuffin had also been partners and now looked at one another, nodded their heads in agreement and sat back with their arms folded across their chests. Gunther Schmidt was a blonde broad-shouldered solitary man, but he leaned back in his chair and looked around the table to see the other's response. He looked at Spann and nodded his head. Joseph Marlett, called Big Joe by most, rested his meaty hands on the edge of the table, reached for one of the bottles and chug-a-lugged directly from the bottle and brought it down with a bang on the boards that startled the rest of the men, then said, "By gum, I'm in! I'm tired of ever'body else gettin' the best claims an' then havin' to work fer them. I wanna work for myself! When do we leave?"

Spann looked around the table and saw the agreement of the others then started, "Let's all meet back at the livery round noon. Bring what supplies an' tools ya' got, then we can figger out what we're gonna need and pool our pokes and git supplied up. If we get it done, why, we can pull out later today or first thing in the mornin'!" declared Spann to the grins and nodding heads around the table. The men rose, knocking over several chairs and kicking them out of the way, clicked glasses together, downed their drinks and left to get their gear.

It was a scruffy bunch that assembled at the Livery. None were well equipped and the assemblage of men and gear resembled one another with broken and patched tools, gear, and the assortment of supplies. As Spann and Big Joe Marlett looked over and picked through the pile of equipment they looked at one another and shook their heads. They were the more experienced of the crew and had a better idea of what kind of gear would be needed, not just for the trip but for their purpose of prospecting and mining for gold. Spann began making a list and turned to the men and said, "Alright, we've got to pool our money to get the supplies and gear we're gonna be needin', so, ante up!" He pointed to the end of the buckboard to indicate where they were to put their money or gold for the proposed project.

There were ample complaints and plenty of grumbling but all knew the necessity of the supplies and each one added to the pot. Spann said, "Alright, I also need to know what kind of rifles and handguns each of you have and what ammunition you have or need. We need to be sure we're ready for any conflict we might run into, white or Injun."

"Injuns! I thought you said them Ute were friendly," grumbled Alex Romero with alarm written across his face.

"Well, they're s'posed to be, but ya kin never tell 'bout Injuns. Better safe than sorry, 'sides, we'll need to be huntin' fer meat, too."

With list in hand of needed supplies, gear, and ammunition, Spann suggested, "Now, me'n Big Joe will go to the store to get started, so how 'bout a couple you fellers harness up the team to the wagon an' get yore pack animals ready and come on up to the store and we can start loadin' up."

The storekeeper was pleased with the sizable order for supplies that filled the wagon and the panniers on two pack-mules and more besides. Little did the storekeeper know that the larger portion of the order that was put 'on account' would never be paid. He had been told by Spann that they had struck a big vein and needed the equipment for the mining operation. After eliciting a promise of a share, signed and delivered, the storekeeper stocked the men with all the needed equipment. It was mid-afternoon when the cavalcade of seven hopeful prospectors left Fairplay behind and turned their faces to the South to start their journey to the distant San Juan mountains and their search for the elusive gold.

Chapter Ten

Shelter

Ty slowly awakened to the sounds of the woods around him. A meadowlark warbled his song from a high branch of a ponderosa, and in the distance, could be heard an overly energetic woodpecker digging for grubs in a grey snag skeleton of a once majestic spruce. He put his hands behind his head and looked at the clear blue sky framed by the tops of the nearby pines that slowly moved in harmony with the morning breeze whispering with the cool air off the remaining snows of the broad-shouldered granite peaks behind him. He turned his head to the side and watched the horse and mule cropping the grass near the white water of the cascading stream. They were content with the lazy morning and showed no interest of leaving the tasty graze.

Rolling out of his blankets, he stood, stretched and started for the creek. He knelt and splashed the ice-cold water on his face and on the back of his neck, rising to take a deep breath of fresh mountain air. Still on his knees at water's edge, he looked upstream at the cascading water tumbling down the steep rocky defile. No more than three feet wide at the widest point, the water it carried was pure, clear and refreshing.

Scattered alongside were clusters of blue lupine with their tall stalks of blue blossoms just now peeking out from their protective buds. An occasional columbine waved its white five-pointed saucer that held the blue and white lace trimmed cup that made up the blossom. The low-lying green crawler plant promised a bounty of strawberries in weeks to come. Ty leaned back on the grassy knoll and savored the clear air, the scent of pine and the promise of a new day. He stood and walked back to the packs on the ground near his bedroll, pulled out the coffee pot, the bag of Arbuckles, and a handful of jerky. He sat the bag and jerky on the log by the smoldering coals of the campfire, put a couple of small logs on the coals and took the coffee pot to the stream for water for coffee.

Seated on the log waiting for the water to heat up, he looked through the break in the pines on the downhill side of his camp and scanned the valley below. The valley paralleled the Sangre De Cristo range but varied in terrain from rolling foothills to wide verdant meadows with a variety of grasses that were inviting to elk and deer alike. Small streams came from the mountains but were insufficient to make a large river. A sizable snake-like creek wandered through the flats, harboring clusters of willow and berry bushes with occasional small stands of cottonwood and alder. With the morning sun stretching shadows that pointed Westward, the contours of the land were exaggerated but few. Ty thought it would be excellent cattle country and with only one cabin farther North in the valley, it invited someone to claim the rich land. His mind took him to a possible future with his own ranch and a family with pastures full of cattle and horses, but the boiling water brought him back to the present. Having previously ground some beans on the nearby stones, he dropped a handful of the grounds into the water and waited for it to brew. He had taken to timing the coffee by the length of time it took to chew a piece of jerky and he was soon ready for his first cup of the day. He poured the aromatic brew and slowly sipped the dark java.

He stood, looked around and started packing up to start the day's trek. He was soon on his way with the trail continuing to hug the shoulders of the tall peaks to his right. The timber was sparser and offered many views of both the valley below and the granite peaks that stretched above timber-line. By habit, he constantly searched the trail for sign of game of other animals or man but this morning the trail held only prints from elk. He was thankful there was no sign of anything with claws. His relaxed expression told of his relief and anticipation that today would be a better day than yesterday.

The trail narrowed and broke from the trees to take them across a wide area of slide rock. A whistle pig sounded an alarm but stood on hindfeet and waved his forepaws at the visitors and chattered his greeting through his two long yellow teeth. The furry and well-rounded marmot watched the visitors to his domain carefully pick their way across the uneven and unstable and often moss-covered slide rock. The clatter of hooves echoed across the clearing and Tyrell was glad that yesterday's grizzly was nowhere near. He looked uphill at the towering and naked peaks that seemed to be supporting the blue sky overhead thinking these were the tallest peaks he had seen in the entire Sangre De Cristo range. Four tall peaks, one with what could only be described as craggy needles that resembled a bony hand, were still holding back the remains of winter's wrath, and towered above the valley floor. Ty calculated them to be as tall or taller than most of the mountains in the entire range. The tall timber at the edge of the slide area seemed to snag the clouds overhead and drag them across the sky to deliver them to the mountain-tops. Ty thought the clouds were growing dark and churning to give warning of a coming rainstorm.

He had been watching for what might be a pass over the mountains and as the trail dropped to cross a gully, he saw a cut between the mountains that appeared to break through the craggy peaks and might be the answer to his quest. The trail followed the contour of the shoulder and brought him to the opening of the steep-sided and deep ravine. A smaller game trail pointed the way into the high walled canyon and Ty gigged his horse to take the narrow trail. Within a short distance, the trail dropped to the ravine bottom and crisscrossed the small creek that bounced over the rocks in search of an escape from the mountains. The steep and rocky hillsides held a smattering of tenacious juniper and clusters of scrub oak brush. Massive outcroppings of rock gave haven to rabbits, coyotes and mountain lion. Ty watched a family of big horn sheep bound their way among the rocks, finding footing where there was nothing but a crack or slight ledge unseen by Ty. Mostly ewes and lambs, with two young rams following as the massive horned herd ram pushed them up the rocks.

Suddenly a cacophony of thunder echoed through the canyon, startling every living creature, Ty included. The roan let loose a chest rattling rumble of concern, the mule stretched his neck and with wide mouth showing all his teeth, brayed his disapproval. Ty watched a jackrabbit run for cover and a coyote, tail between his legs, cower under the low branches of a cluster of sage. Ty searched the hillsides and canyon for any possible shelter and seeing none, gigged his mount forward. "Come on boy," said Ty, speaking to the roan as he gigged him in the ribs, "down in this canyon ain't no place to be if them clouds let loose'a that rain. A flash flood down through here's the last place we wanna be." The V cut between the mountains framed a sudden spear of lightning that struck beyond them but lit the now darkening sky. Ty felt the roan tremble beneath him, but the valiant animal yielded to Ty's urging and did not falter.

As the canyon walls receded and a shoulder of mountain showed itself to Ty's right, he watched the family of sheep disappear over the shoulder into a cleft of rock. He saw a trail leading from the canyon floor over the talus and disappear into the trees. Putting his heels to the roan's ribs, he reined the mount up the narrow trail. Looking to his left, the wide valley beyond was receiving the sheets of rain that were heading toward the mountains. He looked toward the rocks and searched for an overhang, a cave, a thick copse of trees, anything that would give some semblance of shelter. Following the trail through the cleft of rock, Ty had to kick his feet free of the stirrups and lift his legs high for the roan to make it through the cleft. He looked back and saw the panniers of the pack scrape the sides, but the mule successfully negotiated the narrow pathway. What appeared as a box canyon showed several tall spruce and ponderosa toward the back wall and a rock formation that might have sufficient overhang. Thinking the trees would protect the horse and mule, maybe he could find protection in the rocks. Ty, now on the ground in front of his horse and leading the animals on the trail, worked his way forward. Reaching the trees, he tethered the animals and walked on toward the rocks.

He thought of the sheep and realized they had disappeared but his concern was not for them. He focused on the wide ledge leading into the rocks and was startled when a badger hissed at him, turned and ran beneath a large outcropping into his lair. There was a thick cluster of oak brush next to the shear wall of stone and Ty walked around the brush, searching for better shelter. He pushed his way through the thick brush, found nothing beyond and turned back. Something caught his peripheral vision, movement or color, and he looked back toward the brush. He pushed through the branches and saw what might be an opening into a cavern or at least some overhang. He struggled beyond the brush and found a black void that showed promise.

Ty had never liked confining spaces, much less dark confining spaces, but the recurring thunder and lightning reminded of the need for shelter. He grabbed a dry branch of the scrub brush, dug a lucifer from his pocket and lit a torch sufficient for him to see into the blackness before him. He was surprised to see a sizable cavern with a sandy floor, and ample room for him and his animals. He also heard water dripping into a pool in the back of the cavern out of sight. He looked back at the opening and saw it was big enough for his animals to come through and looking around, saw scattered branches that showed this cave had been used before, probably by Indians, and he quickly gathered the wood before his torch burned down and began enough of a fire to keep the place lit until he returned.

He pushed back through the brush, chopping at several branches with his big Bowie knife, and cleared enough to lead his animals through. Returning to the tethered animals, he picked up their leads and quickly returned. It took a little encouragement, but the roan finally yielded and the mule followed as Ty led them into the cavern. By the light of the campfire, he dropped the packs and saddle, made quick halters with the long lead ropes and tethered the animals away from the fire. They nervously pranced for a while but soon started to settle down. The sounds of the downpour came from without and Ty knew they had made shelter just in time. He grinned and grabbed a firebrand to light his way, coffee pot in hand, to the water. He was anxious to have some warm java and a good meal.

Chapter Eleven

Discovery

It wasn't the warm velvety soft nose that woke Ty, nor was it the huff of breath that came from the roan's nostrils, but when the cold snot smacked against his cheek, slumber quickly retreated as he sprang upright. "Red! You sorry no good for nothing crow bait!" The big roan had backed away and gave the man a quizzical look. He probably couldn't fathom why the man was sleeping so late when he was usually up before the sun. Ty wiped his face with his scarf and looked at the horse shaking his head. Standing up, he looked at the filtered sun rays fighting their way through the brush at the mouth of the cavern. He walked to the opening and pushed back some of the branches, tucking them among others to give way to the sunlight. The mouth of the cavern was facing the West, but the morning sun was dancing among the stone walls of the canyon and finding its way to illuminate much of the cavern. The roan now stood behind Ty looking over his shoulder while the mule still stood hipshot and more interested in sleep than sating any sense of curiosity.

Ty reached for the dangling lead rope of the roan's halter and walked back into the interior of the cavern. "Come on, there's water back here," he said as he reached for the lead of the mule as well. The soil of the cavern's floor was loose and sandy and he dug his heels in to gain traction. The pool of water, fed by the overhead drips from the cavern's ceiling far above, showed clear in the limited light. The animals dipped their muzzles and drank their fill. Ty watched and let his gaze travel around the walls of the cavern. Something on the wall behind them caught his eyes and he turned to face it, squinting his eyes in an unconscious effort to see more clearly. Realizing he would have to get closer, he looked at the roan and mule, pulled them back from the water and led them nearer the opening to tether them. The coals of the night's fire still glowed and he reached for a sizable stick that had live coals at the end. He blew on the embers repeatedly until a flame came forth, and being careful to not extinguish the fire, he walked to the back wall.

Drawing near the wall, he lifted the torch and was rewarded with several petroglyphs carved on the surface. There were figures of men on horses, some with long spears, long swords, and what appeared to be helmets. Many stick figures were defending a village and other etchings were hard to make out but appeared to be wickiups. Many of the stick figures on foot were prone, apparently slain. Ty looked at each figure and other emblems that he made out to be the sun and storms and others. He was fascinated at what was before him, especially the men on horses with the long swords and helmets. *Ma told us about the Spaniards coming to the mountains, but that was, what, over a hundred years ago.* He stepped back from the wall and looked at the panorama that apparently told a story, but he shook his head in bewilderment. Lifting the flickering torch, he looked around searching for other drawings. The light reflected from the water and bounced from something to the far side of the pool. *Now what was that?* he thought as he looked at his torch and returned to the fire for another.

Lifting his new torch above his head, he saw what could be enough of a space between the wall and the pool to move around the pool and to the far side to explore the new curiosity. The roof of the cavern dipped along the pathway, but Ty crouched to make his way around the pool's edge. The roof of the cavern soared high and gave the appearance of a larger room. Ty looked in the direction of the object that caught his eye and froze where he stood. A half-buried skull stared at him from the sand, and beyond the skull was the crest of a steel Spaniard's helmet. Typical of the conquistador's armor, the morion style helmet had a pronounced crest with sweeping sides that rose to points on either end. But all that protruded from the sand was the top and the front point. Ty slowly moved toward his find, noticed the whites of other bones that indicated more than one body, and lifted the torch to see. The hilt of a sword lay behind the helmet and skull, bits of aged brittle leather showed from the sand, and a piece of what appeared to be chain mail was also exposed. On the wall behind the skull had been carved a Spanish cross, with the ends squared off. Ty sucked air deep into his lungs, realizing he had been holding his breath as he looked at this amazing discovery.

He quickly looked around, half expecting something or someone, probably in armor and wielding a sword, to leap out of the darkness. He carefully stepped back and lifted the sputtering torch high to illuminate the cavernous room. The shadows cast by the stalagmites and stalactites seemed to move, but he knew it was just the flickering of the small flame that was to blame, but he was uneasy anyway. He retreated to the lesser room and sat down to give thought to what he had seen. He picked up the coffee pot, refilled it and sat it beside the coals. He pushed several more sticks onto the coals and waited.

As he pondered the discovery and all the possibilities, he knew his curiosity was going to get the better of him. Even though the last thing he would usually consider doing was to go into the darkness and start poking around old skeletons, but the history and the story of it all intrigued him. *What if there's more skeletons? What else is gonna be back there? Why were they there?* Many questions fought for his attention and he began to recall some of the history his mother had shared with him. She had purchased every book she could from the different passing wagon trains and from their trips for supplies and she treasured the books of history and always delighted in sharing the tales from the past with her sons. He remembered her telling them about how these mountains had gotten their name.

The Spaniards had built a mission for the priests to convert the Indians, and those that didn't convert, were enslaved and put to work in the nearby gold mines. But one day the Pueblo Indians rebelled against them and fought the conquistadors and even the priests. When the Indians attacked the mission, one of the priests, praying in the garden behind the mission,

saw the red of the setting sun on the snow-capped mountains and muttered the words, Sangre De Cristo, or Blood of Christ, and the few Indians that had converted, remembered that and called the mountains by that name.

Ty pulled the pot aside, dropped a handful of coffee in and returned it to the flames. As he looked at the pot, waiting for it to perk, he thought, *those men in there must have been part of those that enslaved the Indians. I wonder if this cavern was the opening of the gold mine.* He looked around and not seeing any sign of mining, he shook his head and poured a cup of coffee.

Ty took the animals from the cavern, found some graze among the trees and tethered them to enjoy some new grass. He searched for and found a couple of branches from the ponderosa what showed considerable sap and hacked them from the trunk to fashion a better torch. Returning to the cavern, he lit the torches from the still smoldering fire and walked to the larger room. He walked deeper into the large room, looking for more petroglyphs or other evidence of

66

habitation. He found a couple of pick heads, three shovels, another sword, and two more skeletons. He left everything undisturbed and started back toward the first skull when he saw an unusual grouping of stones, that appeared manmade. He walked to the stack of stones that was against the cavern wall, and started moving several at the forward part of the stack. It was then he saw what appeared to be a thick leather covering. Clearing the stones away, he recognized the leather as an escuapil, or the padded leather armor worn by the Spaniards, he was afraid he would find a burial. But as he pulled at the leather, he caught his breath at the sight. Several bars of gold, about a foot and a half in length, three inches wide and two inches thick, were stacked against the wall. Ty fell back on his rump, arms outstretched behind him and the torch falling into the sand. He quickly sat up and retrieved the torch before the flame died.

"Holy Cow!" he whispered as he leaned over the pile of gold bars. "There's a fortune here! Now what am I gonna do?" He spoke in a hoarse whisper as he leaned over and touched the bars. Gold doesn't tarnish, but the dregs of smelting showed on the tops, but not enough to diminish the glimmering gold in the dim light of the torch. He stood up, took a deep breath and looked around. The promise of riches and the lure of the gold fields had never been lingering thoughts to Tyrell and he was not tempted with the wealth, but rather somewhat dismayed. As he considered all the possibilities, he knew his reserves of money were dissipating, but he didn't want to have to deal with the problem of explaining the gold. But he also knew, there could be times in the future that a cash reserve might be useful. *Well, there ain't no way I'm gonna try to pack this all out, but maybe if I just take a bar or two, hide it out and keep it as an emergency reserve or . . .* the sputtering of the torch caught his attention and he reached for his reserve branch, lit it and stood considering.

To The Sangre de Cristo

Chapter Twelve

Dune

The roan and mule picked their way down the steep trail toward the trickle of a stream that wound its way out into the sage brush covered flats. When they left the trail the day before, it followed this same stream with tree lined banks that obscured the cascading waters from view but the cheerful sound of crashing water over the stones filtered its way up the hillside to the lone traveler. Occasionally he would catch a glimpse of the wind-swept flats to his left and he continued to stretch to get a better view of this unusual phenomenon. Finally breaking from the trees, he was surprised at the view before him. He reined up on the roan and sat in his saddle with arms across the pommel looking at what appeared to be a vast wasteland of drifting sand. The wind-carved waves of sand appeared to be scalloped and smoothed by the hand of the creator and held no trace of animal or man. The sandhills rose above him and he could see the back-lit wind-blown traces of sand forming an overhanging lip at the crest of the wave. Each hill had a fine line of peaked sand that appeared as a line drawn across the crest. Ty stood in his stirrups to see farther across the undulating drifts and could only say, "My, my, my, ain't

God sumpin'?" as he bent to stroke the neck of his big roan. Dropping back into the saddle, he kneed his horse along the trail that followed the grass lined bank. Looking at the greenery beside the stream, he saw that the buffalo grass and the few willows and chokecherry bushes served as a barrier to the drifting sands and struggled to keep the encroaching drifts away from the small stream, which he found out later was appropriately named Sand Creek.

He looked at the trail and noted a juncture with another trail that came from the timber uphill of the sand dunes. Looking at the size of the dunes, the long-stretching flats below them in the wide valley, and back to the timber, he chose the trail that disappeared into the timber. He knew the game trails that followed the contour of the mountain's shoulders would almost always lead to water and would stay within the protection of the thicker woods and traveling alone, he knew this would be the safer choice.

With a later than usual start on the day, due to his exploring of the cavern, he pushed his roan and mule to put these desolate dunes behind them. His only mid-day stop was to give the animals a rest and some graze with but a handful of pemmican for himself. The trail had moved in and out of aspen groves, over several small streams, and held at the edge of juniper and ponderosa that climbed the steep hillsides of the towering granite peaks of the Sangres. As they followed the game trails, often having to decide which one to follow by the lay of the land, Ty continuously watched for any sign of big game or Indians. Mid-afternoon they crossed a more prominent trail leading into the tall timber that held many tracks of unshod horses. The tracks were fresh with recently turned small stones that still showed moist dirt on the underside, Ty stood in his stirrups to see the trail that led out of the trees and away from the mountain. *Probably a hunting party returning to their village. But, I'll just stay up here in the trees and out of sight, sure ain't anxious to mix it up with a band of that size, probably 8 or 10 of 'em.* He guessed them

70

to be Ute, but he also knew the Comanche and the Jicarilla Apache were known to hunt in these mountains at the South end of the Sangre de Cristo's. He kneed the roan along the pathway that wound through the aspen before him to begin searching for a camp for the coming night.

A shadow flitted across the trail and Ty looked up to see the broad wings of a golden eagle that searched for his dinner. He stopped and watched through the leafless aspen as the eagle spotted his prey and with a spiraling climb, tucked his wings and swept down to snatch a cotton tail rabbit in his sharp talons and lift the squirming and kicking fluff ball into the air. Then catching a wind current, banked in his flight to return to its nest somewhere above the craggy cliffs on the mountainside. Ty smiled at the sight he witnessed and thought of his father, Caleb, known among the Arapaho as He Who Talks to the Wind, for his ability to flawlessly mimic the call of any animal or bird. The many times Ty and his brother Talon had spent hunting with his father had given Caleb the opportunity to help the twins with their mastery of many of the calls of the wild. Ty had shown considerable skill similar to his father, and often goaded Talon with his ability.

The ponderosa and spruce gave way to the rocky hillsides and the trail wound its way among the outcroppings and massive boulders. With little soil for the taller trees, juniper, cedar and pinion found footing and would often crack massive stone formations with their deep water seeking roots that would pry apart the smallest cracks holding enough soil, usually carried by the winds, and would grow where it appeared there was no possibility that any living thing could thrive. Ty enjoyed the variety of the terrain and held as close to the trees as possible. They soon dropped over the shoulder of a ravine that held a decent stream, but looking to the valley floor, Ty chose to follow the stream up hill and away from the sparse tree cover. With the trail moving alongside the stream and then away from it into the thicker woods, Ty watched closely as the ponderosa and spruce became thicker and the

71

deep ravine still held a trail. Ty looked for any possibility of a camp site with the trail zig-zagging up the hillside. Within a few yards, a small opening offered shelter and protection from view and Ty readily turned into the clearing and started to prepare camp. There was enough graze for the animals and room for his bedroll and a campfire with ample firewood of long dead grey branches and kindling scattered at the edge of the clearing.

After de-rigging the mule and roan, Ty tethered the animals with enough lead that allowed them to reach all the graze and the water. As he looked at the cascading stream, he thought it was inviting him for a refreshing dip and he went to the packs, secured a bar of lye soap and returned to the side of the stream. He could hear the sounds of crashing water below him as he looked for a pool big enough for his needs and walked alongside the chuckling waters toward the sounds of a waterfall. The sheer drop of a cliff showed the waters below and Ty sought a trail that would take him within view. He slid down a steep run-off trail and stepped from the trees to see an extraordinary and peaceful glen. The towering cliffside gave way to the incessant force of water that carved its way through the hard-veined stone to reveal the smooth waterway and the cascades of waterfalls. The upper falls seemed to come from a narrow cleft that appeared as a hole in the rock, and wound its way to bounce again and over the edge above to cascade to a pool of crystal clear water revealing the stone littered bottom of the inviting pool.

Ty sat on the receding shore, removed his moccasins, and waded into the pool. His buckskins turned the darker almost reddish color as he moved deeper into the water. He sat down and ducked under the cold snow-melt water, rising suddenly with a "Whooooeeee! That's cold!" and the shout echoed and bounced around the cliff walls. Ty realized his shout could easily carry through the trees, and grabbed at his mouth as if he could retrieve the sound. Then he whispered, "What was I thinkin'? This ain't nuthin' but ice!" But he knew he and his clothes were long overdue for this dunking. He used the soap under his arms, across his belly and on his trousers, then removed the buckskins, rinsed them thoroughly and tossed them to the bank. He repeated his actions with the faded red union suit, removed it and flipped them to the bank as well. Then he proceeded to thoroughly wash his body, however hurriedly, and his hair and whiskers, rinsed and made his way to the shore. Using the nearby long grass as a towel, he rid himself of most of the water, donned just his moccasins, and walked back to his campsite carrying his duds.

He made quite a sight, wearing only his high-topped moccasins, as he draped his buckskins and union suit on the nearby kinnikinic bushes. He retrieved his coffee pot, coffee, and the remainder of the deer haunch he had been dining on and started making his supper. He knew he was nearing the fort and thought he might arrive sometime on the morrow. He thought he would do a little hunting on the way and replenish his supply of meat, not knowing what kind of provisions would be available at the fort. After his meal, he banked the fire and turned in for the night, wrapped in his blankets while his clothing dried in the evening breeze.

To The Sangre de Cristo

Chapter Thirteen

Ft. Garland

It was a chilly early morning in the dark timber that held the campsite. It was common for spring mornings to be welcomed with a layer of frost on the grasses and brush alongside the mountain streams. This morning's frost added a layer of cold on the clothing that weighted down the branches of the kinnikinic at the edge of the clearing. When Ty saw the frost, he was disinclined to shed the blankets, but he had wisely put a fresh pair of under-drawers beneath the covers and happily donned the muslin garment. After taking a moment to build up his resolve, he quickly threw back the covers and grabbing the frosty and slightly damp buckskins, he shivered into them. Stiffer than usual from the moisture, he knew it would take some time and considerable sunshine for the buckskins to resume their comfortable fashion. Somewhat stiff-legged he walked to the trees for his morning constitutional and soon returned to re-kindle the fire and start the coffee pot of water to boiling.

He sat with a blanket draped around his shoulders as his outstretched and buckskin clad legs soaked up the heat from the almost smokeless fire. What little smoke trailed skyward was dispersed by the overhanging long needled ponderosa and Ty dropped the coffee grounds into the now boiling water. His normal morning routine soon had him prepared for the trail and finishing the last cup of coffee, he threw the dregs on the coals, kicked dirt over the smoldering coals and satisfied, he climbed aboard the roan to start the day's trek, looking at the long shadows of early morning.

He made his way through the thick timber, following the gradual talus slope that led to the aspen that fringed the black timber of the mountain. Spotting a game trail, he reined the roan to the narrow pathway that picked its way through the scattered sage. A broad ravine showed a narrow creek meandering toward the open flats at which stood several deer getting their morning drink. Ty reined up the roan, grabbed his Henry and swung his leg over the rump of the big horse. Shielded by a small cluster of aspen, he rested his shoulder against the nearest one, took a bead on a young velvet antlered buck, squeezed off his shot and was rewarded to see the deer drop to his side, unmoving. The other deer bounded off and quickly disappeared leaving nothing but a brief memory.

Ty led his mount and the mule down the ravine slope to the flat by the stream, tethered them to a chokecherry bush and set about his work of field-dressing the buck. Removing the head, legs and guts, he easily loaded the carcass atop the panniers, secured it and was soon in the saddle again. With occasional glimpses at the three snow-capped peaks that served as his landmarks, it was mid-day when he broke from the trees to cross the flats toward the fort. The rolling terrain was covered with sage brush, buffalo grass, gramma and an abundance of cactus, with cholla and prickly pear the most prolific. The dry soil offered only puffs of dust at every footfall of the horse and mule as the plodding gait brought them nearer their destination. The shallow waters of the Sangre de Cristo creek gave temporary relief to the warm temperatures of mid-day and the cottonwoods provided welcome shade.

As the animals took long drinks, Ty stood beside his roan with an arm resting across the seat of the saddle and looked at the buildings of the fort, less than a mile away. This was his destination, but he wasn't sure he was ready for this dramatic change in his life. His upbringing on the family ranch in the Medicine Bow mountains was a far-cry from serving as a scout for the army in this flat dry Indian country. He wasn't sure he could handle being around that many people, especially with hundreds of men and very few women. Every day of his life had been in the presence of his childhood friend who became his wife, until he lost her and their first child so recently. Now, he wasn't certain about this more structured life and living with so many people. But maybe, just maybe, this is what he needed. To point his life in a totally new direction and putting the past in the past. He drew a deep breath that lifted his shoulders, exhaled and mounted up.

The roadway led along the South side of the many buildings of the fort and brought him to the sally port of the post where he was stopped by a uniformed guard that stepped from the nearby guard shack.

"What is your business here, sir?" questioned the guard holding his rifle diagonally across his chest.

"I want to see General Custer," stated Ty, somewhat surprised at the surly manner of the guard.

"And what business do you have with him?"

"I was told he wanted to have me as a guide or scout for this hyar fort," stated Ty, putting an edge to his response.

"Is he expecting you?" grilled the soldier, notably dropping the 'sir' from his remarks.

"You might say that," answered Ty, crossing his forearms on the saddle horn as he leaned toward the man.

The guard motioned to his left and said, "You can put your animals in the stable yonder and come back. I'll see if the General will see you."

"No," stated Ty flatly.

"No? You mean you won't put your animals in the stable?"

"That's right. I'm not even getting off this horse until General Carson agrees to see me!" affirmed Tyrell as he glared at the soldier. "So, how 'bout you or one of your lackey's just fetch on over to the General and take care of that little matter?"

"I'm not your messenger boy! If you don't do as you're told, you won't see the General or anybody else, buster!" said the guard with a raised voice and a step toward Ty.

"Then it'll be your scalp! Since the General sent for me and should be expectin' me, just what do you think he's gonna do to you when he finds out you wouldn't let that happen?"

"Uh, uh, I, uh, alright, wait right here," he stammered and turned toward the building to his right, "Hey, O'Reilly!" The shout caught the attention of several loitering soldiers that looked to the guard. One man hollered back, "What?"

"Get o'er to the General and tell him this fella's waitin' to see him."

"Who's he?"

He looked back at Ty and showing his irritation, asked, "What's your name?"

"Thompsett."

The summoned O'Reilly waved a hand in acknowledgement and walked around the corner of the building to the commanding officer's room to announce his visitor. Moments later, a uniformed, somewhat shorter than average, man with blonde hair just shy of his shoulders, sporting a somber expression, rounded the corner of the building and walked toward the waiting guard and Ty. He grinned when he saw Ty and said, "Talon! Good to see you. Step down and come on into my office."

Ty swung a leg over the rump of his roan and stretched his hand toward the General and said, "It's not Talon, I'm his brother Tyrell. Good to meet you General Carson."

"Yes, yes, certainly. I remember Talon telling me about you. He said you were well versed in the language and culture of the Ute Indians, is that right?"

"Yessir, I've spent much of my life among the Utes, and some time with Arapaho and Cheyenne as well," answered Ty, standing with the loose rein of his mount in his hand as he conversed with the General. Carson noticed the animals and turning to the man that summoned him from his office said, "O'Reilly, take this man's horse and mule and put them up in the stable. Be sure to rub them down, grain them, and get them to separate stalls."

"Yessir!" replied the trooper and reached for the reins from Ty. Ty handed off the reins and as the General motioned with his head, followed the General to his office. Carson seated himself behind the desk and motioned for Ty to take a seat before him. He began, "I'm glad you made it. I wasn't sure you would come, but after Talon sent a telegram, I've been looking forward to meeting with you. You see, Tyrell, is it?"

"Yessir, but most just call me Ty."

"O.K. Ty it is then. Let me give you a brief picture of where we stand at present. I've been here just shy of 2 months. We have two companies of the 1st New Mexico Infantry and Cavalry Battalion and I have yet to recruit suitable scouts, until now that is. Now, Ty, I've fought the Jicarilla Apache, Kiowa, Comanche, Navajo and Ute. But I'm tired of all the killin' and my main assignment now is to make this entire San Luis valley safe for settlers and to make peace with the Ute and any others that are willing. Now the Ute are mostly on the West edge of the valley, there have been other efforts at forging a peace with them, but as usual, the big wigs in Washington fail to meet the agreement and the Indians aren't too happy about it. There was a Treaty of Conejos that was put in force a couple years ago, but when Washington didn't pay up as agreed, the Ute ignored the rest of it. So, you'll be scoutin' for any patrols that head off in that direction, and just about anywhere else we find it necessary to go.

"We've got Jicarilla Apache to the South of us and Comanche to the East, so there's no tellin' what might arise that would require your services. I'll try to get us some more scouts, but for now, you're our chief of scouts and you'll be bunkin' in the officer's quarters." He stood and walked to the window of his office and pointed, "That building over past that corner of the parade ground, now, you have any questions?"

"Well, nothing I can think of right now. Oh, I do have a fresh venison carcass that I just brought down this morning, could your people use it?"

"Certainly, certainly, the kitchen is just a few doors down that way," motioning with his chin, "and I'm sure they would be glad to have some fresh meat. Which, by the way, anytime you want to use some down time to fetch us some fresh meat, it would be greatly appreciated."

"I'll do that General," said Ty, rising from his seat and turning to the door. He extended his hand again and shook hands with the General and left the office. He walked past the guard, grinned and nodded his head, and walked to the stable to fetch his gear and the venison. *Maybe this won't be too bad, when I'm on a scout I won't have to put up with any of these soldier boys and just have to report to the officer in charge. Hummm, we'll just have to wait and see.*

Chapter Fourteen

Intruders

It was a tired group of travelers that pitched their camp in the ponderosa at the crest of the saddle that separated the Sawatch Range and the Sangre de Cristo mountain range. The oldest maps of the area referred to the mountain pass as Pou Nchay, Ute for foot path. Some called it Poncha pass, the only trail wide enough for wagons that led from the broad San Luis valley to the valley of the Rio de Napestle or the Arkansas river. This route had been used by early Spanish explorers and free trappers from Taos. Kit Carson had guided Fremont through this pass and Colonel Fauntleroy, from Fort Massachusetts, pursued Utes and Apache over this pass, killing many in the resulting battle. But the camping prospectors cared little about those that had been here before them, their only interest was in finding their fortune in gold.

Their horses tethered in the trees, the men were watching the slices of fresh deer meat drip the juices into the flames of the fire, mouths watering in hunger. A large enamel coffee pot rocked on the flat stone beside the fire as the percolating brew danced its way to darkness. These men, from a broad spectrum of lifestyles, were not mountain savvy. With the abundance of plants that would lend variety and nutrition to their meal readily at hand, none would be recognized by any of these men. They understood meat, coffee and beans that were to be had from a trading post or general store, but even making of bread or corncakes was beyond their limited knowledge. Gunther Schmidt had taken to experimenting with the corn meal and flour in their store of goods, but thus far his efforts were not met with the approval of the other men. This meal would amount to coffee and meat before they turned in for the night. The most disgruntled of the group, Big Joe Marlett, leaned forward and grabbed one of the willow branches with a dripping slice of meat and said, "That's done 'nuff fer me! I'm hungry an' I ain't waitin' no longer." He brought the thick slice of meat to his mouth, sunk his teeth into it and jerked the remainder away as juices dribbled into his beard. The raw band of meat had a thin edge of brown along the outside showing its brief acquaintance with the flames. The others looked at Big Joe and followed his example securing their own portions before he tried to consume it all.

Talking around a mouthful of meat, Irish asked, "So, Marcus, ye said you knew about this country, have ye been here afore?"

"No, but I talked to some men that have. They were on a tradin' trip outta Hardscrabble that met with the Utes in these mountains."

"So, what's yer plan?" asked Efe Tuscanny, Irish's partner.

"We're gonna keep doin' what we been doin', that's what. Just cuz our pans didn't show color on any o' the streams so far, don't mean we won't find some," answered Marcus.

"Well, I thought we was gonna go to the San Juans where them Spaniards found their gold, like you said," whined Curtis Tuffin.

"That's the general idea, but why pass up what might be a better discovery? It don't take much effort to wash a pan or two whenever we come on a stream. An' if'n we find some color, why we just follow up on it to see what shows. If it ain't nuthin' to shout about, we move on to the San Juans."

There were several grumbles between bites and slurps of coffee, but most agreed with his plan. Anxious to get to the San Juan mountains, the source of many fabled stories of Spanish gold, they were also reluctant to pass up any closer possibilities. After all, it didn't matter where you found gold, just that you found plenty of it. The dark timber and long shadows of sundown soon beckoned the tired men to their bedrolls and before long the sputtering racket of snoring men rattled the cones on the nearby pines.

Having eaten the last of their venison the night before, breakfast consisted of Gunther's third attempt at corncakes and a fresh pot of coffee. Marcus Spann led out and kicked his horse to a canter to put him far enough ahead of the group to give a good scout. Big Joe handled the team and wagon while Irish and Efe led the heavily laden pack mules. The other men had been assigned the job of panning the creeks as they came to them, while the rest of the party would continue on the trail. The easy trail led down the slight decline from the summit of the pass and followed a small stream that meandered lazily through the green meadowland. Thick clusters of chokecherry and buffalo berry bushes lined the creek banks and a mantle of dark blue timber sat on the shoulders of the nearby snow-capped peaks that scratched the blue arc of sky. With less than a mile behind them, the men were startled by the sound of a rifle shot from well in front of them. Curtis said, "Ah, prob'ly jus' Spann shootin' a deer or sumpin'." The men looked from one to the other and nodded heads indicated agreement without alarm and kept up their pace.

Less than a mile from their camp, they found Marcus dressing out a nice sized doe that would provide meat for the men for a couple of days at least. He motioned below him to a confluence of three creeks and said, "I'll finish this, how 'bout you three tryin' them creeks fer some color?" The three, Alex

Romero, Curtis Tuffin, and Gunther Schmidt, nodded their heads and gigged their horses forward to try the small streams. Big Joe, Irish and Efe reined around the downed doe and proceeded along the trail that followed the San Luis creek. They were used to disappointing results from the panning of the creeks and didn't expect any different from these. One of the small streams trickled from the beginning of the Sangre's, one followed the valley from the crest of the pass and the third came from the lower hills to the West. This would be the first stream off this watershed for the men to try their luck on and Gunther jumped down into this creek with a little more than usual enthusiasm. But his results on this first stream were no different than the others, with the only color being the sparkle of fool's gold, or iron pyrite, on the brown sandy bottom.

Travel was slower than the days before with several creeks coming from both sides of the valley. Those that cascaded down the steep mountains of the Sangre's ran full with snow melt that fed the many streams with ice cold water. Another stream paralleled the San Luis creek and caught the watershed of the mountains, causing the prospectors to split up with Romero and Tuffin choosing to pan the streams off the mountains. They believed the prospects from the towering granite peaks were better than the streams that came from the lower hills on the West of the valley. Gunther was content with working solo and gladly took his time to pan several locations on each feeder stream.

The wagon road stayed on the high side or West side of the San Luis creek and the men chose to munch on the smoked meat for their noon meal and not take the usual break at mid-day. As the sun touched the West horizon and dusk was ushered into the valley, Big Joe reined up the team alongside a thick cluster of chokecherry bushes at the edge of the stream, tied off the reins to the brake handle and jumped down to start unhitching the team. Without any words exchanged, Irish and Efe followed suit and started removing the packs from the mules and prepared to tether the horses. The animals gave a good shake and a roll in the grass before walking to the Creekside for water. There was little firewood nearby and Irish volunteered to walk upstream of the feeder creek to a finger of tree covered hillside for the needed wood. Gunther had already started his panning of the feeder creek and Irish saw Gunther's tethered horse alongside a cluster of chokecherry. Gunther was squatted streamside and busy washing a pan of creek bottom soil and didn't hear Irish approach.

"Findin' any color, Gunther?" asked Irish, startling the big blonde.

"Just started, don't know yet."

"Well, I'm gonna fetch us some firewood, how 'bout after you wash a couple pans, you grab an armload when you come back to camp. We're just down yonder at the bottom there."

"Jah, Jah," agreed the big German and continued with his circular motion, washing the light weight sand and small stones from the pan.

When Irish had his armful of wood, he started back toward the camp and noticed Gunther had moved to another spot further upstream. He grinned at the diligence of the big man, then walked on to the camp.

Marcus hung the carcass of the doe from the side of the wagon to finish the butchering and deboning of the meat. Big Joe had sliced several steaks from a rear haunch and was draping them over the fire to start broiling. Irish and Efe found some wild onions they wanted to try together with steaks and washed them off and lay them across a flat stone near the fire. The coffee pot was beginning its percolating dance and the aroma of the dark brew filled the camp. Alex and Curtis had joined the group at the camp after tethering and de-rigging their horses and now sat on a long grey log, waiting for their portion of meat. Irish looked up and saw Gunther leading his horse to where the others were tethered, but he was holding a gold pan at his side with a conscious effort to not spill the contents. Irish watched the German set down the pan, tether the horse and drop the saddle and gear with the others, then pick up the pan and walk to the fire. He carefully sat the pan on the large end of a downed log, and looked at the men as Irish asked, "So, whatcha got there Gunther?"

"Come see," he replied with a wide grin splitting his face.

Irish cocked his head to look at the man, stood to his feet and walked to his side. He looked down at the pan and was surprised to see a small arc of gold flakes hugging the far side of the pan. He looked at the German and back at the pan then hollered to the others at the fire, "Hey fellers, come look at this!"

With curiosity but little excitement, the men sauntered over to see the source of interest. Marcus grabbed up the pan and fingered the gold flakes, looked at Gunther and asked, "This was just one pan?"

"Jah, jah. One pan."

Marcus passed the pan to the others, each one touching the gold flakes and looking back at Gunther. Irish asked, "Was it a pocket? Or was there more?"

"The first two pans showed color, but this was the best."

If gold had been taken in just one location, it was possible it was just a rich pocket and could easily be exhausted without much profit. But when gold was found in more than one panning, it was possible the gold had washed downstream from a rich vein somewhere higher up the mountain.

"Whoooeee, Hot diggity! Finally! Color!" shouted Alex, then looking around at the others asked, "Think there'll be 'nuff fer all of us?"

"Only one way to find out! That's foller the color upstream and see what we get. But a pan like that? That's mighty promising!" declared Marcus as he took the pan and fingered the gold again.

Chapter Fifteen

Scout

As Ty entered the large barn and stables of the fort, he paused for his eyes to adjust to the dim light, and breathed in the odors of the horses and their feed. Several troopers were busy cleaning out the stalls and shoveling the manure into the carts, others were tossing hay to the horses in the stalls and loading another larger cart to take hay to the horses in the outside corrals. Ty asked one of the men, "You fellas seen a long legged strawberry roan and a mule that was brought in here just a bit ago?"

One trooper stood upright, leaned on his fork and pushed his cap to the back of his head as he looked at Ty, then answered, "Yup, they's back yonder in the two last stalls. An' yore stuff's stacked in the corner b'side 'em."

"Thanks!" answered Ty and started toward the rear of the barn. Before he went more than a couple of steps, he was stopped by a question from the trooper, "Say, you gonna be a scout fer us?"

"That's right."

"Ain'tchu a little young fer that?"

Ty chuckled and looked back at the man with the questions, noted his salt and pepper hair peeking from under the cap and answered, "Would you want a young man that knows what he's doin' or an old man that doesn't?"

"Hmmm, got a point there. But do you know whatchur doin'?"

"Yup," answered Ty without further explanation, turning to go to his animals. The trooper watched him leave, then resumed his work in the stalls. Ty was not surprised at being questioned because of his youth, but he was confident his years of experience in the mountains and with Indians would far outweigh the doubts of soldiers whose only experience was with the fighting in the civil war and none with Indians or the ways of the wilderness.

He found his animals, checked on the feed for Red and spoke to the roan as he patted his neck. He hung the saddle from a loop of rawhide that was attached to an overhead beam, draped the halter and bridle on the saddle horn and began putting the pack saddle on the mule. With too much to carry, he loaded the mule with the panniers, parfleche, saddle bags, bedroll and rifle and scabbard and led the mule, Maggie, to his quarters. He tethered the mule at the hitchrail and started carrying his gear into his quarters. He was pleasantly surprised by the spacious room that held a single bunk, a small chest of drawers, a simple desk and chair, a flat top stove for heat and sufficient for brewing coffee or even cooking, and a set of shelves. As he was finishing the unloading of the mule, a woman came from the quarters next to his and smiled as she said, "So, you're the new member of our corps?"

"Uh, well, I guess you could say that. I'm not a soldier as you can see, but I am the new chief of scouts for the post," answered Ty. "My name is Tyrell Thompsett," he said as he retrieved the last of the panniers. The added weight of the gold bar in the bottom of each of the panniers made the maneuvering of the large canvas containers more cumbersome than usual and he sat it on the ground to get a better grip. The woman walked closer and extending her hand said, "I'm Elizabeth Barrett. Lieutenant Barrett is my husband," as she waited for Ty to shake her hand. He was stepping forward when she said her name and at his hearing 'Elizabeth' he caught his breath and slightly stumbled before catching himself and taking her hand lightly for a simple get acquainted shake. She noticed his reaction and asked, "Did I say something wrong?"

"Oh, no, no m'am, I guess I'm just a bit clumsy after riding all day," explained Ty as he looked at the woman. Her blonde hair was stacked in a pile of curls with two hanging to the side and dangling near her shoulder. Her dress was a green plaid gingham with a lace trimmed collar that sat just below her chin and the long sleeves sported the same lace at the cuffs. She was a pretty woman, young, and with a friendly smile enhanced by her blue eyes. A hint of freckles graced her nose and cheeks and lent a girlish aura to the woman.

"Will your wife be joining you, Mr. Thompsett?" she asked.

"Uh, no m'am. I, uh, I don't have a wife," stammered Ty, uncomfortable with the question.

He turned and reached for the pannier and she said, "Well, when my husband returns, I'll introduce you and maybe we can have dinner together one of these evenings."

"That will be fine m'am, just fine," replied Ty and started for the door of his quarters. "Now if you'll excuse me, I've got to get my stuff put away. Nice meeting you m'am."

"Of course, don't let me keep you," she answered and stepped back through her doorway.

It didn't take Ty long to put his gear away, leaving the bars in the bottom of the panniers with the panniers stacked in the corner beside the bed. He went to the Cavalry dining room and enjoyed a fine meal of fresh venison, potatoes, beans and cornbread and a steaming cup of java that would melt a horseshoe, just the way he liked it. Small talk with a few of the cavalrymen started his round of getting acquainted with the men, most of whom had a skeptical manner regarding any new men to the company. But Ty knew the nature of people and had experienced the poor manners of many when the various wagon trains came through the Cherokee trail and passed near his family's ranch. Although he understood being skeptical, he never understood bad manners, and many of the soldiers came from a life that was totally devoid of any teaching regarding manners. But soldiers were neither taught nor concerned with manners, just the fighting ability of the man beside him, for that man held the life of his companions in his hands and each one wanted to know they could trust the other with that responsibility.

He returned to his quarters just as a group of soldiers gathered on the edge of the central parade ground and Ty heard the sounds of music coming from the group. He leaned on the hitchrail and looked toward the group to see a lanky redhead tuck a fiddle beneath his chin and begin to pull a bow across the strings as he tuned. Another man held a squeeze box and began fingering a tune as he drew it back and forth. The fiddler joined in and soon the group of men began singing. The melancholy men sounded out with the tune and words to Blue Eyed Maiden, a favorite with the men.

All bless the blue-eyed maiden, with curls of auburn hue,

Whose voice comes music laden those rosy portals through;

Though graceful, light and airy, too gentle to be vain,

All bless thee smiling fairy, All bless thee blue eyed Jane;

The men continued to sing, sounding out with all three verses interspersed with a chorus between each one. After a short pause, they struck up again with The Old Log Hut or as it had become known, Row, Row, Row Your Boat.

With a pleasant harmony, the men enjoyed the singing and the growing crowd of officers and their ladies applauded each number. The sun shared the last of its light by painting the Western sky with broad strokes of gold and orange held by the wispy clouds of evening, then soon tucked itself in for the night to let the stars share the black velvet canopy.

The men of music returned to their quarters and the Barrett's, noticing Ty at the rail, walked over to join the newcomer. Elizabeth introduced her husband, "Mr. Thompsett, this is my husband, Lieutenant Barrett. David, this is Mr. Thompsett, the new chief of scouts."

"Pleased to meet you, Lieutenant," said Ty as he extended his hand to shake.

The lieutenant took his hand and replied, "And you as well. Chief of scouts, huh? Aren't you a little young for such a title?" The lieutenant wasn't much older than Ty, but he was a recent graduate of West Point and quite proud of the fact. He looked upon anyone, officer, trooper or civilian with a certain element of disdain thinking himself more accomplished and certainly more intelligent.

Having heard about the lieutenant from the troopers at dinner, Ty was ready for his judgmental airs and readily responded, "No, actually lieutenant, I'm quite experienced and much older than I look. When anyone has had the opportunity to live two or three lives in a matter of a few short years, his wilderness education gives him certain advantages and knowledge that cannot be had by other means."

"Well, surely you don't think a little experience with this wild country would equal a true education."

"Why no, of course not. An education of practical experience and real life would far surpass anything that could be gained from a bunch of stuffy professors that have never stepped out of the halls of higher education. You see lieutenant, this 'wilderness education' is more what you might call 'graduate school' and there is plenty for everyone to learn, me included."

The lieutenant stood with his mouth slightly agape and showing his perplexity at the scout's response. He did not expect this mountain man in buckskins to be so well-spoken and so ready with a comeuppance. Little did he know that his wilderness education was just beginning and professor Thompsett would be giving the passing or failing grade.

The lieutenant sputtered for a moment then said, "Well, Thompsett, you will be scouting for our patrol that will leave first thing in the morning, day after next. The General has tasked me with a patrol to the Northern part of the valley. There will be one platoon of cavalry, two wagons of supplies, and we'll be gone a week to ten days, perhaps more. Do you have any questions?"

"No, first thing in the morning, huh?"

"That is correct. You will not need any supplies except for your own ammunition. If you need any, you can draw it from the post sutler on account." He turned on his heel and taking his wife's elbow in hand, walked back to his quarters without looking back at Ty, who was smiling at the lieutenant's retreat. He chuckled to himself and went to his quarters, looking forward to his first night in a bed.

Chapter Sixteen

Preparation

Ty rolled from his bunk before the sun crested the mountains East of the Fort. He reached for his pocket watch that lay open on the small bedside table, saw the time as 5:40, snapped the case shut and slipped it into the waist pocket of his buckskin britches that hung on the chair. He stretched, rubbed the sleep from his face and gathering his tunic and britches, returned to the bed to slip them on and pull on his high-top moccasins. Having already hung the Bowie across his back, he reached for the belt that held his holstered Remington and the extra cylinders and decided to leave it hanging on the chair. The tomahawk rested on the seat of the chair but Ty thought he would leave it as well. He grabbed his brown felt hat, doffed it and walked out of his quarters to see the first long rays of sun bending over the mountains. He walked into the sunlight on his way across the parade ground towards the Cavalry dining room and noted the absence of any movement around the barracks. He didn't know what time they served breakfast, but he hoped to at least get some coffee.

He stepped into the dining room and found it empty. There was noise coming from the adjoining kitchen and Ty walked to the doorway. Two cooks and their helpers were busy with the morning's preparations and the bigger of the two noticed Ty at the doorway.

"Sumpin' we can do fer you mister?"

"Well, I'd like to get some coffee if it ain't too much trouble," answered Ty.

"Humph," growled the cook, then motioning to the sideboard against the wall said, "Grab yoresef' a cup and pour yore own. It's on the stove yonder," he waved a long spoon dripping with some batter toward the cook stove.

Ty looked in the direction indicated, stepped into the kitchen and followed the cook's directions, pouring himself a cup of steaming java. From behind him came the gravelly voice of the cook, "So yore the scout, huh? Ya gonna be bringin' in anymore meat?"

"Yup, I'm the scout. An' I'll be sure to bring you in some meat, time to time. But, the lieutenant tells me we're goin' out on patrol tomorrow and we'll be gone a spell, but when we get back I'll see 'bout fetchin' you in some meat."

"Which lieutenant?" asked the cook, scowling at the intruder to his kitchen.

"Barrett," answered Ty.

"Humph, you watch that greenhorn, he's liable to gitchu all kilt!"

"Well, Kit told me my job was to keep him outta trouble, so that's what I aim to do."

"Kit? You mean the Gen'l, don'tchu? Don't let them wet-behind-the-ears officers hear you callin' him Kit! They'll come unglued if'n they hear you do that."

"Well, since I answer to the General, I'll just take it as it comes. What's for breakfast?"

"Flapjacks n' sidemeat, same as ever' Sunday," answered the cook.

"Sunday? So that's why ever'body's sleepin' in, why I plumb lost track of what day of the week it was."

Ty walked back into the dining room and heard the bugler sounding reveille to bring the camp awake.

> *I can't get 'em up*
> *I can't get 'em up*
> *I can't get 'em up this morning;*
> *I can't get 'em up*
> *I can't get 'em up*
> *I can't get 'em up at all!*
> *And tho' the sun starts peeping,*
> *And dawn has started creeping,*
> *Those lazy bums keep sleeping,*
They never hear my call!

Listening to the lonely call of the bugle, Ty sat down at the end of a long corner table and nursed his coffee. He thought about this new chapter of his life and wondered about his choice. As his father told him, *Son, sometimes what we need most in life is a radical change. I think serving as a scout for Carson will be a good experience for you. You'll see some new country, meet new people, both good and bad, and you'll see how a good part of the rest of the world lives.* Ty nodded his head and thought it just might be good for him although he wasn't looking forward to some of 'the bad' his Pa had referred to, but he knew it would be a learning experience.

Cooky stuck his head through the door and said, "Got some flapjacks ready if you wanna git a head start on them lazy troopers."

"Why thanks, Cooky, I'll just take you up on it."

Ty was finishing up his breakfast when the troopers started filing into the dining room grabbing their trays, filling them and seating themselves at the benches alongside the long tables. Those that sat at his table were all non-coms and he was quickly informed this table was reserved for those with a rank of at least sergeant. The man directly across the table from Ty had been doing the speaking for the rest of the men and continued, "So you see, since I don't see any stripes on your sleeve, I guess you shouldn't be sittin' here."

"Well, Sarge, since I'm the chief of scouts, I can sit where I please, but since I'm done, I'll leave you 'gentlemen' to your flapjacks," and picking up his tray, he stood to leave. "Enjoy!" he said as he walked away from the table without looking back. He heard the men talking among themselves and heard one of them address the talker, "First Sergeant, you're gonna get yourself in trouble, you know a chief of scouts is the same as an officer!" Ty did not hear the top-kicks response, but chuckled as he walked out of the dining room.

He started across the parade ground to return to his quarters when he was hailed by a voice behind him. He turned to see Carson standing at a hitchrail in front of his office and motioning for Ty to join him. With a hand on Ty's shoulder, the General ushered the young man into his office and walked to the far wall that exhibited a large map of the area.

"Ty, this map is the closest thing we have to a description of this area, although not real accurate, it does give us an idea of what's around us. As you know, I've been in this area and served as a scout, in my younger days, so I've made a few corrections to what the cartographers originally laid out. But it will suffice to let you know what I have in mind. Now, first off, you're goin' out with Lieutenant Barrett, and he's a good man, just green. He's from the East and a recent graduate of West Point, so he thinks he knows everything, but his only experience was the trek from Sante Fe up here to Ft. Garland. I don't think he's ever seen an Indian, 'cepin for a few we passed when we came through San Luis, but they were fallin' down drunk. So, you're gonna have your hands full, but if you're anything like your Pa and your twin brother, I'm confident you can handle it. Now," and he turned back to the map and pointed, "you'll be goin' up to the North end of the valley, crossin' over and . . ."

The General spent some time detailing the patrol's route and purpose, sharing his concerns and any possibilities that Ty should be watchful about. He finished with, "Oh, and you should get a Spencer Carbine from the Quartermaster, we have ample ammunition for the Spencer and we're a bit limited on ammo for your Henry. Feel free to pack 'em both if you want, and if you happen on another prospect for a scout, sign 'em up. We can use some more 'cuz we'll have patrols going in several directions at once and you won't be able to cover 'em all."

After getting his instructions, Ty excused himself and walked to the Quartermaster to secure his supplies. After selecting a new Spencer carbine and scabbard, sufficient ammunition for both the Spencer and his Henry, and powder and lead for loads for his Remington, he returned to his quarters. He picked up his Bible and walked out, waving at his neighbors as he left the post for a short walk of about half a mile to the trees that lined the banks of the Sangre de Cristo river to the West of the fort. He thought it would be a good place to spend some time in the Bible and with his Lord.

He found a nice grassy bank overlooking the clear chuckling waters of the stream and under the shade of some tall cottonwoods. Taking a few minutes just to enjoy the solitude and the sounds of creation, the stream, a meadowlark nesting overhead that sounded his singular melody, and farther away he heard the kee, kee, kee of a circling falcon. He opened his Bible to the book of Psalms, flipped to chapter 8 and read about man having dominion over all the beasts of the field and the fowl of the air and couldn't help but let a light laugh escape his lips, thinking of all the animals that he enjoyed eating. *I guess that's one way of having dominion,* he thought. He considered the change in his life, the instructions from the General, and the anticipated patrol and started to pray. He had been taught about prayer at the side of his father and mother, and practiced the same principles as he began to pray about the coming patrol, the lieutenant, and the troopers and more.

He was sitting with his elbows on his knees, head dropped with chin on his chest and as

he finished his prayer, he lifted his head as he heard someone approaching from behind him. The steps were not tentative and he knew whoever it was, wasn't trying to sneak up on him. He slowly turned his head to see Lieutenant and Mrs. Barrett walking towards him. He stood and turned to face them and said, "Mornin' folks, takin' a little stroll, are you?"

They walked hand in hand and as they drew near, the lieutenant responded, "Mornin' Thompsett. We saw you walkin' this way and my wife was curious, especially when she saw you carryin' your Bible. It's not often we see someone with God's Word and naturally she wanted to know more."

Ty looked at the Bible in his hand and back up to the curious couple and explained, "I've always tried to spend time in the Word every day. I find it's counsel always very timely. I asked around and the troopers said there wasn't a chaplain or any type of services, so I just decided to have my own."

"Well, we'd be pleased if you would include us the next time you decide to 'hold services' with the Lord. We miss the times with other believers and it would be encouraging. I think there are a few others that would appreciate a time together in the Scriptures, that is, of course, if you wouldn't mind."

The demeanor of the lieutenant had changed considerably as he spoke and Ty motioned for them to be seated on the grassy knoll with him. As the lieutenant helped his wife to be seated, Ty said, "Well, I'm no preacher that's for sure, but it might be enjoyable to be with others that appreciate the Word and could share. Maybe when we get back from our patrol, we might just do that."

The rest of the morning was spent in pleasant get acquainted conversation and the lieutenant was pleased to share his knowledge about the fort and the personnel as well as his plans for the patrol. It was readily evident, his experience with any Indians was non-existent and Ty knew he had his work cut out for him.

Chapter Seventeen

Patrol

Ty leaned against the hitchrail in front of Officer's row watching the confusion and commotion as the troopers led their mounts into the parade ground. As agreed, Ty had been waiting since 'first light' having taken an early breakfast in the Cavalry dining room, stored his gear aboard Red and tethered his now hipshot horse at the rail while they waited on the lieutenant and his men. He was surprised when so many men and horses began assembling in the parade ground at the center of the fort. When the General had said 'patrol', Ty thought it would be handful of men, but the sergeants were assembling what looked to be enough troopers to invade a sizable fortress. But what Ty watched was the assembling of 1st and 2nd platoons of A Company, 1st New Mexico Cavalry, consisting of about 50 men, 25 to a platoon counting the sergeants. *And we're supposed to go patrol the entire San Luis valley, unnoticed. Might as well send a brass band, cuz ever' Indian in the mountains will know when we're comin' and how many there are before we even leave the fort!* thought Ty to himself, shaking his head in consternation.

He watched and listened as the sergeants barked their orders, and the frustrated men labored to obey them. It was obvious that several of the troopers were green, if not wet-behind-the-ears, and fought with the horses as they started to mount. Finally, four rows of troopers sat astride their mounts waiting for further orders. When Lieutenant Barrett rode to the front of the formation, Ty slipped the reins of his roan from the rail and mounted up to wait for the troop.

Ty hadn't noticed the General and other officers that exited their quarters and stood behind the hitchrails watching the assembled troop. When Lieutenant Barrett saluted the General and crisply reported, "A Company, ready for patrol, sir!" the General returned the salute and firmly replied, "Proceed as ordered, Lieutenant, and Godspeed."

"Thank you General," answered the lieutenant, then turned to the First Sergeant and ordered, "Move 'em out, 1st Sergeant!" The First Sergeant barked, "Column of twos, wheel left, Ho!" and the troops as one, reined their mounts left and by twos followed the Lieutenant and First Sergeant from the post. Ty watched and followed, kicking his mount up to a canter to catch up with the Lieutenant and pulled alongside. "Mornin' Lieutenant, looks like a right dandy day for a patrol."

"Morning Thompsett, and yes, it appears we have a fine day on our hands."

"Do you have anything in particular in mind for me, or shall I just scout on ahead and keep you apprised of anything goin' on up yonder?"

"I trust you know where we're going?" asked the Lieutenant, sitting stiffly erect on his McClellan saddle. Ty sat comfortably in his full seat with a Mexican style tree and leaned on the pommel as he looked at the Lieutenant and said, "You know, Lieutenant, we've a long way to go and it'll be easier on your back if you just relax a bit. I know it ain't all that easy on that McClellan, but you're not on the parade ground now an' all these greenhorns are watchin' you an' followin' your example."

"As you said, Thompsett, I'm setting the example for my men and we are a cavalry unit on patrol, even if we're not on the parade ground."

"Whatever you say, Lieutenant. And yes, I know where we're goin' but do you want to stay out here in the open, or would you prefer to be up in the trees and under cover?"

"Why would we want to be under cover? I see no threat before us, and I believe we will have easier traveling on the flats."

"Suit yourself," replied Ty and pointing to the front of the column, he continued, "This trail you're on is the old Spanish trail and it leads North right alongside the edge of the mountains. I'll be scoutin' 'bout two miles ahead an' if I bag any game for supper, I'll leave it in plain sight for your troopers to pick up. Savvy?"

"Savvy? What do you mean?" asked the bewildered Lieutenant.

"Uh, savvy means, understand. Do you understand?"

"Of course, I understand!" retorted the West Pointer.

Ty dug heels in the ribs of Red and the big horse stretched his head forward as he lunged into a full out gallop, leaving the troopers in a small cloud of prairie dust. Both Ty and the long-legged horse reveled in the morning run, it had been some time since they really stretched their legs. Ty lay along the neck of the big horse with the mane whipping in his face and feeling the bunching and stretching of the muscles beneath him. He watched the flat terrain before him carefully scanning for any obstructions and shortly reined his horse to a walk and sitting erect, he looked over the slightly undulating plains, seeing nothing but miles of sage, gramma, and cactus. To his right, the Sangres caught the morning sun that climbed the blue sky behind them and brightly shone on the remaining snow that was slowly melting with the coming summer heat. Stretching out to the West and away from his left, the flats of the San Luis valley showed little life to the casual observer, but

Ty saw big-footed jackrabbits, scurrying lizards by the dozens, and an occasional diamondback that slithered from the trail.

The valley was home to buffalo, antelope and in the timbered slopes that framed the valley would be found mule deer and wapiti in abundance. But on this sunny morning, the bigger game chose the cooler climes of the trees, even the shaggy buffalo hung around the edges of the timber to take advantage of the only shade offered. The Eastern edge, nearer the Sangres, had fertile land that supported grassy meadows that were well watered by the Spring runoff, and the route of travel would take the troop North into this greener portion of the valley. Their first day out with fresh and frisky mounts, brought them just North of the Sand Dunes and they found Ty waiting at the edge of the timber with a deer carcass hanging in a nearby tree and Ty sitting on a patch of grass beside the small stream, his horse grazing beside him.

As the troop reined up and stopped, at the order of the First Sergeant, Ty stood to watch as the orders began to fly, troopers dismounted, and the camp began to gain some order. The Lieutenant walked over to his scout and said, "Good campsite, well done, Thompsett," as he looked around the area with a critical eye. Ty responded with, "Uh, why don't you call me Ty or Scout, instead of being so stiff with the last name and all."

"Alright Scout, well done. And that fresh meat will be enjoyed by all, I'm sure."

"By the way, I thought you oughta know, I cut the trail of a bunch of Indians, probably a hunting party, back South of the dunes. Looked like they were headed Southeast, maybe Comanche goin' home."

The Lieutenant stiffened and asked, "Should we be concerned?"

"I don't think so, the sign was a day or two old and they were headed away from us, but I thought you'd wanna know."

"Certainly, certainly, but you said you thought they were Comanche, I thought this was Ute country."

"It is, but the Comanche and even the Jicarilla Apache come up this way on huntin' trips occasionally. But the further we go, I don't think we'll see anything but Ute."

"We were told the Ute were friendly, but what do you think?"

"There are several different bands, or tribes, of the Ute people. Each one has different leaders and are not bound by the agreements or treaties made by the others. If one band has a leader or leaders that want to fight against the invaders, or the whites, then that band will fight. Or, it might be they have a leader that wants to make peace, then that's the way the band will go," explained Ty.

"And what bands or tribes are around here?" asked the curious Lieutenant.

"Along those mountains yonder," Ty waved his arm toward the Eastern mountains, "are the Mouache and Caputa bands. Both are thought to be friendly, but nothing is certain. Further South are the Tabaguache and the White River, while further North are the Yamparika."

"And do they all speak the same language?" asked Barrett.

"Mostly, but there are always variations brought by neighboring tribes, though all use the universal sign language."

"And do you speak their language?"

"I do," replied Ty without explanation.

Ty had made his camp at the edge of the trees and had started a small fire with the grey branches of a standing snag of pine. When the lieutenant left to join his men, Ty started his supper by pulling some of the coals away from the flames and dropping his harvest of plains vegetables into the smoldering embers and ashes. Yampa root, cattail root and wild onions would supplement his fare of broiled deer steak and coffee. He sat waiting on the log when the Lieutenant came back to observe the mountain man's camp. He looked at the bedroll

103

on the thick grass with a saddle for a pillow, and at the deer steaks suspended above the flames that licked at the droplets of grease, and the green shoots of the baking vegetables, then said to his Scout, "I was going to invite you to join us for dinner but you seem to have your own preparations underway, which by the way, smell wonderful."

"You're welcome to join me, Lieutenant. There's plenty."

"I'm tempted, but I didn't bring my service," he replied, referring to his service ware of utensils.

"You've got your fingers, that's all you need," said Ty with a grin. He reached for one of the willow withes that held a steak and stretched it out to the Lieutenant to take. He pulled on the green stalks in the ashes and brought out a Yampa root, extended it to the man and said, "You'll want to peel off that top layer, but I think you'll like that. That's a Yampa root, has kind of a nutty taste, but good."

The surprised officer from the East took a seat on the log opposite Ty and accepted the offered fare. He bit into the steak, tearing the portion from the rest, and grinned as the juice, a mixture of fat grease and blood, trickled down his chin. He wiped his chin with the back of his hand and grinned at his host, then holding both the willow and the stalk of the Yampa, he peeled off the skin and took a bite of the roasted root. Around the mouthful of meat and root, he mumbled, "That is good," and chewed with delight. When he had a free hand, Ty passed his guest a cattail root and an onion, then continued with his own repast. It was a pleased and filled Lieutenant that bid his host good night to return to his own blankets, in anticipation of an early start on the remainder of their patrol.

Chapter Eighteen

Soak

It was a crisp morning that brought the patrol from their blankets to stand beside the re-kindled fires. Most stood with blankets around their shoulders staring into the flames as they waited for their morning coffee. Behind them the Sangres donned a fresh dusting of Spring snow that gave the granite crags the appearance of an old man in his pajamas with the cape laying loosely atop the tall timber. The morning breeze drifted off the mountains and chilled the troops, none of whom expected to awake to snow, as they stood stomping their feet to bring warmth to their toes.

Ty rode his roan through the camp of troopers and nodded his head with a grin at the shivering soldiers. The lieutenant and first sergeant stood with outstretched hands to their fire and Ty stopped his mount beside them. "Today's route will take us further North along the mountains, but we'll be in greener pastures where the trail follows the creek. You'll find the horses will tire sooner, especially the teams at the wagons, because even though it doesn't look it, we'll be climbing higher in the mountains. If I run into any difficulties you need warnin' about, I'll try to get off three quick shots, comprendé?"

The lieutenant nodded his head in understanding and Ty gigged his horse to start the day's scout.

Just past mid-morning, the big roan tossed his head and let a chest rumbling nicker escape as he pranced a step to the side, giving Ty warning of something ahead. Since he was traveling alone, Ty stayed closer to the tree-line and that elevation above the floor of the valley gave him an excellent view of anything below him. As he scanned the area in the direction of the pointed ears of his horse, he saw two turkey buzzards circling overhead and some movement below. He reached behind the saddle and pulled out the small brass telescope his father lent him and searched the area of concern. Three wolves were arguing over their dinner that was scattered in the grass near the willows that lined the stream. Their focus on their meal had prevented them from seeing the approach of the man and horse while they continued their snarling and snapping at one another. With the scrapping wolves fighting over their dinner, Ty gigged his horse to move along the game trail they were following in the edge of the timber. When they were at the nearest point, Ty took another look with his scope and saw the gut pile that had been left for the wolves and thought, *that means someone else made the kill and left the guts for the scavengers, coulda been whites or Indians and that kill was probably made early this mornin'.* The nervous horse kept watching the wolves as they passed, well back in the trees.

With a brief stop for noon and a rest for his roan, Ty was again on the scout but had dropped down to the valley floor and was now riding through belly deep grass which his roan didn't hesitate to take a mouthful on the move. The day had been a typical Rocky Mountain spring day with the mountain meadows showing their new coat of green and the aspen anxious to display their pale green shoots that contrasted to the white thin barked trunks. The air was fresh with the chill of the previous night's dusting of white, and Ty basked in the beauty around him. He saw movement at the edge of the trees and reined his horse to the side of the thicket of blooming buffalo berry. He sat still and watched as he peered over the scraggly bushes and saw the tentative steps of a cow elk as she stepped from the timber, carefully surveying the field before her. She stepped into the clearing, followed by a calf and two more cows and while he watched the assemblage increased with a spike bull, all pushed by a bigger bull with velvet covered antlers. They began grazing and moving slowly toward the meandering stream. Ty slowly pulled his Henry from the scabbard, swung his foot over the rump of his roan and stepped down. Slowly, he made his way beside the brush and dropped to his knee to take a sight on the group. He debated between one of the younger cows and the spike bull, settled for the first of the younger cows, drew a bead and slowly pulled the trigger. The Henry barked and jumped in his hands, but he was surprised by another shot from off to his right, that sounded like an echo of his kill shot. He watched as the cow stumbled, and dropped to one knee, and fell to her side. The others had spun around and retreated to the timber, all except the spike bull and Ty noticed it had also fallen.

Realizing what he heard was not an echo of his shot, but the report of another rifle, he quickly jacked another round into the chamber and moved back into the brush as he quickly scanned the hillside and field to his right. At the corner of his right eye, he caught movement, swung his head in that direction to see a figure step from behind another cluster of chokecherry and buffalo berry brush. The figure was unmistakable and Ty rose from his cover to greet his friend, Grey Wolf.

"Well, look at you! I thought you'd be a fat and sassy old married man by now, but you're just as skinny as ever!" declared Ty as he walked to meet his friend.

"Well, I'm still workin' on it, white man. Aren't you a little far from home?" answered Wolf as he stretched out his hand to greet Ty.

The friends clasped one another in a firm hug, patting each other on the back and then pulled back to look at each other.

"So, where's your woman, I wanna meet the one that clipped the wings of the great Grey Wolf!"

"What makes you think I have a woman?"

"The grin on your face, of course. I never knew you to hold a smile longer'n a minute or two and you've been smilin' since you pulled that trigger," observed Ty, letting a grin split his face.

"Well, there's a few of us came down to the hot springs yonder, and there's a woman there that has taken a shine to me. You know the pretty ones never could resist a real man like me," he laughed as he shared the news. Ty looked in the direction he indicated and could only see a slight wisp of what apparently was the cloud of steam rising from the hot springs.

"Hot Springs? I didn't know there were any here, I could use a good soak."

Wolf looked at his friend, sniffed the air, and said, "I'd say you could."

Ty slapped his friend on the shoulder and said, "But first I think we need to dress out some elk before the wolves come. I ran onto some a ways back, so no sense takin' any chances."

The friends helped each other and were soon finished with the field dressing of the elk. Wolf helped Ty hang the four quarters of meat from a high branch of a ponderosa at the edge of the timber, and Ty helped Wolf secure the two quarters on his pack horse and one on his mount and volunteered to put the last front quarter behind his saddle and help him back to the hunting party. They left the gut piles in the open, made an arrow of stones in the middle of the trail for the troop to see, and Ty followed Wolf through the grassy field to return to the hot springs.

When Ty was introduced to Walks Far Woman, he could easily understand what was keeping the smile on Wolf's face. She was a very pretty, young lady, proud, and apparently quite taken with Grey Wolf. Ty stayed and visited with the group for a while, but they were anxious to return to their village with the fresh meat and soon departed into the trees East of the valley en route to their village. Ty looked over the hot springs, bent down and tested the water, looked at the sun and said to himself, *Yup, you need a good hot soak, Tyrell Thompsett.* He picketed his horse, shucked his clothes, lay the rifle at water's edge and waded into the aquamarine steaming water.

The troop was starting to make camp when Ty returned to the grassy meadow that was the scene of the elk kill. The First Sergeant was cutting portions of meat from the elk carcass and the Lieutenant, seeing Ty, waved him over.

"Hello Scout!" then turning to motion to the elk carcass continued, "You've made a hit with the men today, they're all excited about that elk you left for us. I made sure the top kick set aside a fair portion for you. I think he said something about a back strap."

"Sounds good to me. I've got another surprise for you, if you're interested."

"Of course, what is it?"

"There's a mineral-hot-springs just over that little rise yonder, and it makes for a real soothing soak for sore muscles and stiff joints, not that you'd have any, of course."

"Here? In the wilderness? I can't believe it, really?" asked the Lieutenant incredulously.

Ty just chuckled and hung his head to hide his laughter and looked back at the man and nodded his head. "It ain't big enough for everybody at once, but if you all kinda spaced out your dips, I think you might enjoy it."

The Lieutenant looked at Ty, thought for just a minute, hollered at the first sergeant and said, "First Sergeant, have the first two squads of first platoon form up on me, immediately!"

The first sergeant was surprised and looked quickly around to see any immediate danger and seeing none, barked orders to the two squads. They scrambled for their mounts, now picketed in the tall grass, and soon formed a double line in front of the Lieutenant. He looked at Ty, grinned, and said "Lead off Scout!"

All the men enjoyed the refreshing soak in the soothing mineral hot water, although a couple grumbled as baths were not a normal part of their routine, but their sore muscles won the argument and they were soon enjoying their dip. The squads switched off duties, one standing watch while the other dipped and they soon were mounted and ready to return for their delayed elk steaks.

The evening hours saw the relay of soaking soldiers and as the sunlight was chased from the valley by the encroaching darkness and the myriad of stars that marked the milky way, the relaxed and relieved troopers filled the valley with their cacophony of snores. Ty lay awake pondering the reunion with Grey Wolf and his happiness with Walks Far Woman. He was glad for his friend but concerned about the shared news of the encroaching white men prospecting in the canyon not too far distant. But, *sufficient unto the day is the evil thereof* and tomorrow would have to take care of itself. Now was a time for rest.

Chapter Nineteen

Gold

The prospectors got an early start. With gold fever in the air, no one bothered with anything but coffee for breakfast while they stood around the dwindling cook fire planning the day. All agreed they would leap-frog their panning until consistent color showed, then they would work the stream in earnest. Dreams of finding the mother lode filled the heads of every man for greed is seldom satisfied with initial findings. When someone is poor, a dollar is wealth, but when that dollar is in hand, visions of bags of dollars become the goal, until greed consumes the dreamer and the whisper of demon riches drives on and on until greed becomes an evil task-master, unsatisfied until it consumes its prey. When Gunther pointed out the creek bank where he brought up the rich pan, the men jumped from their horses, leaving them to wander the tall grass with reins dragging, and Big Joe jumped off the wagon and left the horses standing in their harness. The race was on to the creek and the excited men plunged into the water, dipping pans in the sand and eagerly washing the mud and silt searching for the first glimmer of gold.

Marcus trotted a short distance upstream, saw a ripple of water over some rocks and a bend in the creek, and splashed into the knee-deep ice-cold water to wade to the sand-bar and undercut bank to try his luck. A shout from downstream brought everyone's head up to see Irish pointing to his pan and hollering, "I've got color! It's gold! Gold!" The others froze in place for just a moment, then bent to their work for their own discoveries. The once crystal-clear stream quickly turned to muddy silt and the pans dug in the stream bed. Soon Efe shouted, "Me too!" to be followed by Alex, "I've got some!" The easy finds drove the group of men into a frenzy as they dug a pan, moved to another spot, dipped another and continued until enthusiasm gave way to the realization that what they were doing was actually hard work. The cold water did its work of numbing the toes and fingers of the panners until they had to find dry ground and warm up. Soon the bank was lined with stretched out men gasping for breath and rubbing their fingers to restore circulation.

Big Joe sat up and looked at Gunther still in the stream and Marcus farther upstream. He watched as Marcus waded back to shore, grinning all the while and looking down stream to the men now resting on the bank. Gunther also made his way to the shore, carefully carrying his pan. Marcus came with his pan pushing against his waist and looking at something with his free hand. He looked at the men as he approached and said, "Take a look at this, fellas," holding out his right hand, palm up. Nestled in the middle of his palm was an oblong shining gold nugget about the size of the first digit of his little finger. Curtis Tuffin plucked it from Marcus' palm, hefted it for weight, looked closely at it and handed it to Irish. "That's at least two, maybe three ounces!" said Curtis.

"More'n that, I'd say closer to five, that thing's heavy!" declared Alex, now turning it over between his thumb and index finger.

"Men, I'm thinkin' we need to change our plans," said Marcus, getting the immediate attention of all men. "I know

112

we said we'd leap-frog our pannin' an' work our way upstream, but I think we need to go 'head on an' set up our rockers, and pan out every pocket as we work upstream. This stream is rich with gold that's just beggin' us to take it!"

"I dunno, Spann, I wanna find that mother lode," declared Big Joe.

"Well, I dunno about the mother lode, but I'd sure like to dig out some nuggets like this'n and bigger too!" added Efe.

"Here's what I'm thinkin' fellas. There ain't nobody else around but us, and we can clean out this stream all the way up. And when we find the source of the gold, then we can start some serious minin', but until then, I don't want to pass up certain riches in hopes of possible riches," explained Spann. Several of the men nodded heads and looked at one another, then Gunther spoke up, "Jah, I agree vit Spann. Let's try if for a day or two, an' then decide." Nodding heads and mumbled agreement spurred the men to action. The wagon held the needed tools and the disassembled rockers that would get the men started on their hopefully lucrative day and all of them set-to and began unloading.

"Gunther, how 'bout you head up a crew of say, Irish, Efe and Curtis. I'll take Big Joe, and Alex. We'll start up there where I was pannin' and your crew can clean out this stretch. If you get it cleaned out, then leap-frog above us."

"Jah, Jah, dat's goot," answered Gunther and motioned for his crew to set up the rocker near the bank. Big Joe and Alex carried their gear and followed Spann to the rocky riffle site and began setting up. By noon, both crews had shown good results with the accumulated gold covering the bottom of a pan with Spann's pan holding three small nuggets. While Gunther's pan held about 15 ounces, Spann's with the nuggets probably tipped closer to 20. It was a good day's haul and the day was only half over.

The men were tired and the enthusiasm had been tempered by determination, but all were willing to break for a noon meal. All pitched in to gather firewood, make a fire, and get some

113

venison steaks broiling and coffee perking. Irish worked on a batter of cornmeal and flour and fried up some passable corn cakes to complete the meal. They made short work of the venison and corncake with each man consuming two or three thick slices of the lean meat and a healthy chunk of corncake, washed down with blacker-than-sin coffee. They scattered about, some under the wagon, others on the shady side, and enjoyed a short snooze. With dreams of riches robbing them of a good night's sleep the night before, it didn't take long for the tired prospectors to nod off.

Spann walked around kicking the feet of the men and encouraged them to "Rise and shine men, day's a wastin' and gold's a waitin'."

By the end of the fourth day, the crew had made little progress upstream, but had taken a considerable amount of gold. They split the take each night and every man held their own poke with each one growing in weight. Now they had a semi-permanent camp back away from the stream and tucked in among the trees. As they progressed up the stream, they were careful to hide any evidence of their prospecting by returning the washed rocks and mud into the streambed and clear off any residue from the creek bank. It wasn't perfect, but at least wouldn't draw any undue attention from the rare visitor to the valley.

After an especially profitable day, and a good supper of fresh venison and Irish's improved corncakes, the men broke out the whiskey to have a bit of a celebration. As the whiskey flowed, stories were told, dreams were shared and ideas exchanged. The more Big Joe drank, the more sullen he became and the rest of the men did their best not to rile him, knowing he was too big for any one man to take on in a fight. When several men broke out in laughter at an amusing story from Efe, Big Joe stirred from his stupor and muttered, "We need some wimmin! Where's the wimmin?"

"There ain't no women, Joe. Here, have another drink," said Spann offering the bottle to the big man. Big Joe slapped away the offering mumbling, "Don't wanna drink. Wanna woman! Where they at?" as he tried to stand and fell back, mumbling incoherently and drifting off into his drunken stupor. Alex looked at Curtis and said, "I could use a woman too, maybe we should get us one o' them Injun gals. Ain't them Ute s'posed to be friendly? Mebbe we could find out how friendly?"

"Oh, shut up, you crazy ol' man. You wouldn't know what to do with a woman if you had one!" replied his partner, Curtis.

The only one of the men that was not totally drunk, was Gunther, who suggested, "How 'bout ve all turn in and dream about gold instead of women. It'll be healthier for all of us!"

No one answered Gunther, but all rolled or crawled into their bedrolls and were almost instantly sound asleep. Twice during the night, one of the men staggered away from the camp and the sounds of upchucking carried back to the camp as a reminder that they all had too much to drink.

To The Sangre de Cristo

Chapter Twenty

Visitor

Ty stretched himself awake, bent to stir the coals of his cook fire and standing erect saw a man riding boldly into the camp with but a trace of light coming from the grey morning behind the granite fingers of the mountains. The visitor, seeing Ty's camp showing the only sign of life, walked his mount up the slight rise and reined up a short distance below the smoldering fire. A wide sombrero held his face in shadow, but he pushed it off his head letting it drop behind his back and hang on the throat cord. He leaned forward, rested his forearms on the wide saddle horn that told of the craftsmanship on the Mexican saddle. His short jacket, matching his tapered and snug fitting trousers, was black with silver and white embroidered decorations at the corners and down the arms and legs. The tapaderos of the saddle hid his boots, but Ty was certain the boots accented the outfit. Ty looked at his visitor and said, "Step down if you're friendly."

"Si, si, I am friendly," he spoke as he swung a leg over the rump of his horse and dropped to the ground. "I am also hungry, and could use some coffee. I see you have just awakened, may I get the water for you?" he asked as he motioned to the trickle of water cascading from the mountainside by the camp. Ty nodded to the man and cut several thin slices from the elk back-strap, hung them on willow withes and suspended them over the now flaming cook fire. He pushed a small handful of Yampa root into the coals, sat back and watched as the visitor sat the now full coffee pot on the flat stone beside the flames.

"So, what's a fella like you doin' wanderin' around Indian country all by yourself?"

"Senor, it is not I who is wandering, but you and these men. The land where you sleep is part of the Baca land grant and the reason I am here. I work for the Baca ranch, but there is no one here and it has been sold and re-sold and no one is left here but me. Now, I must leave because there is no one to pay me."

"The general told me about some old Spanish land grants up this way, but we didn't see anything that even looked like a ranch."

"Ah, that is because the only building is a small ranch house that sits back in the trees and back up a wide draw through the timber. If you don't know where eet is, eet is hard to find," explained the visitor. "My name is Luis de la Vega Montoya, but my friends call me Louie," he said as he extended his hand for a greeting. Ty took the offered hand, and as he shook hands with Louie he said, "My name's Tyrell Thompsett, I'm the guide for all these soldier boys." He looked at the sizzling meat, stretched out for one and motioned for Louie to do the same. As they ate, they became acquainted with Ty asking most of the questions.

"So, Louie, did you come up here from down South a ways?"

"Si, I came from Taos Pueblo, my home."

"Taos Pueblo? I heard of Taos, but . . ." started Ty to be interrupted by his visitor.

"Si, most have heard of Taos, it is the town near our Pueblo, but our Pueblo was there long before the town. Taos Pueblo is where my people, the Pueblo, live."

"But your name, it's Mexican, ain't it?"

"Si, si. Mi Padre was Mexican, but mi madre is Pueblo. She is called Blue Spider woman and my Pueblo name is Elk Running, but it is easier to go by Louie."

"Say, do you speak any of the Indian languages around there, you know, Comanche or Apache?"

"Si, si," answered Louie between bites of elk meat and Yampa.

"And you know this area pretty well, don't you?"

"Si, si," he replied and looked at Ty wondering what he was thinking.

"How 'bout taggin' along with us? We're gonna be headin' back to the fort in a day or so, and the general said if I found somebody that might work out as a scout, to put 'em on. How 'bout it?"

"You mean work for the soldiers? Like you?" he asked leaning forward toward Ty, showing his interest.

"That's exactly what I mean. Ya interested?"

"Si, si. That would be good, I think I would make a good scout."

They were finishing their breakfast when the Lieutenant walked up to Ty's camp, noticed the tethered horse and seeing the visitor at the camp fire said, "Morning Scout, I see you have a visitor."

"Mornin' Lieutenant," and turned toward Louie and said, "This is Luis Montoya, our new scout, but he goes by Louie. Louie, this is Lieutenant Barrett, the man in charge of this outfit."

The wiry man stood with outstretched hand and said, "Good to meetchu, senor."

The lieutenant shook his hand, looked at Ty and said, "Is this your doin'?"

119

"You could say that, although he came here kinda surprisin' like early this mornin'. He worked for the Baca ranch," and motioned with a wide sweep of his arm, "the land that we are currently on is part of the Baca ranch. But Luis was fixin' to leave and since he knows the area, I thought he'd make a good scout, so as the general suggested, I hired him."

Louie shook his head, grinning in agreement as he looked from Ty to the Lieutenant. Barrett looked at the new man, turned on his heel and went back to his cook fire to join the first sergeant. Ty turned to Louie and said, "Don't mind him. You answer to me and there's quite a few greenhorns in this bunch, not just the lieutenant." Louie grinned and sat back down for another cup of morning java with his new friend and employer.

When the troop was ready to move out, Ty and Louie were long gone. After getting more first-hand information from Louie, Ty determined to reach the upper end of the valley to the North and hopefully make the bend for the return leg of the patrol.

The noon break saw the pair in the shade of a lone ponderosa overlooking the headwaters of Rock Creek. Their view of the valley stretched to the lesser mountains to the East and the long stretch of the San Luis valley that faded away in the haze in the distant South. The green meadow below them, watered by both Rock Creek and San Luis Creek, hugged the western cape of the Sangre de Cristo's and faded away where Ty calculated lay the Sand Dunes. As they surveyed their scouting domain, Ty noticed movement across the valley near the far tree line. He walked over to retrieve his brass telescope for a better look. He leaned across the saddle and scanned the sage flats and the shadows of the juniper and pinion that dotted the hillside. He waited, and was rewarded with the lumbering forms of buffalo. As he watched, first four, and three more, came from their beds in the cluster of juniper and started their afternoon graze.

As he watched, he spoke to Louie, "Looks like we found our supper."

"What do you see, amigo?" asked the new scout, rising to join Ty.

"Looks like a small herd of buffalo. It's been a while since I've had a good hump roast, how 'bout we work our way along that hillside above 'em and see if we can't bag a couple?"

"Si, si, we can do that. When we get closer, we can come from both sides and get one each. That should feed those troopers for a few days," agreed Louie.

They bided their time working their way around the upper end of the valley, across several small streams that spilled into the San Luis Creek, and higher on the mountain side in the darker timber. As they neared their objective, they tied off their horses and Ty directed Louie to move across the near ravine and work his way through the timber to an outcropping that overlooked the grazing woolies. Ty said, "I'll move down this ravine and should be able to find a spot within view of yours, I'll signal you when I'm ready, and you take the first shot. I'll take mine after yours, comprendé?"

Louie nodded his head in understanding and started across the ravine intent on making the rocks. Ty started down the slope on his side, slipped on some loose rock and slid part way on his rump, kicking up some dust. Unseen by Ty, the buffalo stopped their grazing and looked in his direction, and although buffalo are not as flighty as deer or elk, they were restless, but didn't move away. Moments later, Ty made his way to the ravine edge, peered over to see the buffalo less than thirty yards away staring in his direction. He froze in place, watched the animals and waited until he thought none were looking his way and brought up the big Spencer, chosen because of its bigger slug for the buffalo, and took aim. He could see Louie prone on the rocks awaiting his signal, raised the palm of his hand for the signal, and was rewarded by the boom of his rifle. Without waiting, Ty let loose his missile of death to see the cow buffalo drop straight down as if she had been poleaxed. The rest of the

121

herd jumped in alarm and thundered farther into the sage flats to make their escape. The young bull that was the target of Louie staggered to follow but a second shot from the new scout dropped the bull before he made three more steps.

The pair of scouts met at the carcass of the young bull, that fell not more than thirty feet from the cow, slapped each other on the shoulder and laughed together. Louie said, "Now our work begins, senor."

"You got that right. Ain't much o' nothin' harder'n dressin' out these woolie boogers."

But the men found they worked well together, both experienced and ready to do whatever was necessary. They started with the long cut from gullet to tail, and with one man using one of the horses to pull the two uphill legs back, the other pulled the innards from the carcass, saving the heart and liver. They started skinning the top half, used the horse to first pull the hide back then pull the carcass over to the other side, and skinned the other half. Ty used his steel bladed tomahawk and split the carcass down the back bone, and they lay the halves together on the hide. The tedious work was repeated for the second carcass and by the time they finished, they saw the approaching troop coming down the flats at the edge of the trees.

The top kick, or first sergeant, was the first to spot the two scouts finishing their work on the fresh meat and reined his horse over to inspect the kill. His wide grin told of his satisfaction with the work of the scouts and hollered over his shoulder to the lieutenant, "We're gonna be eatin' good tonight!" which prompted the lieutenant to mount his own inspection. When he reined up to the pile of meat and guts, he saw the two scouts pushed up sleeves revealing bloody arms, and with grinning faces, also bloody. He wasn't sure what the carcasses were until he saw the cast aside heads, recognizing them as buffalo and said, "I've never had buffalo before. Is it as good as elk?"

The first sergeant looked at his lieutenant and at the scouts, shook his head and said, "Lieutenant, you ain't had good eatin' till you've had fresh buffler," and he turned to the scouts and asked, "Ya got any gall to go with that liver, youngun'?"

Ty pointed with his Bowie to the gut pile that lay next to the heart and liver on the edge of the hide and nodded. Top kick quickly dropped from his mount, walked to the liver, cut a slice and dipped it in the gall and sunk his teeth into the raw meat with, "MmmmMmmm, been a long time!"

The Lieutenant watched his top kick with mouth agape and said, "But it's raw!"

"Shore is!" answered the first sergeant, cutting another slice. He turned to Ty and said, "You know younker, when I first saw you, I had my doubts. But not no more, if'n you keep ridin' with us, we're all gonna be so fat an' sassy we won't wanna ever go back to the fort!"

Ty just grinned and finished his butchering, stood up and motioned for Louie to follow, and the two men went to the small trickling stream and washed up. The first sergeant had the wagon pull nearer the carcasses and with the help of several troopers they loaded it up and pulled to a nearby flat that was partially sheltered by a smattering of juniper, cedar and pinion. It wasn't as grassy or protected as the previous camps, but this side of the valley had sparser cover and the tree-line of black timber was farther up the hillside and less accessible.

Once again, the men turned in with full bellies and sore muscles, but the feast dulled the pain and they looked forward to a good night's rest. Ty had just dropped off to sleep when he was awakened by the sounds of distant gunfire. He sat upright and listened, pistol in hand. The rattling of rifle fire bounced around the hills and a low echo could be heard from across the flats. He marked the direction of the shots and was immediately concerned, as it came from the direction where Grey Wolf said the village of the Mouache Ute lay in the Eastern mountains. It was not an extended battle, *maybe a quick raid by another band looking to steal horses,* thought Ty.

He stood, walked to the side of the nearby trees and looking in the direction of the sounds, listened for any more shooting. Hearing none, he started to turn, only to see Louie at his side. The new scout asked, "What do you think it is?"

"That's the direction of a Ute village, maybe it's just another band of Indians on a horse-stealing raid. It didn't last long, so probably nothing to be concerned about," he said as he started back to his bedroll. Louie looked again in the direction of the shooting and followed his friend. "Maybe, maybe," he said, and followed Ty's example and crawled back into his blankets.

Chapter Twenty-One

Raid

"Grey Wolf, Grey Wolf!" shouted Bear Chaser, the brother of Walks Far Woman, as he brought his horse to a sliding stop in front of the wickiup of his family. Grey Wolf was crafting a bow from the dried wood of an Alder that Walks Far Woman had selected and given to the man she had chosen for her mate. Although the two had yet to follow the ceremony of her people, the Mouache Ute, all understood that Walks Far had made her choice and Grey Wolf would soon become a part of their family. When the younger brother of his woman raised such a ruckus with his return from his scout, he attracted the attention of all within earshot and they started drawing near the scene of commotion. He and two of his young friends had been on a scout of the area searching for any game animals. Grey Wolf stood and motioned with his hands for the young man to settle down and asked, "What is it that has my brother so excited this early in the day?"

"Buffalo, Grey Wolf, buffalo! There's a small herd in the flats beyond the creek that talks!" Everyone knew the creek that came from the tall mountain behind their camp and cascaded down the steep mountainside with several small waterfalls as the creek that talks because of the many cascades.

"How many?" asked Grey Wolf, still trying to calm his friend, though unsuccessfully.

He looked around for a comparison and responded, "More than we have lodges in the village, many more!" Wolf scanned the village seeing more than thirty lodges and looked back at the young man, "More than we have lodges?

"Yes, many more!"

At his answer, Wolf looked at the gathering villagers and announced, "We hunt buffalo!"

The men of the village, young and old, shouted for joy and most ran to retrieve their weapons and their favorite buffalo horse. Most of the proven warriors had at least one horse he used mostly for hunting buffalo, as it took a proven mount that would run among the thundering herd of woolies and get close enough for his rider to get a kill shot with a bow or a thrust with his lance. The hunter depended on the sure-footedness of the animal and trusted the horse with his life.

It was a short while later when the men were gathered near the wickiup of Tall Bear, the father of Walks Far Woman, and the leader of the village. He stood before the lodge and surveyed the large group of warriors and showed pride in what he saw. Because of the nearness of the herd and the semi-permanent nature of the camp, he had told his people they would not move the village as they so often had in the past for an extended buffalo hunt. Although most of the men were prepared to hunt, and the women to butcher the kills, there were several of the women and old men that would stay behind with the children and tend the cook-fires and other duties of the village.

It was a joyful and excited band of Mouache that rode from the village for their first hunt of the warm season. Several young men were especially enthused as they looked forward to their first buffalo hunt. Although not all the hopeful would be allowed on the hunt, they would serve their village in other ways, most by assisting in the skinning and butchering of the massive beasts. These young men rode together and bragged about the kills they hoped to make while the women and their pack horses with travois trailed the men and chattered excitedly among themselves.

It was less than an hour of travel that brought the group of hungry hunters to the far side of the Creek that Talks below the high ridge that obscured the herd from view. The advance scouts were hunkered behind a cluster of sage that rode the crest of the ridge. When they saw the rest of the hunters cross the creek, they crabbed their way beneath the crest and trotted back to the group. Tall Bear moved to the front of the crowd and listened to the report of the scouts. He had been the leader of this village for many years and was well respected as a hunter and warrior and as he began to give commands to the hunters, all willingly took his lead and waited his cue to move forward on their hunt.

Just a handful of the men had rifles, most were muzzle loaders, and Tall Bear instructed Grey Wolf to lead them in a wide arc that would take them out in front of the herd. After they were in place, the other two groups would be ready for the first fusillade from the rifles and as the herd turned to flee, they would attack from both sides and take their kills on the run. At the cue of Tall Bear, merely a nod, Grey Wolf led his group of four and started their wide sweep to the front of the herd, following a low swale that hid them from the woolies. Although the eyesight of the buffalo is not as good as most other animals, they do rely on their sense of smell for any warning of danger. Wolf had positioned his men and had barely raised his head for his first look-see, when the suspicious herd bull spotted his movement and tossed his head, throwing a long slobber over his shoulder as he pawed the ground. His actions alarmed the herd and every head rose simultaneously. Wolf signaled his men and allowed them to pick their shots and start the kill. The staccato of the rifle shots rattled and echoed from the mountain behind them, startling the herd to action. It was an amazing sight to see the massive brown mounds that appeared to have spindly legs, drop their shoulders as they turned to flee and with tails waving like flags of alarm, the herd raised a thick cloud of dust and stormed over the sage and grass in their desperate flight for escape. As a large cow wheeled to make her run, Wolf's big Spencer bucked in his hands and the cow dropped to her side. Two others had fallen and a third staggered from its wound but struggled to make its escape. With the other men trying to re-load their muskets, Wolf jacked in another round, cocked the hammer and fired a slug that dropped the wounded animal. Wolf hollered to his companions to "Get mounted, we will give chase!" The men struggled to get their loads in and primed, then mounted up and dug heels to their mount's ribs and took off at a dead run into the choking cloud of dust in pursuit of the herd.

Within moments, they came across a few downed animals with the feathered fletching of arrow shafts protruding from their sides and necks. One was struggling to get up and Wolf dispatched it with a single round from his Spencer. They had slowed to a canter as the dust slowly dispersed and they could see the action before them. The herd had been diminished by the kills, but several men continued the chase and sought additional kills. As Wolf reined up and watched, one hunter's horse stumbled, throwing his rider head over heels to land awkwardly on his side to lay unmoving. The horse limped with a broken leg, trailing its rein and showing its fear with wide eyes and tossing head. Wolf quickly moved beside the horse, dropped to the ground and grabbed the rein to steady the animal. He spoke softly to the brown and white paint, stroked his neck and looked at the contorted and broken leg. He pulled his big Walker Colt from the holster at his belt, cocked the hammer and placed it behind the horse's ear and pulled the trigger. The explosion startled his own horse that tossed his head and backed a couple steps, as the paint horse dropped to its side, dead.

Wolf went to the still unmoving man, knelt at his side and felt his chest for movement and the man's eyelids fluttered as he moaned in pain. A quick glance told Wolf that the downed man had at least a dislocated shoulder and maybe a broken arm. He kept his hand on the man's chest and said, "Stay still, Big Raven, your arm's hurt, maybe broken. I'll get the women to tend to you." The man nodded his understanding and looked at his horse and back at Wolf. "His leg was broke, I had to shoot him." Big Raven's eyes flared and he sucked air, let it out and nodded. It was not easy to lose a proven hunting horse, raised and trained for years and always faithful.

Wolf stood and looked over the wide swath cut by the herd and saw many carcasses and the large group of women leading their packhorses to begin their work of butchering the buffalo and harvesting the meat. Most of the meat would be smoked and much of it would be made into pemmican. Many of the fruit bearing bushes had an early crop and the buffalo berries and chokecherries would be mixed with the smoked meat and tallow to make the nutritious pemmican. But there would be a large feast in the village on this night and all were excited about the great bounty that would give the people sustenance for many days and into the summer.

Dusk whispered its exit beyond the Western Mountains and the first stars of the Southern sky winked at the last of the Mouache as they finished securing the bounty on the travois and started their return to the village. It would be a long night, with their late return, but it was a happy group that started the trek. It was a well-traveled trail and easily seen in the dim light of the rising moon with Tall Bear leading the way. The tired horses and tired men, heads hanging, plodded along the moon-lit trail thinking only of the waiting blankets and a good night's rest.

The sudden staccato of rifle shots from beyond the ridge and from the village startled men and horses alike. Looking at one another, wide eyes reflecting moon-light and fear, they kicked their mounts to a run to try to reach the village before it was too late. War cries were shouted, women wailed, and the clatter of hooves on the hard-packed trail echoed through the trees as the long line of angry and fearful warriors readied themselves for battle with an unknown enemy.

As they neared the village, flames from burning wickiups licked at the black sky and the wails of grief lifted from the shadowy figures that ran between the lodges. Dust rose from the trail that led away from the village, but they must first look to those that had remained in the village. Crying and naked children were running among the lodges, and in the firelight, bodies could be seen sprawled in unnatural positions with others kneeling by the prone figures, pleading for life. It was a macabre scene that filled the eyes and minds of the returning hunters.

Chapter Twenty-Two

Crazed

The big man stomped his way past the small cook-fire, grabbing some meat from the fire with his bare hands and immediately chomping down it without wincing at the hot grease and blood that dribbled into his beard. He continued his tear, spewing his anger at anything that resisted his will, grabbed a shovel and plodded to the stream. His head ached from his excess of the night before and the night before that, and his gut gnawed at him as if a wolverine had taken up residence inside. He started shoveling gravel from the creek bed to a pile beside the rocker, bellowing at the others that were waiting on their steaks to cool and the coffee to perk. They waved their hands at him and turned back to their breakfast as Big Joe grumbled, "If we had us some wimmin, they could tend to the cookin' an' them lazy whelps could be workin' at gettin' us some more gold!"

For several days, he had been resolute in his thinking about having a woman. He thought about going to some settlement and find a hurdy-gurdy girl at one of the dance-halls, but he knew the closest settlement was over a week in any direction. His mind turned to his earlier thoughts about the

Indian village nearby. He didn't know exactly where the village was, but they saw a group of Indians, including several women, that had visited the hot springs and passed by the entrance to their valley with the gold-bearing stream they now worked. They had seen plenty of sign of Indians traveling a trail that followed the far ridge, and he was certain the village was just beyond that large ridge that led up to the far mountain just West of their camp. He thought, *Mebbe we could go to that village and get us a couple them Injun wimmen, have them do our cookin' an' cleanin' an' such. I'd like to have me one o' them young squaws for my own, yessir.*

The rest of the men sitting around the fire looked at the sullen bear of a man that shoveled the gravel and grumbled and Spann said, "He just can't get the idea of havin' some women in camp outta his head. What're we gonna do? Any ideas?" He looked around the circle of men and the only response came from Alex Romero, "Mebbe we need to find him a woman, find us some women! We could use the company. What good's all this gold without some women to spend it on?"

"Have you gone plumb loco, Alex? Look around you, do you see any women just waitin' for an invitation from that big ox?" said Spann as he motioned toward the valley with his arm.

Alex dropped his head and mumbled a "No, I s'pose not."

His partner, Curtis Tuffin, a wiry man with a scruffy beard and dirtier than usual ragged clothes, grinned wide and showed his mostly toothless smile and said, "We could allus get us a couple them Injuns. Ain't there some o' them squaws in that village yonder?" and cackled at his own remark, with his shoulders bouncing with the effort.

Alex looked at his partner and grinned as an expression of recognition and remembrance crossed his face. The two men had been partners for several years and knew one another's proclivities regarding women. They had been driven from more than one town and dance hall because of their treatment of the women, and they nodded their heads to one another as they thought about another opportunity to have their way with a woman. Alex slowly drew his knife from his belt sheath and fingered the blade and cackled. Curtis grinned at his partner and savored their secret.

Their behavior, though brief, had been watched by the others and looks of disgust and alarm painted their faces. Irish and Efe looked at Spann and Efe asked, "How 'bout you Spann, any ideas? If we don't do somethin' Big Joe'll drink ever'thin' we got and tear most ever' thin' else to bits."

Gunther said, "Just leaf him alone, hide the vhiskey and maybe he'll come out of it."

Spann chuckled and said, "You don't know Big Joe. When he gets somethin' set in his mind, he gets more stubborn than a pair of Missouri mules and meaner'n a wounded Grizz. The only women around are those Injun women an' I don't think they're gonna be real excited about just comin' back to camp, not with Big Joe actin' like he is, uhuh."

"Let's just see if ve can vork him out of it, before we do somthin' crazy," suggested Gunther. "Hide da vhisky, before he comes back. He likes his drink vit his lunch."

"Alright, we'll give it a try, but I'm thinkin' it ain't gonna work," replied Spann as he rose from his seat to go to the wagon and their store of whiskey. He took the wooden crate that held the four bottles, walked to the trees to hide the box, and returned to the group at the fire. "There ya go, now let's all get to work and get us some gold. From what we saw yesterday, we're gettin' close to tappin' out this spot, and we might have to move upstream later."

None of the men responded to what they already knew to be true.

When they took their noon break, Big Joe didn't bother with looking for the whiskey and the men thought they had succeeded with their plan, but as Big Joe finished his meal, he reached behind his bedroll and produced a bottle of whiskey, took a deep draught and put the bottle back in his bedroll. He stood and stomped off to his work, without speaking to any of the men. They looked after the man, at one another, and resentfully followed Big Joe to the diggings.

They usually worked until dusk dropped its apron across the creek and they could no longer see to use the rocker. Determined not to let even a few flakes of gold get away, they would stop work as the shadows lengthened. But with Big Joe thrashing and throwing everything that got in his way, they determined to call it a day when late afternoon showed no color in the rockers. They washed out the ripples of the rockers, packed them back to the wagon and joined Gunther, who had been tasked with preparing the evening meal. When Big Joe plodded back into camp, he looked at the strips of venison hanging over the flames, the corn cakes cooking in the frying pan and threw his tin plate down and rumbled, "I'm gonna get me a squaw that knows how to cook sumpin' 'sides that hog slop!" He headed to the tethered horses and hollered back over his shoulder, "Anybody else want a squaw?" Alex and Curtis looked at one another, grinned and jumped up to follow the big man to the horses. The others looked at each other with none of them making a move to join the three squaw hunters, until Efe Tuscanny said, "Maybe I better go along, you know, to keep 'em outta trouble," as he rose and started after the three.

When the four mounted men led their mounts to the wagon, Spann joined them and said, "Well, if your'a goin' you better go armed. I don't think that village'll be too anxious for you to take some of their wimmen folk." He reached into the wagon and brought out four rifles, two Spencers and two Henrys. He handed each man a double handful of ammunition and added, "Don't be bringin' any trouble back to camp. If they're followin' you, head to the timber till you lose 'em. I don't want to lose all the gold we've got over a couple Injun squaws."

The four men started off and Spann reached back into the wagon to get three more Henrys and a couple of boxes of ammunition for the men that stayed behind. He walked back to the campfire, handed out the rifles and ammunition and said, "I'm thinkin' we might oughta be prepared, just in case."

As they expected, the trail led straight to the village, but the men hung back near the top of the ridge in the thick timber to look over the activity of the encampment below. Big Joe was anxious, but cautious as he watched the people in the village. From what they could see, the only ones outside the wickiups were old people and children. He mumbled, "Ain't nuthin' but old men and older squaws, and them chillun'," as he watched several children running among the lodges. Alex said, "Ain't none o' them ol' ones worth takin'!"

Curtis said, "Wait a minute, lookee yonder," as he pointed to the edge of the village by the stream. Three young women, probably in their teens, were busy thrashing clothes against the stones in the water, rubbing them with yucca root for suds, then scrubbing them against the stones, all the while chattering among themselves. The other men grinned at Curtis' discovery and Big Joe said, "Yeah, that's what we want. Alex, you an' Curtis come at 'em from round yonder," motioning toward the far side of the stream, "An me'n Efe'll just ride straight on into the camp. We'll give you time to get there, but don't do nothin' till we cause a ruckus o'er here."

Big Joe and Efe rested their rifles, cocked and ready, across their thighs behind the pommel of their saddles and walked their horses straight into the village. When the children saw the men coming, they ran to the old men and shouting and pointing sounded the alarm. The old women pulled back into the wickiups, dropping the blankets over the openings, and the men rode to the stream, where Alex and Curtis held the three women huddled together between their horses under the barrels of their rifles. Joe barked, "Get 'em on your saddles, you sit behind 'em and hold onto 'em." He jumped down from his saddle and grabbed his choice from the trio and threw her belly down over his saddle and stepped up behind her. Efe was the only one without a woman and Joe growled at him to lead the way back through the village.

They wheeled their mounts and kicked them up to a trot and started back through the village, that now appeared abandoned. Suddenly a blanket was pushed aside, an old man stepped out with a fully drawn bow and let loose an arrow that buried itself to the feathers in the chest of Efe. The impaled man grabbed at his chest and slumped forward, grabbing the mane of his horse to stay aboard. The sudden attack inflamed the already pig-headed Joe who spurred his horse forward. The animal leaped at the dig and knocked over the old man and as the Indian fell beneath the horse, one hoof caved in his chest. A scream from the entry further enraged the big man and he fired at the source of the scream to see the woman fall across the body of her man. Others pushed aside their door covers and another arrow sailed through the air, narrowly missing the cheek of Big Joe. He reined his mount around and jumped down to grab a firebrand and ran to the side of the nearest wickiup and torched it. He remounted his horse, holding the torch and went from lodge to lodge, spreading the flames. The woman on the saddle before him screamed and kicked until he chopped at the back of her head with the edge of his hand and knocked her unconscious.

The flaming wickiups emptied and people were running in all directions, Joe saw two small children running, hand in hand, and spurred his horse to trod them underfoot. He reined around in time to see Alex shoot a woman that was running away, dragging a child and saw her drop on her face. Curtis fired and another man, about to loose an arrow, fell into the side of a burning wickiup. Alex shouted to Big Joe, "We better get outta here! There's bound to be some others somewhere, an' they'll hear them shots!"

Joe answered, "Yeah!" and turned to fire at another old man, hitting him in the leg and causing him to fall backwards. An old woman rushed to the side of the wounded man and fell to her knees beside him only to have Joe shoot her in the side of the head, knocking her across her man's struggling body. Screams were filling the air as others tried to flee. Children chased after the old women that tottered away from the flames to escape from the view of the invaders. The smoke and the coming darkness added to the confusion and the attackers, now together, looked to Big Joe for orders. "Alright, let's get outta here!" He gigged his horse and led the way from the village.

To The Sangre de Cristo

Chapter Twenty-Three

Discovery

Ty let his gaze linger on the painted sky that rested on the jagged fingers of the Sangre de Cristo to his left. The wispy clouds of night had been colored with the broad brush of sunrise and the entire Eastern sky looked like a broad blanket of muted orange that had just been lifted from the treasure of the mountains. He was riding alongside Lieutenant Barrett as they discussed the route for the day that would take them around the broad finger of foothills and back against the green timbered mountains that framed the Western edge of the valley. The days of travel had been enlightening to the lieutenant from the East. His homeland was thick with the leafy hardwoods and tangled undergrowth with incessant rains throughout the summer months. This wide expanse of sage and cactus covered flats surrounded by snow-capped mountains and the dry climate was radically different than the woods of his youth.

The animals, the majestic elk, big eared mule deer, antelope and the bear, black and grizzly, were an education of their own. But he was also learning the people of the West were men of backbone and character, rugged individualists determined to conquer the wilderness. And the Indians, the few he had met or been around, were difficult to understand, but the white man's response to the red man was as varied as their experiences and he realized he would have to make his own judgments and acquaintances. He continually quizzed Ty on his knowledge of the different tribes that he had first-hand experience with and knew their language. But there were other tribes to the South, the Jicarilla and the Comanche, that he must learn about. But Ty was impressed with the lieutenant's eagerness to learn and he hoped the rookie lieutenant would willingly gain his own knowledge and not be influenced by the hatred or prejudices of others.

"Well, Scout, so far we've seen very little of the Ute people. Are they staying hidden because they're afraid of the cavalry?" asked the curious lieutenant.

Ty chuckled and responded, "Most Indians have little fear like the white man. You see, lieutenant, we know fear because we're afraid of death and what might bring that death or terrible injury. When an Indian thinks of battle, they see it as a place to gain honors. If they are injured, their only fear is that they failed to show courage. And if they die, they look forward to walking with their fathers in a place that has nothing but good to look forward to and to dwell forever."

"Kind of like when a Christian thinks about Heaven?"

"Yes, but I have found the Indian really believes in their type of Heaven and the white man, though he says he believes, doesn't live or fight like he really believes. You see, I think if a man truly believes that he has a home in Heaven, it will change the way he lives here on earth."

Their conversation was interrupted when the first sergeant said, "Lieutenant! There's a man back there that's trying to catch up with us, he looks injured," as he pointed to the rear of the column. A man, slumped on the neck of his horse, bounced with the rough gait of his animal and waved his hand as he tried to holler for their attention. Ty and Barrett reined their mounts around as the lieutenant raised his hand to stop the column. The two men, followed by the first sergeant, rode back along the column to intercept the struggling man as he neared.

The man, Ira O'Callaghan, Irish, struggled to sit up and as he lifted from the neck of his horse, revealed the fletching of an arrow that fluttered with the movement as it protruded from his chest, and caught the attention of the lieutenant. "My word, man, you've got an arrow in you! What happened?"

Irish slumped back to the neck of his horse and slipped off the saddle to fall on his side on the ground. Ty, Barrett and the first sergeant quickly stepped down and Barrett knelt at the side of the wounded man. "What happened? Tell me!" He turned to the first sergeant and ordered, "Get the medic up here!" Irish struggled to talk and muttered, "Injuns, it was . . . Injuns. Hit us early . . . killed all . . .up Kerber . . ." his breath left him with a long sigh and he fell limp in the lieutenant's arms, eyes staring sightlessly.

The lieutenant lowered Irish to the ground, and pulling his arm from beneath the dead man, rose, looked at the blood on his hands and up at Ty with a question on his face. Ty said, "I'll back track him and see what I find. I'll leave sign so you'll know." The lieutenant nodded wordlessly and watched Ty mount up and with a signal to Louie, the two rode along the tracks of Irish to find the scene of whatever battle took place. Ty looked at Louie and said, "I guess that rifle fire we heard last night and early this morning wasn't a bunch of young bucks on a horse stealin' raid, like I thought."

"No, no, I think this is worse than stealing horses," agreed Louie.

They rode in silence, keeping vigilant of everything around them, although the tracks were following the same trail the troopers traveled and was well away from any cover that might shield an attack. The wide draw that cradled Kerber creek was almost a mile across and lay between the foothills covered with juniper and pinion and many rock formations. As the duo rounded the rocky knob, Ty reined up, stood in his stirrups to survey the terrain before them. He dropped back into the saddle and kneed his horse forward. A couple of miles into the wide draw, a shallow ravine joined the creek and a knob of a hill pushed into the narrow valley. As they came up out of the ravine, Ty saw what he thought might be the remains of a burnt wagon on the opposite side of the creek and back near the tree line. He pointed it out to Louie and said, "Look sharp, they could still be around," as he stood in his stirrups and scanned the creek bottom.

Moments later, the two men, now on foot and leading their horses, walked the scene of the battle. The carcasses of mules lay at the edge of the trees, and the bodies of the men were scattered. Two had been tied to the wheels before the wagon was set afire and their burnt bodies were recognizable only by their outstretched legs. Ty didn't know their names, but Spann and Gunther lay behind the rocks that had circled their camp fire. Apparently, this had been their cover against the attack, but now their bodies, stripped and mutilated showed little resemblance to what they once were. Those against the wagon wheels were Big Joe and Alex, and the body of Curtis lay nearby. The previously wounded Efe had apparently tried to run away and was caught. The broken shafts of several arrows remained in the torso of his body. All had been stripped, scalped and mutilated. Whatever had been in the wagon had been taken and unknown to Ty, their horde of gold lay buried nearby, never to be found.

"Whoooeee, those Ute musta really been mad at these gringos!" said Louie, shaking his head as he looked around the site.

"Why do you say that?" asked Ty, thinking he already knew the answer.

"When they tie them up like that, and set the fire, they want them to suffer. They must have done something bad to these Indians to be treated that way. These others, not so much," as he waved his hand at the scattered bodies.

"Yeah, well, we better get back to the troop and let the lieutenant know. I'm a little concerned about what that rookie might do," cautioned Ty as he started to mount up. Louie nodded his head and climbed aboard his mount to follow Ty. As they rode away from the scene, Ty said, "Don't look or do anything, but we were watched from the trees back there."

"Si, si, I saw them too. How many do you think were there?"

"I spotted at least three, maybe more, but I think they just wanted to see what we would do. Don't say anything to the lieutenant, but keep your eyes open. I'm sure we'll be comin' back this way," cautioned Ty.

They met at the mouth of the draw and Ty gave the lieutenant a report of what they found. "And lieutenant, you need to be prepared, what you're gonna see up there ain't purty." But nothing he said could have prepared the green horn easterner for the carnage of the scene. The stench of burning flesh hung heavy on the hillside of blood and death. The bloody and mutilated bodies caused the lieutenant and the toughened first sergeant to cover their noses and mouths with their kerchiefs as they stumbled among the corpses. Anger filled the lieutenant and he thought only about retaliation when he said, "What kind of animals could do this? These are white men and those animals desecrated their bodies!" He stomped back to the men assembled at the bottom of the hill, followed closely by the first sergeant. He turned and started to order the first sergeant to action, but Ty stepped forward and said, "Lieutenant, maybe it'd be a good idea if we scout out the trail toward the Indian camp. When we were here earlier, we were watched by several Indians back in the trees yonder, and they know we're here. If we storm off with some sort of vengeance in mind, we might run into trouble."

"He's right about that, lieutenant. This is their country and they know ever rock and tree an' we don't, so it would be good to scout 'em out. Maybe he could even find out what brought this on, cuz these Injuns were s'posed to be friendly,

143

an if this is friendly, we're in trouble," drawled the first sergeant.

The lieutenant looked at his first sergeant and replied, "We can't let them get away with this! Our job is to make this valley safe for settlers and others and this is not what I call safe!"

Ty stepped forward and said, "You're right, Lieutenant, but we need to get all the facts before we jump in the lake that might end up bein' bloody water, don't you think?"

Barrett looked at his scout, reading his expression of concern, and thought about what had been said, then spoke, "Alright, you and the Mex go scout things out and report back. I'll get the men busy with a burial detail and we'll wait for your return."

As Ty mounted up he said, "And Louie is more Pueblo Indian than Mex," and the two reined their mounts to the trail that led over the near ridge toward the deeper timber. Unseen but felt, three of the Mouache warriors trailed behind and hung back in the black timber, out of sight. Within less than two hours, Ty and Louie sat silently on their mounts in the tall pines as they surveyed the village below. They could hear the keening wails of women rise from near the wickiups and Ty knew they were grieving the loss of a family member. He was determined to know what had transpired the previous night that brought so much death and grief.

Chapter Twenty-Four

Report

"Well, the only way we're gonna find out anything is to just go on down there," said Ty as he looked at his partner. Louie looked at the chief scout and said, "Are you sure you want to do that? I think they might still be in a killing mood."

"Well, you can come along and protect me," suggested Ty with a wide grin.

"Who's going to protect me?" asked Louie.

"Since those fellas," motioning back to the trees and the warriors that followed, "have been followin' us anyway, they know we're here so we might as well go on in, 'fore they decide to take us in strapped over our saddles," said Ty as he gigged his horse back to the trail.

As they approached the village, several warriors lined the way with arrows nocked and rifles lifted. Ty and Louie kept their empty hands raised and looked around at the many burned wickiups and heard the wails of the grieving. Ty greeted them in the Ute language then said, "I want to speak to your war leader, your chief."

A voice came from beside a wickiup, "What makes you think he'd want to speak to you, white man?" Ty turned to see the grinning face of Grey Wolf and he dropped his hands as he turned in the saddle, started to get down and was stopped by the uplifted palm of his friend. "You better sit still before one of these Mouache use you for target practice." Ty sat back and looked around at the gathering crowd and noticed a commotion near a wickiup before them. A tall and rather imposing figure of a man was followed by several others as he walked toward the visitors.

Tall Bear stepped before the horses of Ty and Louie and looked at the men with a stoic expression on his face. Grey Wolf stepped nearer and said, "Tall Bear, this is my brother, Tyrell Thompsett, he has come in peace to talk with us," then looking at Ty said, "My brother, this is the leader of the village, Tall Bear."

"Were you with the men that dig for gold?" asked Tall Bear.

"No, but I am with the Cavalry from Fort Garland and General Kit Carson," explained Ty. He saw the expression of Tall Bear change slightly at the mention of the name of Carson and he continued, "I am here to understand what happened between your people and those that are now dead."

Tall Bear motioned for them to dismount and follow him to his lodge. Ty and Louie quickly dropped to the ground and looked at Grey Wolf as he motioned for a young man to take the horses. Wolf walked beside Ty as they followed Tall Bear to the lodge and entered before him. They were seated around a central fire pit and Tall Bear indicated for Ty to begin. "All I know is one of the men caught up with the troop and said Indians had killed them. When we went to their camp site we found the rest of the men, mutilated and burnt. Now, last night early I heard rifle fire and then early this morning, more. That's all we know. But I know if the lieutenant isn't satisfied with an explanation, he's gonna come stormin' in here bent on revenge and it won't be pretty."

Tall Bear, Big Raven, Grey Wolf and others looked at the scout and at one another before Tall Bear began, "Our people, the warriors and most of the women, left yesterday for a buffalo hunt. Before we returned, those men had come into the village, taken three of our young women and when our old men tried to stop them, they began killing. Two of our elders, three of the wise women, and three children were killed and many of the lodges burned. Our warriors went to their camp and brought justice to these killers of old men and women and children."

"What happed to the captives?" asked Ty.

"One was beaten and used badly before they cut her up and killed her. The others fought back and were beaten before they were taken back by our warriors," explained Grey Wolf.

"Did you know these women, Wolf?" asked Ty of his friend.

"The one that died, was the sister of Walks Far Woman and the daughter of Tall Bear," explained Wolf, nodding to the chief.

Ty looked at the chief and said, "My heart grieves with you for the loss of your daughter. You have done what I would have as well. I'm not sure the lieutenant will see it that way, but I'll try to explain it to him. Would you be willing to talk with him if I bring him back with me?"

Tall Bear looked to Grey Wolf and as Wolf nodded, he turned back to Ty and said, "I will speak with this man."

"Good, good. We will go and bring him back with us. I think it will be good to talk instead of fight," said Ty. The chief nodded and started to rise, causing all the others to rise as well. The chief motioned for Ty to go to the doorway and the others followed the scout out into the clearing before the lodge. As Ty mounted up, Grey Wolf stood at his side and Ty bent down to speak with him quietly in English, "This lieutenant is a greenhorn from back East and he's never been close to an Indian, so you might need to prepare the chief for this meeting." Wolf nodded in understanding and bid his friend good-bye.

It was nearing noon when Ty and Louie rode off the ridge to rejoin the troops, now lounging near the trees and partaking of the rations of left over buffalo meat and corn dodgers. The lieutenant stood as Ty approached and greeted him with, "Finally! I thought those Indians might have done you in too."

Ty grinned at his assumption and began his report with, "As I suspected, lieutenant, this," and motioned across the hillside to indicate the battle, "was the result of some poor choices on the part of the prospectors."

"Poor choices? You better explain that a little better, scout."

"These fellas decided they needed some women and last night they raided the Indian village and took three women captives. They also killed several old men, women and children. And after they got their women here, they used them, killed one and beat the others. When the villagers came for their women, they fought it out and lost."

"So, the Indians just took the law in their own hands and hunted them down like animals and butchered them?" asked an incredulous Barrett.

"What law? Lieutenant, there's no law in this land. It's not like they could go down to the corner and get some constable to go arrest them. And even if they could, then what? There's no courts. That's the way it is in the West, lieutenant. Men have to work together and do what's right. When a wrong is done, it's punished, and life goes on, hopefully for the better. Indians have never done anything but handle their own problems like they've had to do for centuries before you and the cavalry showed up." As Ty spoke, he paced back and forth, with his confused mount having his head pulled to and fro as Ty slapped the reins against his palm to emphasize his point.

"But we can't let them get away with the slaughter of these men!" said the exasperated lieutenant. "Besides, how do we know they're telling the truth? I've heard some say you can't trust the Indians."

148

"Lieutenant, how 'bout you comin' with me and we'll go back to that village. You can see the evidence of what happened. And when you hear the women grieving for the children these men rode their horses over, and for the elders of their village, then maybe you'll see things a little differently. Will you do that? Come with me?" pleaded Ty, anxious for a peaceful resolution.

Lieutenant Barrett looked at Ty, then at his first sergeant, and back at Ty. He dropped his gaze and turned away to look at the graves at the edge of the trees and the other signs of battle. Then shaking his head, he said, "I'm not sure what would be the best thing to do. How 'bout if we just take the whole troop there, just in case they want to fight it out or something?"

"If you take the whole troop, they'll know about it long before we get there and they'll be long gone, or laying in ambush to wipe us out. Where their village is, they will have all the advantage and when we ride into the location of the village, we'll have about that," and he snapped his fingers for effect, "long to live. No lieutenant, it's you and me or . . ." and he let the thought linger while the rookie considered his options.

Barrett nodded his head, motioned for a trooper to bring his horse and when he mounted, he said to Ty, "I hope you know if I don't make it back from this patrol, my wife is gonna be real mad at you." Ty grinned at the more relaxed mood of the leader of the troop and said, "And if neither of us make it, who's she gonna be mad at?"

"Oh, she'll find somebody. Maybe the general or someone, that's just the way she is," explained the greenhorn as the two started up the trail.

To The Sangre de Cristo

Chapter Twenty-Five

Truce

Lieutenant Barrett let his eyes rove around the circle of men seated at the fire amid the common area for the village. These were the leaders of this village and their most notable warriors. Directly across the circle sat Tall Bear, their chief and recognized leader of this band of the Mouache. Ty had given Barrett a summary of the structure of the Ute's, specifically the Mouache and the Caputa that lived in this area, and he understood the different villages had their own leadership, but the Mouache tribe recognized a council of leaders from the different villages. Although seldom was an individual given the right to lead the entire tribe, there were occasions when they chose a singular dominant leader or chief.

Tall Bear had Grey Wolf give an explanation of the attack and the resulting punitive raid in English so the cavalry leader would understand. When Wolf finished, he asked the lieutenant, "Do you understand why our people had to go after the murderers of our old men and children?"

"Yes, I believe I do. I understand why you had to recover the captives, but the murder and mutilation of the men I don't understand. What you've done is start a cycle of retribution that could take many lives before it is done. We are to make this country safe for any and all white men, settlers, ranchers, miners, all of them. If your people continue with this mayhem, where will it end? This mutilation, it's barbaric and disgusting!" As he spoke, his voice raised and he became more agitated and angry, his frustration pushing him almost beyond control. Ty reached over and touched his arm to try to settle the man down, but he yanked his arm away and turned on Ty with, "No, I will not tolerate it!"

His anger caused a ripple of uneasiness and concern to spread around the circle and the faces of the Ute mirrored his anger and Ty was fearful of both the lieutenant's actions and the possible response from the Mouache. Grey Wolf, seeing the tensions rise, stood and looked at the cavalry leader and started, "Perhaps if I explain," he began and with sign directing Ty to translate for the Ute, Ty nodded and Grey Wolf continued, "Our people have a simple way of keeping the scales balanced, when one does wrong, he is punished with the same deed that he has done. In this case, those men murdered many of our people, so they had to die. But what you seem to be troubled by is what you call mutilation. I'll explain. Our people have a strong belief in the future life on the other side," he motioned with his hand toward the sky to indicate the afterlife, "and that when we cross over, we can expect all of what we do here, only better. We will be able to love and mate, hunt and ride, and all other things of pleasure. But to do that, we must leave this world with what we need. That's why you see our 'burials' as you call them, with weapons, possessions of pride, something of our loved ones, even our favorite horse. But for an enemy, especially those that have done great evil, we want to deprive them of the ability to enjoy the afterlife. That's why we take scalps, not just to show off our bravery and keep a trophy, but the way the hair of our people is worn often shows the tribe, but is also where we wear our 'honors', eagle feathers earned in battle and other feats, and the war bonnets of our leaders that show earned honors of great bravery. That honor is deprived when a scalp is taken. Also, when other things are done, eyes cut out, genitals taken, fingers or hands removed, all are done to deprive the evil one of pleasure and honor in the afterlife." He paused as he watched the reaction

152

of the lieutenant and summarized, "So you see, lieutenant, it is what you might call a 'spiritual' issue regarding our strongly held beliefs of right and wrong, even into the next world."

Wolf sat down and the other Ute nodded their heads and mumbled their agreement. The lieutenant looked to the ground, up at Wolf and to Ty and said, "I think I understand. So, what you're saying is this was just an act of justice on those that had done your people wrong, and that it is done, no additional attacks or anything like that will be coming?"

Wolf translated for the other warriors and Tall Bear stood to speak. "We have done that which our people have always done, when evil is done to our people, we must repay that evil so there will be no more." As he spoke, he also used sign and when he finished, his sweeping gesture was like a profound statement that ended the explanation. But he was interrupted and startled by a commotion at the edge of their camp, and he looked at the lieutenant as if he expected betrayal and an attack by the cavalry. But seeing nothing but curiosity on the face of the cavalryman, Tall Bear motioned to his other leaders and they rose to see the source of commotion.

A group of riders, Ute, were entering the camp, but the reaction of the villagers was one of curiosity rather than fear as they watched the visitors ride into the village. They were led by a broad chested stern figure, young yet visibly dominant, with long braids that fell down his chest. He held his head high and slightly back causing him to look down on anyone around him. The villagers spoke to one another and began trailing after the group of visitors. When their leader reined his horse to a stop before Tall Bear, both men looked at one another and the visitor raised his hand, palm forward and greeted the village leader, then introduced himself, "I am Ouray, chief of the Uncompahgre and Tabeguache." Tall Bear answered, "And I am Tall Bear, chief of the Mouache, you are welcome. Join us," he said, motioning to the council fire where blankets were spread around the circle.

Ouray and his followers slipped from their mounts, handing the leads to one of their younger men who led them from the circle to the edge of the village where other horses were grazing. Following the others to the council fire, Ouray was given a place of honor to the right of Tall Bear and was seated. It was then he saw the uniformed lieutenant and the scout beside him. His expression gave only a slight indication of his surprise at seeing white men here but he turned to Tall Bear to await an explanation. Tall Bear motioned to the two and said, "This is lieutenant Barrett and Tyrell Thompsett from the Fort of Kit Carson, Fort Garland," he motioned to the two and continued, "Lieutenant, Thompsett, this is Ouray, chief of the Tabeguache Ute."

As Ty translated for the lieutenant, Ouray watched with interest as this white man spoke their language. Ty spoke directly to Ouray and said, "We are honored to meet the chief of the Tabaguache."

"I have come to visit with the Mouache, what I have to say does not concern you," said Ouray by way of dismissal. Ty nodded and explained to the lieutenant they were being dismissed and started to rise. Before they left the circle, Ouray spoke to Ty, "You are from the Fort and you know this Carson?"

"Yes, I know him."

"I also know him and wish to speak with him. Tell him we will visit soon, there is much to talk about," directed Ouray.

"Do you wish to speak of peace?" asked the lieutenant.

"There is a treaty in place, the Conejos treaty, but it must be fixed," proclaimed the chief.

Ty nodded to the chief, and with a motion toward the lieutenant, turned to leave. The lieutenant looked at Grey Wolf and said, "Let this be the end then." Wolf nodded and turned his attention back to the council as Ty and the cavalryman left the circle, surprised to see a young man waiting with their

154

horses. They mounted up and left the village with no attention given to their departure.

When the trail was wide enough for the two men to ride abreast, the lieutenant said, "Interesting, interesting. I've learned a lot today, but I still have a hard time accepting the mutilation of corpses like they did, it's just barbaric."

"But you see lieutenant, these people have lived this way and held these beliefs since long before any white men came to these mountains. Even before there was a white man step on those Eastern shores of this land, these people and others like them had established their way of life that served them well, until we interfered."

"Yeah, but, it's just so different," started Barrett to be interrupted by Ty with, "We don't have to agree with them, nor do we have to change them. But it would serve us well to try to understand them. But what happens is some do-gooder politician from the city that has never met a real Indian, thinks we need to push 'em aside, or put 'em under, just so more white men can come and take their land and try to make the rest of 'em into farmers an' such. I think we need to just leave 'em be an' quit takin' their land. Why this whole San Luis valley belonged to them and everything was fine till ol' Coronado came along lookin' for them Seven Cities of Gold, and started tryin' to make good little converts out of 'em. So, it's been goin' on now for nigh onto three hundred years," spat Ty with disgust. The lieutenant looked at his scout, shook his head in surprise at the revelation of his historical knowledge, and followed his lead to return to the troop.

To The Sangre de Cristo

Chapter Twenty-Six

Return

The cluster of adobe buildings was a welcome sight to a very tired Tyrell and Louie. The last week of scouting and hunting for the patrol had been hot and dusty and trying on their patience with the stumbling greenhorns that made up the cavalry patrol. Following the contour of the eastern mountains that framed the valley, they traveled South until striking the Rio Grande River. The cottonwood lined banks were a refreshing sight to the dust choked troopers and the patrol followed the Rio Grande until reaching the Sangre de Cristo river which led them back to the fort. Seldom did Ty enter a conversation with the lieutenant that the rookie from the East didn't complain and grumble about the way the Utes reacted to the attack on their village. The lieutenant struggled with a culture that was so dramatically different from the civilized gentry of the East, and would usually end any conversation with a comment about his desire to return to civilization. Ty and Louie did their best to avoid the cavalry leader and willingly rode out on their hunts for an escape. Now they looked forward to sleeping in their bunks and eating at a table, but that was the height of their desire for any civilization.

No longer needed in their role as scout, Ty had Louie accompany him to the commandant's office to meet General Carson. Kit was pleased to see the returning troop and was anxious to talk with Ty to get a report of their patrol. The official report would be forthcoming from the lieutenant, but he was more concerned about the first-hand observations from the scout. When Ty and Louie entered the General's office, he greeted them both with a friendly handshake, directed them to be seated and as Ty started with, "General ..." he was interrupted by the uplifted hand of Carson as he said, "Ty, call me Kit. This general stuff is fine if you're in uniform, but between us scouts, it's Kit. Continue," he instructed.

"O.K. Gen . . .uh, Kit, first let me introduce you to our newest scout, Luis de la Vega Montoya, or Louie. He was a part of the Baca Ranch up North, but he's from Taos Pueblo and he's half Pueblo and speaks Spanish, Apache, and Comanche." Louie stood and nodded his head as he stretched his hand out for an introductory handshake. The General accepted his hand without rising and motioned for him to be seated.

"Good, good, that's real good, Ty. I'm sure Louie is going to make an excellent scout. Now, about your patrol," asked the General.

"It was a good patrol, kind of an educational time for a lot of those greenhorns, but a good one. The only excitement was a bit of a run-in with the Mouache Ute, but even that was a good education for the lieutenant."

"Well, would you give the lieutenant a passing grade for this education?" asked Kit.

Ty nodded his head and grinned, "Yeah, I would. But he's still not ready to graduate, if you know what I mean?"

Kit grinned at his explanation, nodded his head and said, "I think Barrett could make a good officer if he could just cut the cord that ties him to the way of life back east. But, I think he won't last without getting his wish and going back to the civilization that spawned him. Too bad. Now, tell me about the Utes!" he ordered.

Ty spoke while Louie fidgeted and the general leaned forward to hear the tale. As Ty concluded, he added, "And Ouray says he's gonna come visit with you."

"Ouray? He's not Mouache, he's Uncompahgre or Tabeguache. So, he's a chief now. Well, that could be a good thing. How soon's he comin'?" asked Carson.

"He didn't really say, but I think he's gettin' some of the other leaders together before they make their visit. He was visitin' with the Mouache and 'peared to me he was goin' to meet with some others."

"Well, good, good. We'll just have to wait 'til he comes, then. In the meantime, we've got some trouble brewin' down south we might have to take care of, seems some mustered out confederates made off with some British Enfields and are comin' this way. Not sure what they've got in mind, but it can't be good. But, enough about that. We'll talk more tomorrow, Ty. You and your new scout probably wanna get a good meal under your belts and a few hours in your bunks!"

"You're right about that, Gen . . .uh, Kit. I'll see you in the mornin'," shared Ty as he rose to leave, motioning Louie to follow. The two men picked up their gear left piled outside the General's office and started for their quarters. They were anxious to stow their gear and hot foot it back to the chow hall for something besides camp-fire seared venison. They were especially pleased to find the cook had prepared some fresh beef-steaks, from the Trinchera ranch, and all the fixings for a welcome for the returning patrol.

Ty and Louie leaned their ladder back chairs against the adobe walls of the BOQ, Bachelor's Officer Quarters, where they had adjoining quarters. The long day was heralded with a brilliant colored sunset that cast an orange glow on the West facing buildings and the bugler sounded Taps as the flag was lowered from the tall mast in the center of the parade ground. It was a pleasant end to a long patrol and as Ty let his reminiscences take him away, he was suddenly brought back by the voice of Mrs. Barrett, "Good evening, Mr. Thompsett," she spoke as she stood with her arm through the crook of her husband's arm and looked at the lounging scouts, "I just wanted to thank you for bringing my David back, safe and sound."

"You're entirely welcome," began Ty as he stood to speak to the visitors, "but I assure you, I had very little to do with his safe return. You have a very capable man at your side, m'am."

The lieutenant let a smile begin, caught himself, and looked to his wife, "Dear, we should continue our walk and let the scouts enjoy their solitude."

She looked at her husband, smiled and looked at Ty as she said, "Well, thank you anyway, Mr. Thompsett, and who is your friend?"

"I'm sorry m'am, allow me. This is Luis de la Vega Montoya, or Louie for short. He's our newest scout." Louie, now standing, gave a bit of a bow and said, "Very pleased to make your acquaintance, m'am."

"Why, thank you Mr. Montoya," said Elizabeth and turning to her husband, she said, "Let us continue, David."

The two scouts watched them walk away to make their customary stroll around the compound, a route they would follow for at least two rounds before turning in for the evening. As they moved away, Louie looked at Ty and said, "So, she's why he wants to go back to civilization?" Ty looked at his friend, grinned, and replied, "Yup." They sat back down and after a short while of idle chit-chat and with the sun dropping below the horizon, they turned in for their long-anticipated rest on a real bed instead of a rocky hillside.

After a refreshing breakfast of eggs and bacon, biscuits and gravy, shredded potatoes, and piping hot coffee, Ty strolled to the General's office for his agreed upon meeting. He was directed to the commandant's quarters and was warmly received by the general's aide, Lieutenant Calloway and ushered into the general's office that he kept at the front of his quarters. As he stepped into the hallway, he was surprised to hear the laughter of children but soon realized the general had the privilege of the company of his family. Five children, ranging in age from three to fifteen, had accompanied Carson and his wife, Josefa, to Ft. Garland and she had made a comfortable home out of the commandant's quarters where the children now frolicked freely, chasing one another from room to room.

Ty waited by the window that over looked the compound with a southerly exposure. The blue sky of the Colorado morning gave Ty a melancholy mood as he thought of his own Elizabeth and the child they would have enjoyed, had they lived. They had often talked about their plans for a large family and a home of their own, but now, the voices of children playing brought a touch of sadness to the young man. His mood was interrupted with the entrance of Carson with a, "Morning Ty, morning! It's sure a fine day out there, isn't it?"

Ty turned from the window and took the offered chair in front of the General's desk and replied, "Just another fine day, General, like so many we enjoy in this beautiful country."

"Yes indeed. We should enjoy every day the Lord gives us, we never know how many we'll have, do we?" asked Carson. He turned from his desk and stood by a large map on the wall behind his desk and motioned for Ty to come closer. He pointed at the map and directed Ty's attention to the Eastern edge of the San Luis valley and started, "Now, let me further your education regarding our Indian friends. What I'm going to tell you comes from the many years I spent as a scout and leader of the cavalry in many conflicts with these very Indians. Now, over here," pointing at the mountains North of the San Juans, "we have the Capote Ute, they are allied with the Olleros band of the Jicarilla Apache. Down here," pointing further south on the same range, "we have the Mouache Ute, that you are more familiar with, and they're allied with the Llaneros band of the Jicarilla. Now Ouray's own father, Guera

Mural, was a Jicarilla." He dropped his hand to the lower part of the map, pointing at the southern edge of the valley, "and this," moving his hand across the lower part of the map, "is all Jicarilla Apache. But East of them are the Comanche. The Yaparuhka Comanche have been known to ally with anyone that suits their purpose." He turned around and directed Ty to be seated after seating himself.

"Now, I understand you had a good breakfast of bacon and eggs, am I right?" asked Kit.

Ty nodded and answered, "Yessir, we did, and it was mighty fine," with a wide grin.

"Well, we get those from a farmer and trader that has a place just south of San Luis. He also trades with the Indians a lot and he passed the word along to us that there might be trouble brewin'. It seems there's some mustered out confederates that are lookin' to trade some rifles to the Apache and maybe even the Comanche. Now, in my book, when you add some disgruntled Indians, all of which are sort of allied together, and some rifles with some trade whiskey, we've got trouble. But the good news is, I don't think the rebels have made it this far North yet, and we might just have a chance at interceptin' 'em."

"How'd this farmer find out about all this?" asked Ty.

"Good question, but from what I understand is he had some of his Indian friends askin' him about some traders coming with guns. When he asked about 'em, they wouldn't tell him any more than they were expecting some traders with lots of guns. Now when I got word from

General Grant's office about the theft of goods from the warehouses at Brazos Santiago and to be on the lookout for British Enfields, I just put things together and you know what I'm thinkin' don'tchu?"

"So, what do we do now?" asked Ty, already suspicioning the answer.

"I think that's a job for you and your new scout," answered Kit.

Chapter Twenty-Seven

Investigation

First light saw Ty and Louie on the road South to San Luis. The cool morning nipped at their ears as the horses stretched their legs at a brisk ground eating gait. It was a pleasant day and the men looked forward to a few days on their own without the need of scouting and hunting for the troop. The flats of the southern part of the San Luis valley were dry and empty, save for the usual sage and cactus and an occasional blossoming wildflower. Ty watched a coyote give chase after a scampering jackrabbit that twisted and turned around every clump of prickly pear and cholla, finally disappearing down a whole that left the coyote, tongue hanging out and showing his exasperation. He chuckled at the drama of the desert as Louie said, "Señor Ty, I have a question for you," leaning on the big flat saddle horn of his Mexican saddle. "I see you many times, reading your Bible and praying, but I never see you with the beads, why?"

"The beads?" asked Ty.

"Si, si, the beads, you know like I see the padres at the mission use when they pray."

"Oh, those beads. Well, Louie, a long time ago my father told me, 'Son, if it's somethin' you need to be doin' it's in the Bible. If it ain't in the Bible, you shouldn't ought to be a doin' it.' And I've found that to be good advice. If I ever find in the Book where I should be usin' beads to pray, then I'll just get me some," drawled Ty as he looked at this friend. The rocking gait of the horses caused Louie to twist in his saddle as he looked at his friend and asked, "I am, how you say, curious about what you believe. Now, we Pueblos have a belief in a Great Spirit or the creator of the world and in the sacred rivers where live comes, but I dunno, I just dunno . . ."

"Well, Louie, do you believe in Heaven? I'm sure the padres taught about Heaven."

"Oh, si, si, it is not different from when a Pueblo crosses over, it is a beautiful place."

"But, do you believe you will go there one day?" asked Ty, curious about his friend's beliefs.

"See, that's what I don't know. How can anyone know they're going to go to Heaven?"

"I know, because the Bible tells me so. See Louie, it says we're all sinners and we deserve to burn in an eternal hell because of our sin," started Ty.

"Oh no! I thought we were talking about Heaven," exclaimed Louie.

"We are, see, we deserve Hell as payment for our sin, but God loves us and doesn't want us to go there, so He made a way for us to go to Heaven and that's through His Son, Jesus. So even as rotten as we all are, if we just confess our sin to God and ask His forgiveness, and really mean it in our heart, then He says that since Jesus paid the price for our sin on the cross, we can pray to accept Jesus as our savior and we'll go to Heaven," explained Ty, watching the reaction of his friend. Louie was concerned and asked, "We'll go to Heaven right now? When we pray?"

"No, Louie," chuckled Ty, "after we die, not right now."

"So, if I pray that prayer, to ask Jesus to be my Savior and confess my sins, I can be sure of Heaven, just like you?" asked Louie.

"That's right, Louie, that's what the Bible you see me reading, says."

"Look! There's San Luis! Didn't the General say the farm of Diego was Southeast of the town?"

"That's right, but we'll have a looksee around town and see if we can learn anything first," explained Ty as the men came to the edge of town.

San Luis was the oldest town in the Colorado territory and sat between to interposing ranges of foothills. With scattered Juniper, pinion, and cedar on the nearby hillsides, the rising hills brought a pleasant change to the flats of the valley. The Rita Seco creek flowed through town and met Culebra creek just South of the village. To the east many ravines and ridges pointed bony fingers to the Sangre de Cristo mountain range that fed the streams with snowmelt. Ty looked to his right where a flat top mesa sheltered the town from the incessant dust-bearing winds off the flats. Typical of western towns, the first building they came to bore a crudely lettered sign that hung on squeaky hinges that said, *Livry Stabel.* Ty hadn't expected the town to have so many businesses and his survey showed three saloons, two general stores, one hardware store and gun shop, two hotels and a butcher. The names on the signs of the bigger businesses were, *Fred Meyer and Co., General Store,* and *Auguste Lacome, Gunsmith,* and *Mazers and Rich, General Store.*

Louie had been to San Luis before, when he traveled North from Taos Pueblo, and he reined up in front of the first saloon, *The Crazy Rooster,* and told Ty, "This is the best place to get something to eat. We might pick up some information also, if that's what you want, Señor?"

"Well, right now I'm more interested in something to eat. Information can wait," answered Ty as he swung his leg over his mount's rump and stepped to the ground. They tethered their horses at the rail and walked through the doorway into the dimly lit interior of the adobe building. Ty stepped to the side of the door and waited for his eyes to adjust, with the only light coming from the door and a single window at the side of the building. Three shelves lined the wall behind the counter, which was nothing but a couple of planks on upturned barrels, and held an assortment of bottles, glasses, and jugs. A middle-aged woman with long black hair streaked with grey, stood behind the bar and grinned at the visitors. "What would you gentlemen like today?" she asked with a wide and welcoming grin.

Ty and Louie made their way to a table to the side of the window, noted they were the only ones in the place, seated themselves and Louie spoke, "We would like something to eat, señorita, if you please?"

"We have Huevos Rancheros, Chili Rellenos, Tamales, Frijoles and tortillas," she stated listing the day's menu.

"Si, si, we will have some," answered Louie.

"Some of what?" replied the confused woman.

"All of it. We are hungry, señorita. And some coffee, por favor."

She put hands on hips and went through the door beside the shelves and into the kitchen at the rear of the building. Within moments, she returned with an armful of platters, food piled high, and sat them on the table. She spun on her heel and returned to the kitchen for more and within moments, the table before the two men was full of platters of food and cups of coffee. Louie looked at the woman with a broad smile and said, "It smells wonderful, muchas gracias."

Ty took off his hat, bowed his head for a quick prayer of thanks, and both men started putting away the ample meal.

As they finished and the woman, Juanita, refilled their coffee cups, Louie motioned for her to join them. With no other customers in the place, she brought out a cup of coffee for herself and pulled up a chair to join the two young men.

Louie started with, "Señorita, my friend, Ty, this is his first time here. Would you tell him about this place, you know, the people, the town, the businesses, the Indians, all of it, por favor?"

Juanita smiled and began her explanation with the history of the town, founded by the early Spanish explorers, the growth of the town with trade from the Sante Fe trail, and about the Indians, "The Jicarilla have their rancheria on the South end of San Pedro mesa and the Comanche have villages along the West side of the Sangre," she explained with dramatic hand motions in the directions indicated. "But, they are usually no trouble, except when too many come into town and trade for whiskey. They don't wait to drink until they are out of town. They start right away and when they are drunk, they litter the place with everything."

"I didn't think they were supposed to get whiskey from town?" asked Ty, knowing that when there was a will there would always be a way and Indians were no exception.

"No, no, but there are many traders that have whiskey, and between you and me, there are a couple of the saloons that don't care. They trade out the back door and think no one knows."

"Have there been many traders through here lately?" asked Louie with a nonchalant air.

"No, no, but I heard the other day there were some coming from Texas that wanted to trade with the Indians, and I think they have guns. I hope not, because Indians, guns, and whiskey mean a lot of trouble. But, what can I do?" she shrugged her shoulders and took another sip of the black brew.

Ty stood to leave and said to Juanita, "M'am, that was a mighty fine meal, and I thank you for the company, but we've got to pick up some supplies before we move on, so if you'll excuse us?" he dropped some coin on the table to pay for their fare and tipped his hat to the smiling woman. Louie followed Ty from the saloon and cantina and asked Ty, "Now what?"

167

"How 'bout you goin' to the blacksmith, pick up some horseshoe nails, and see if you can find out anything more. I'll go to the butcher shop yonder," he motioned with his chin as he loosed the reins from the hitchrail, "and get us some pork belly and see what I can find. We'll meet up on the road goin' South."

An hour later, Ty stood beside his horse in the shade of a tall cottonwood by the creek bank, and watched Louie ride up on his tall black and step down from the saddle. "So, find out anything?" asked Ty.

"Nothing new, but I did find out how everybody seems to know. The traders sent a scout ahead to find the Apache and Comanche villages, and he went into the saloon asking questions and let it be known they wanted to trade with the Indians and needed to find them. Also, he wore the uniform pants of a confederate soldier," explained Louie.

"Well, you found out more than I did. The butcher didn't know nuthin' an' if he did, he wasn't sayin'," said Ty. "But, he did have some good smoked pork belly. So, let's go on out to the Diego farm and see if he knows anything more. We need to find out when they're comin' so we can let the General know." With a nod, Louie mounted up and the two men gigged their horses to the road leaving San Luis, bound for the farms on the well-watered wide valley.

Chapter Twenty-Eight

Meeting

Three wagons were parked near the trees that held the picket line for the horses. The group started with four wagons, loaded to the top with trade goods and Enfield rifles, but when a broken axle forced the men to abandon one beside the roadway, they combined the loads in the three, cached the excess goods which was mostly great coats and frock coats from the warehouse, and continued their Northward trek. Camped near a small creek with grass and several cottonwoods, the men were slow in rising this morning. This was the first camp in over a week that had fresh water and shade trees and they were wont to leave. Just last night, Jasper Wolfton, "Wolf", had returned from his scout and the men were relieved to know they were less than a day from a town that had three saloons and three hotels. It was only the promise of booze, a bed, and maybe some señoritas that motivated the men at all.

T.C. hollered at the men, "Come on and get your lazy rear-ends outta them bedrolls! We gotta get on the road if you wanna get inta that town!"

He was met with the grumbles of four men as each rolled out of his blankets, stumbled erect and made their way to the trees for their morning constitutional. T.C. stirred the embers of the cookfire to life, added a few sticks and grabbed the coffee pot to go to the stream for fresh water. When he returned, Dodo had a pan of side meat cooking and had set several cornbread biscuits on the flat rock near the fire to catch a little heat. When T.C. sat the coffee pot near the fire, he dropped to a log and looked around as the men drifted back to the fire. Bull Dominguez looked at Wolf and asked, "Didchu find where them Injun camps are?".

"Well, near 'nuff. They said the Apaches are up on a big mesa called San Pedro, an' the Comanch' are up in the Sangre's, them mountains yonder," he replied, pointing to the long line of snow-capped peaks to the East.

Bull grunted and mumbled, "If'n ya hadn't killed them other'ns, mebbe they coulda tol' us!" When the group was transferring the load from the broken-down wagon, two Indians came around asking for whiskey and when they got bothersome, T.C. shot both of them.

Jalen Ramsey, "Mouse", looked to T.C. and asked, "How we gonna hook up with them Injuns, anyway, T.C., surely not like you did the last bunch?"

"I'm not sure right now, Mouse, I know we can't just go walkin' into their camp, they might get a little touchy if we do that. But, I'll figger out sumpin', maybe find us somebody that can take us there. You know, somebody that has traded with 'em afore, or somethin' like that," answered the leader of the crew. He had set everything else up, recruited the men, got the supplies, and made the freight company at least look official with the signs and painted company name on the wagons. The crew of former confederates looked to him for answers and were willing to follow him if things went as planned. But other than the anticipation of a sizable profit, they had no other loyalties to the man. The war had given the men their fill of obeying orders with little return and they felt no other obligation to Terrel Careington than to share in the profit of this venture.

"Well, I'm anxious to get me a good meal, some good whiskey and a bad woman," said Mouse as he stood with a cornbread biscuit in one hand and a coffee tin in the other. The others laughed but agreed and all rose to ready things for the day's travel. They followed what they had been told was a cutoff that would take them through a wide but fertile valley that lay between the foothills of the Sangres and the flat-top mesas to the East. Their previous route followed the Sante Fe trail, but this cut-off would be easier travel and they had their fill of the dusty trail that led through the sage and cactus flats. They passed a few farms with fields of corn, large vegetable gardens, ramshackle buildings, adobe homes, and scrawny livestock. Unseen by the would-be traders, three Apache were shadowing their progress. The farmer/trader to the South of San Luis that supplied the Fort, also traded with the Indians and had told the Apache of the traders that were looking for their camp. When two of their number approached the wagons, asking for whiskey and were killed, the nearby watchers had taken word back to the rancheria of the incident and that the cargo of the wagons held many cartons of rifles. Now they were watched closely by the Apache.

None of the farms held enough appeal to cause the men to waver in their mission to make the town with the saloons. It was close to mid-afternoon when they came to a crossing of Culebra Creek near the confluence with Ventero creek. The crossing was easy, but when the freight wagons pulled up after the crossing, they were surprised to see two men, sitting horseback and watching the crossing. One of the men while the drivers of the wagons stopped to watch.

T.C. reined up short of the two watchers and spoke first, "Afternoon. You fellas coming from San Luis?"

Ty looked at the man, nodded his head and answered, "Ummhummm."

T.C. said, "Well, maybe you could help us. Are we apt to run into any Injuns on this road?"

"Probably not, they pretty well keep to themselves up in the mountains yonder."

"And what kind or tribe of Injuns are in these parts?" asked T.C.

"Well, there's some Apache and some Comanche, might even run into a few Ute. Why?"

"Why? Well, we want to be prepared. We have a considerable investment in our goods here and we don't want to lose them," answered T.C.

"Gonna start a store, are you?" asked Ty, "cause if you are, San Luis already has a couple general stores and one hardware store."

"Is that right? Well, I was actually thinkin' 'bout tryin' to trade with the Injuns, if they're friendly, that is."

"Whatchu got there that Injuns would want?"

"Oh, lots of things, you know, pots, pans, material, beads, a few old guns, just trade stuff. Say, would you fellas know of someone that speaks the Injun's language that could guide us up to their village? We'd pay, of course."

Ty looked at Louie who had been sitting silent, saw a slight nod from his friend, and looked back at the rebel leader and said, "Well, my friend here speaks Apache and Comanche, I can speak a little Comanch."

"Do you know where the Injuns camp is, you know, their village?" asked a very interested T.C.

"Not 'xactly, but we could probly find 'em."

"Well then, let me make you a proposition. We're going into San Luis, get us a good meal and a nice bed, but tomorrow we'd like to go to the Injun camp. If you'll lead us, we'll give you, say, ten percent of whatever we trade. How's that sound, pretty easy money, don'tchu think?"

Ty looked at Louie, back at T.C. and said, "I think you've got yourself a deal," and reached out a hand to seal the agreement, "I'm Ty and this here's Louie, and you're . . ."

"I'm Terrel Careington, and this is my freight business," motioning to the emblem with the T.C. Freight painted on the freighters. "I'll introduce the others when we get to town. I think this is going to be a very profitable partnership, Ty."

As the small caravan of trade wagons and men made their way toward town, Ty and Louie followed along. Shortly after crossing the last creek, Louie looked at Ty and whispered, "Did you see . . ." and nodded with his head toward the cluster of juniper on the hillside of the flat top mesa. "Yup, three of 'em, I think."

"Si, they have been following us, watching . . ." replied Louie.

Ty spurred his horse forward and pulled alongside T.C. and asked, "I thought you said you didn't know where these Apache were, but they sure know where you are. We've been followed by a small party of Apache, any idea why?"

T.C. looked around in alarm trying to see any Indians and back at Ty and asked, "Where? Where are they?"

Ty said, "Be calm, they're not about to do anything just yet. It 'pears they're just watchin' an' maybe waitin' for somethin'. Any reason for them to be hangin' around?"

"No, no, no reason," declared T.C., but he was overheard by Dodo driving the nearest wagon and the man asked, "What about them two we done in back yonder, T.C.?"

Ty looked at T.C. as the man started stuttering and said, "Aww, they were nothin' but drunks. They don't matter none. Would they?" he asked as he looked at Ty.

"Maybe not, but word had gotten around 'bout you fellas comin' up the trail, and if the people in the village knew it, the Apache probably did too and mighta sent out a scout to check out your load."

"How'd the village know about it?" asked T.C., bewildered.

"Well, for one thing, your man was askin' everbody where the camps were and that you wanted to trade with 'em."

173

T.C. grumbled and shaking his head asked, "You don't think they'll do anything this close to town, do you? I mean, we still wanna trade and mebbe you two could tell 'em that," suggested T.C.

"Might work, course it'd be a mite more dangerous if they were looking for vengeance for you killin' their men and they might not be in a talkative mood. You just never know about them wiley Indians," answered Ty.

"You think we'll be alright for the night if we stay in town? You and your partner there could have a day or so to make peace and set up the trade," offered T.C. with a hopeful expression on his face.

"Might work. I'll talk to Louie 'bout it and maybe we'll be able to head out early in the morning to try to find their camp and talk to 'em."

T.C. dropped his shoulders and visibly relaxed with a grin and turned his thoughts back to the anticipated night in the town of San Luis.

Chapter Twenty-Nine

Confrontation

The rattle of trace chains, the creaking of ungreased wheels, and the groaning of the mule teams announced the arrival of the freight wagons to the townspeople of San Luis. As they approached the livery at the edge of town, Ty and Louie separated themselves and hung back away from the group. T.C. asked the liveryman, "Got a place where we can keep our wagons and teams for the night, maybe two?"

"Sure, sure, ain't got room in the barn, but you can park your wagons 'round back an' put the teams in the corral. There's hay 'n water, but you gotta toss the hay to 'em," answered the scrawny livery man with a big grey handlebar moustache that kept filtering his words. He absent-mindedly pushed it aside repeatedly as he spoke and never changed his slouching stance as he leaned against the upright at the edge of the door.

"What's it gonna cost me?" asked T.C. waving his hand toward the wagons.

"Ya wanna board them saddle horses too?" asked the man.

"Yes, all the animals and the wagons," explained T.C.

175

"Hummm, I reckon bout a buck, four bits'll do it."

T.C. motioned to the men to pull the wagons around and start unhitching as he stepped down from his mount to pay the keeper of the livery. Rastus McKinnon stretched out a callused palm for the coins and on bowlegs hobbled back to his cubby-hole office in the far corner of the barn. T.C. motioned for Ty and Louie, still astride their mounts and hanging back from the wagons, to come forward for a confab. As they approached, T.C. said, "Are you fellers plannin' on stayin' at the hotel with the rest of us?"

"Nah, we had our time on the lumpy mattresses, we prefer to have the stars for our roof," replied Ty as he motioned to a cluster of pinion a short distance behind the livery. "We'll just roll out our bedrolls over yonder after we get us a good meal from the cantina."

"Well, me 'n the boys ain't had a good meal or a good bed since we left Texas, so we're gonna enjoy it while we can. Since you're gonna be nearby, how 'bout keepin' an eye on things over here?"

Ty nodded to the man and answered, "We can do that. Don't see no need to keep a guard up or nothin' but we sleep pretty light."

"That's fine. I'll check with you fellers in the mornin' 'fore ya head out to find them camps," instructed T.C. as he turned to watch his men finish with the teams. He knew he would have to bankroll their night on the town and he wanted to keep tabs on his men. What with all the planning and traveling so far, he didn't want something to go wrong due to some foolishness on the part of the men.

* * * * *

Fleches Rayada or Striped Arrows was the undisputed and respected leader of the Llaneros Jicarilla Apache. They called themselves the Gulgahén or Plains people of the Tinde, the people. Striped Arrows had been their leader for almost two decades and stories were still told of his bravery and leadership when the Apache went against the bluecoats at the Battle of Cieneguilla and defeated the many bluecoats and captured many horses and weapons. But since that time, the Jicarilla had continually been pushed off their sacred lands and away from their sacred rivers, the Rio Grande and the Arkansas. Even though they were allied with the Mouache band of the Ute, they still raided and fought against the Kiowa, Comanche, and the white settlers. When they made a treaty with the whites and Governor William Lane of the New Mexico territory, they peacefully took up agriculture, which they had been known for before, but the government betrayed them and no longer paid them or provided supplies. Now their crops had failed and they resorted to raids for survival.

The elders of the village were gathered in council when Striped Arrows stood to speak. "Once again, the whites have betrayed us. Two of our young men were killed when they approached the trader wagons, the same wagons that we were told were bringing supplies to us and to trade with us for new rifles. Now they have gone into San Luis instead of coming here. It is with a heavy heart that I say we should go and take the wagons with the rifles." As he looked around the circle, the white-haired leader of the Tinde watched the reaction of the other elders. He seated himself and waited for others to speak.

Another elder struggled to his feet, brushed the loose white hair from his brow, and began. "I believe our ancestor, whose name I carry, Killer of the Enemies, would say as I do. We must punish the whites that have killed our young men and to survive, we must capture the supplies that are in those wagons. Our people will go hungry come winter if we do not. The leader of the whites has broken the treaty and they do not give us the supplies we must have. We have no choice but to take what is ours." In the early years of the treaty, the government would send wagons of supplies, mostly food and seed, to fulfill their promises of the treaty. When the Apache saw the wagons,

177

and heard of the man wanting to know where the Apache were camped, they were certain these wagons carried the much needed and promised supplies.

White Stone Man stood, he was younger than most but was a respected leader, and began, "I fear what may happen when we raid the town of San Luis. They will tell the blue coats of Fort Union and maybe even Carson of Fort Garland. If the blue coats come, more of our people will die. Our warriors are few and they are many."

Killer of the Enemies spoke up, "Our warriors have told of many boxes of rifles that are on those wagons. When Striped Arrows led us against the blue coats at Cieneguilla we only had old rifles and bows and arrows. With more rifles like the blue coats, we could go against the Comanche and the Kiowa!"

As Striped Arrows watched the elders begin to discuss the different opinions, he nodded his head and listened. When the murmuring stopped, the elders looked to their venerated leader as he slowly stood. "Without our crops, without more supplies, we have no choice but to take what we need. If there are many rifles and the needed powder or what else we need, it will be good for us to be better armed. When we are stronger, we can better defend ourselves and we can have better hunts. With the buffalo on the move, we need better rifles. I say we make the raid this night to take the wagons and whatever else we need."

Again, the elders turned to one another to discuss their leader's remarks and as they chattered, a young war leader, Antonio, stood and spoke. "If we go against the town, more rise against us, but if we make a raid to take just the wagons, we will need fewer warriors and we could take them without them knowing until morning comes."

Grins and laughter broke out among the leaders and it was evident this last suggestion was well received. All the leaders were nodding their heads and looking to Striped Arrows. He also grinned and agreed, "Antonio speaks well, you will lead the men to take the wagons this night."

Ty and Louie returned to *The Crazy Rooster* to be welcomed by Juanita, "Señors, so good to see you again. Are you hungry?" she asked as she watched the grinning faces and nodding heads of the two men. Louie answered for them both with, "Si, si, señorita. We just couldn't stay away."

"Tonight, we have Chili Rellenos, Tamales, Frijoles and tortillas and I have added Pollo enchiladas al la crema!" she explained with a broad smile showing her white teeth. "Si, si," answered Louie as they took a seat at the nearest table. They soon were enjoying a sumptuous feast with plates piled high and more offered. Juanita seated herself by the men and enjoyed watching them sate their appetites.

"Did you find the villages and the traders you were looking for?" inquired the friendly woman while she poured them another cup of hot java. As she looked up at them she saw curious looks on their faces as they looked at one another. "Well, didn't you ask me about the villages?"

"Uh, no m'am, but you told us about them and all about the history of this place, but we didn't ask you about the villages," answered Ty as he looked at their hostess.

"Oh, oh, that must have been the other man that was in here that day," explained Juanita.

When Ty and Louie finished their meal and rose to leave, Juanita bid them goodbye with "Vaya Con Dios," as she watched them leave. The men led their horses down the street and behind the livery to make their camp in the trees beyond the corrals and buildings. The copse was about two hundred yards distant from the corrals and their camp well hidden. With no need of a fire, the men spread their bedrolls near the trees and as darkness began to share the heavens with stars and a sliver of moon, the men lay with hands behind their heads and listened to the night-sounds. Somewhere farther up the hillsides came the lonesome cry of a coyote that was answered by another roaming loner. A great horned owl questioned the darkness from his perch in the eve of the barn. Cicadas filled the flats with their scratchy sounds and a whiff of a skunk was carried on the evening breeze. The peaceful sounds of the evening ushered sleep to the reverie of the two friends and their mounts stood silent and hipshot behind the pinions.

It was well after midnight when Ty's eyes opened. He lay perfectly still, looking around without moving his head, listening to see what had awakened him. He heard his horse stomp and snort, but not from alarm. Louie was not moving, and there were no night sounds. Something had disturbed the night, but what? Ty's grip tightened on his Remington and he slowly pushed aside the blankets, sat up and pulled on his moccasins. Looking over at his friend, he saw the whites of eyes alert to his movement. Ty whispered, "Something's wrong, I'm going to move around and see if I can see what it is." The sliver of moon gave just enough light to see the nod from Louie and Ty walked to the edge of the trees to look toward the livery.

Seeing movement among the animals in the corral, Ty froze in place to watch and try to discern what was happening. A sliver of light came from the barn and the silhouette of Rastus and another shown in the doorway of the barn. Ty recognized the other man as an Apache, the loose-fitting clothing and the long straight hair bound by a scarf was the giveaway. The Apache held a pistol to Rastus and the liveryman was carrying an armful of harness. As Ty's eyes grew accustomed to the darkness he saw three other Apache were leading horses from the corral to be harnessed. Ty turned to Louie, now by his side, and whispered, "The Apache are going to try and steal the wagons, we can't let them get those rifles!"

"Si, but what can we do?" asked Louie.

Ty directed his friend to approach from the uphill side beyond the edge of the corral and he would approach from the blind side of the barn. "I don't know how many there are, nor where the rest of them are hidin' but we gotta try to keep them from gettin' away with them rifles. I'm gonna try an' get to the barn and maybe hit 'em with somethin', don't rightly know what, but . . ." and he let the thought lie in the darkness. Louie started out through the black night to reach his designated site, while Ty hunkered down and trotted toward the barn. He knew it would take a little while to harness the animals and hook up the wagons, but he hurried to find something to stop them.

Ty reached the side of the barn, moved stealthily to the corner and looked around to see an Apache standing in the dark recess near the door, apparently on watch. The Indian looked toward the town, back to the interior of the barn, then moved to the far corner. Ty saw his chance and quickly but quietly moved behind the man, coming up behind him just as he started to turn. The long blade of Ty's Bowie slipped between the Apache's ribs as Ty's left hand covered his mouth. The weight of the man hung on the knife blade and Ty slowly let the man drop to the ground. He looked around the corner to see others harnessing the teams, two were leading animals from the corrals, two were following whispered orders from Rastus, still with a gun held on him by the same Apache, to harness the team. *There's got to be more somewhere,* thought Ty as he turned to look into the barn. Empty.

Keeping to the shadows, Ty felt his way along the stalls toward the corner office of Rastus. A light glimmered through the cracks by the door showing the way. *Maybe I can use a lantern . . .* thought Ty as he worked his way to the office. He listened at the door and slowly pushed it open to see it empty. Knowing the light would also reveal his presence, Ty dropped to hands and knees and moved inside to search for another lantern or an oil can, something that he could throw and set the wagons on fire. Nothing. He heard movement outside and stood to flatten himself against the wall behind the door. But the only sounds that came to him were the movements of the horses and men with harnesses. The Apache were talking in muted tones and Ty could hear the jingle and clinking of the trace chains that told him they were hooking the harnessed horses to the wagons. He had to move.

He moved more silently than the Apache and stepped to the side of the big door that led to the corrals. Just as he started to look around the tall door post, he came face to face with an Apache that was coming to investigate the light in the office. Before the Apache could sound the alarm, Ty thrust his knife into the Indian's gut just above his crotch and ripped the razor-sharp blade upwards. Simultaneously with the knife thrust, Ty's hand smothered the Apache's cry and the man crumpled to the ground with his guts spilling out. Suddenly a cry came from another Apache sounding the warning to the others and a pistol shot broke the silence and the slug threw woodchips at the face of Ty, ducking away and back into the darkness of the barn. The Indians were no longer concerned with silence and their shouts hastened the hooking of the teams to the wagons. Ty ran to the office, retrieved the lantern and ran back to the door. Just as the second wagon started to pull away, he threw the lantern at the back end of the wagon and watched it explode in a ball of flame on the rear of the cargo. The first wagon was already on the move and headed into the darkness away from town.

A shot came from the trees beyond the corrals and Ty knew Louie had announced his presence as his well-placed shot brought a cry from an Apache that fell from his horse. At a glance, Ty could tell that each wagon was driven by one man, with at least two more riding their horses beside the team to help guide the horses away. The handling of a four-up team was not as easy as some would believe and the Indians knew they would have to help by practically leading the team. The warriors on each side of the team reached down to grasp the lead lines at the side of the bits held tight in the horse's mouths and struggled with the horses to get them away from town.

The third wagon was now starting out and Ty grabbed his rifle that hung on his back from the sling around his shoulder. He fired at the driver, but the darkness hindered his aim. He fired again and again, hoping to strike the ammo he knew was in the wagon. He levered another round into the chamber, fired, levered another, fired at the same target that was moving away. He levered another and fired again and was startled at the resulting explosion as his bullet had struck the cache of powder and caps and exploded. The blast lifted the back of the wagon off the ground and shook the earth beneath Ty's feet. He watched as the flames licked at the remains of the wagon and the driver was drug by the frightened team. Darkness enveloped the scene but lights began to blossom across the town and curious townspeople, all armed, stepped from doorways to see growing fire of the destroyed wagon that littered the street at the edge of the small town.

With all the attention focused on the burning debris in the street, a second and more distant explosion told Ty his shattered lantern had completed its assigned task, but it would be morning before he was able to determine just how much of the second wagon was destroyed. Louie joined Ty as he stood at the corner of the livery and said, "It looks like you stopped a couple of them anyway."

"Yeah, but they got the other'n and we don't know how many rifles and ammo that one held. Maybe we'll find out from him," said Ty as he motioned toward T.C. who was running their direction.

To The Sangre de Cristo

Chapter Thirty

Pursuit

"Those were my wagons!" screamed T.C. at Ty and Louie. "You were supposed to be watchin' 'em!" he continued with his tirade, waving his arms in the air as he stomped his way to stand in front of Ty. T.C. was used to intimidating men with his threats and demeanor and was surprised when Ty sat his rifle butt first on the ground, leaned on the barrel and looked at the shouting man and said, "We watched 'em. Watched the Indians hook 'em up, watched 'em pull away, watched a couple of 'em blow up. Yup," and he looked at Louie with a grin, turned back to face T.C. and said, "we watched 'em."

"Why didn't you stop 'em?!" said T.C. still shouting.

"We stopped a few of 'em," said Ty, motioning behind him with a head nod, "but there was more o' them than there was of us an' we couldn't get 'em all," casually shrugging his shoulders.

"Wait! You said there were two of 'em that blew up, did they take the other'n?"

"Yup, got clean away with that'n," replied Ty as he looked down the road in the direction of the Indian's escape.

185

"Do you think we could catch 'em and get it back?" asked a hopeful T.C.

"Probably not. We couldn't track 'em till daylight, an' by that time they'd probably be back at their rancheria or they'd have unloaded what they wanted and skedaddled," said Ty, maintaining his casual attitude.

T.C. looked at Ty and Louie, shook his head and stomped off in the direction of the hotel where the rest of his men waited. Ty looked at Louie and said, "I'm goin' to follow after them 'pache. I want you to stay here and as soon as you can roust out the telegrapher, I want you to send a message to Carson 'bout what happened here and what we're doin'."

"Just what are we doin'?" asked Louie.

"Well, I'm goin' after 'em, and you're sendin' the message," explained Ty.

"Do you want me to follow you when I get the message sent?" asked Louie.

"Sure, I could probably use some help 'bout then, 'specially since I don't know their lingo. I'll leave plenty of sign so you can follow, but if I don't get started, we'll never find 'em," added Ty.

Ty turned back to the stable and walked through the building to the distant grove of trees to retrieve his horse and gear. Within moments he emerged from the trees astride his roan and took to the road at a canter. The starlight and the little glow from the sliver of moon gave just enough light to follow the trail of the big freighter and the many Apache ponies. Less than half a mile from the edge of town, the roadway crossed the Culebra Creek, a shallow sandy bottom creek, and even in the dim light, Ty could see the deep tracks of the heavy loaded freighter where they crossed. His roan splashed through the water and continued on the roadway that followed the edge of the sloping hillside of the big mesa. Ty slowed the roan to a trot and leaned down to reassure himself the tracks were still on the roadway, sat erect and slowed the anxious long-legged mustang cross to his ground eating walk.

The last thing I want to do is come up on that bunch of hair-liftin' Apache before it's light enough to see 'em good. 'Sides, this here road doesn't cut back up to the top of the mesa for a ways yet. It'll probably be full light by the time it starts up thataway. Ty knew he could not be too careful because contrary to popular opinion, Indians, and especially Apache, were intelligent and crafty fighters. It would not be unlike them to have some of their number hang back to guard their backtrail and Ty moved his horse to the softer ground to the side of the road. The last thing he needed to do was to announce his presence with the clatter of shod hooves on the hard-packed roadway.

The stars faded and the Sangre de Cristo's were shadowing the slowly greying horizon to the East. The scattered stubby pinion were casting long shadows as the eastern sky lightened and Ty reined his roan behind a cluster of juniper. He dropped to the ground and stepped to a large outcropping of rock to survey the terrain before him. He would wait until full light before continuing. Now less than three miles from the creek crossing, Ty watched as the rising sun illuminated the trail that left the road to follow the dry gulch to the top of the mesa. If the Apache were to hide out to attack any pursuers, this area with the many cry sandy creek bottoms and coulees would be the perfect spot. Ty retrieved his telescope and examined the area before him but there was no sign of the wagon nor the Apache. Remounting, he reined his horse back to the roadway and kicked him up to a canter to follow the tracks of the wagon.

The high bluffs of the mesa gave way to a saddle cut by the run-off of ancient storms that carved the gullies and coulees. The trail followed a wide rounded ridge that twisted its way toward the top and slowly narrowed to a single trail. Ty reined up and leaned down along the neck of his mount to look at the tracks and was surprised when there were no tracks of the wagon. He started to straighten up when the whisper of an arrow and the searing pain in his shoulder made him drop further along the neck of his horse, quickly swing his leg over

187

its rump and with his left foot still in the stirrup, he slapped his horses neck and coaxed him off the trail and down the slope away from the attack. He heard the screamed war-cry as three Apache warriors gave chase. Ty reached across the cantle of the saddle, grabbed his Henry and dropped to the ground behind a cluster of rock, sage and cactus, narrowly missing landing butt first in the big prickly pear patch. The screams of his attackers came loudly as he jacked a round and fired from his hip at the nearest one as he leaped from a rock toward Ty. The Apache buckled in the middle as if he had taken a kick from a mule and fell to the ground in a puff of dust. Ty quickly jacked another round but the second attacker kicked the rifle aside and started to bring his tomahawk down to split Ty's skull. Ty blocked the tomahawk with his forearm and reached for his Bowie with his other hand, slipped it from the sheath that hung between his shoulders behind his head and brought it down in a chopping motion that sliced through the shoulder and collarbone of the attacker. Ty brought the blade down across the chest of the Apache that screamed at the sudden pain and blood trailed the knife down his chest. Ty had clasped the arm of the Apache that held the tomahawk with his left hand and now drew the Bowie back and plunged it to the hilt into the Apache's stomach, just below the ribs. The warrior looked at Ty with hatred and a snarl to his mouth as he slumped to his knees. Ty released the arm and held to his knife as the Apache slid to the ground.

The sudden pain to the back of his head shocked Ty as he tried to keep from falling, but his legs weren't responding. He heard the scream of an Apache but he didn't see his attacker. He tried to turn to face the Apache, but his head was spinning. He tried to lift his arms to catch himself but they wouldn't move. A blackness was drawing across his eyes from the sides, an excruciating pain coursed down his neck to his shoulders and he felt himself falling and darkness coming. He saw his roan moving away, eyes frightened and reins trailing. *That's strange, I don't hear anything,* he thought as everything went black.

When Ty opened his eyes, he was confused. Lying on his stomach on a blanket, his eyes focused on grass. He heard the chuckling of water over rocks that told of a nearby stream. He tried to lift his head but was stopped by the throbbing pain that seemed to drive his head back to the blanket. He heard a horse stomp, snort and start munching on the grass but he couldn't see anything for all that was before him was grass and a chokecherry bush. He tried his fingers, they worked. His hand and his arm had feeling and moved at his slight impulse but he remained still. He wasn't bound but it seemed as if he had a heavy weight on his shoulders then he felt a sharp pain and remembered the arrow that cut his shoulder. Now it was coming back to him, the knife fight with the Apache and then the blow to his head. *Must be the Apache have me, but why am I not bound?*

"Oh, you are coming around I see," said a familiar voice that took Ty a moment to realize it was Louie. Again, he tried to raise his head and chose instead to roll to his side to try to locate his friend. Louie was sitting on a grey log that was the remains of a long dead cottonwood. He grinned at Ty, took a sip of coffee, and said, "It's about time. I was beginning to wonder if you were going to sleep all day, amigo."

Ty struggled to sit up, grabbed at his head to try to stop the world from spinning and closed his eyes as he dropped both hands to the ground to keep from falling over.

"You are dizzy. No wonder, that war club the Apache hit you with was a big one. It had a stone head, this big," he held his hands out before him to indicate the size of the war club's head, "it's a wonder he didn't bash your head in. You must have moved just enough to make it a glancing blow. Lucky for you I came when I did, he was rearing back to clout you a good one but my bullet hit him harder. He won't use his war club again, I theenk."

Ty crawled to the log and struggled to seat himself on it. Placing his elbows on his knees, he dropped his head into his hands and asked, "Got'ny coffee left?"

"Si, si, I'll pour you a cup, my friend."

"How long have I been out?" asked Ty.

"Oh, less than two hours," replied Louie handing Ty his coffee. "I brought you down from the ravine," motioning with his head toward the ravines and gullies that cut the bluff, "so I would have some water to try to bring you around and some shade also."

"Thanks. Say, you were supposed to send a telegram to Carson, what happened?"

"I didn't have to wait. The townspeople were so scared about the Indians, the telegrapher opened up and wanted to send for help from the Fort. I told him what to say and who to send it to, so he did. I saddled up and came after you, and it's a good thing I did. I think that Apache would have your scalp on his lance if I didn't."

Ty grinned at his friend and sipped at the coffee. It hurt to bend his head back to take the coffee, but he was almighty thirsty for the hot brew and he savored the cupful. "Thanks, I owe you one. Did you get a response from the Fort?" asked Ty.

"No, I figgered by the time they woke somebody up and went through the ranks it'd take too long, so I lit out," answered Louie. "So, what are you thinking amigo?"

"Near as I can figger," started Ty, shaking his head to clear his thoughts, "if Carson sends a troop out first thing, they could get here as soon as mid-day or so, maybe a little later. That gives us a few hours but what with them raiders losing three of their own, no tellin' what they'll do. By the time the troop gets here, the 'pache'll have that wagon unloaded and those rifles handed out. So, I don't think you'n me'll be able to do much against the whole rancheria of Apache, 'specially not knowin' how many there are and such. So, here's what I think we should be doin'," he started explaining as he leaned over and drew in the dirt beside the coals of the fire. "How 'bout you takin' that trail yonder," he pointed with his stick to the trail that followed the edge of the steep sloping hillside away from the bluffs, "and see if there's another way to the top that might have more cover, instead of all exposed like that trail they got me on. I'm still too light-headed to ride for a bit, so I'll wait here for them soldier boys. Now, don't you go gettin' yourself in trouble, ya hear? Just find a possible trail and come on back. Then we'll let the boys in blue decide what they want to do next. Got that?"

"Si, si. I'm pretty sure there's another trail up through the trees. I've been through this area before when I came up from Taos Pueblo. I haven't been to the top, but I've seen a trail. It won't take me long to find it."   Ty started to nod his head, stopped himself and grinned, then watched as Louie tightened the cinch and stepped aboard his tall black. Louie nodded to Ty as he reined his mount around and started on his scout.

To The Sangre de Cristo

Chapter Thirty-One

Troops

Ty sat on the log with his head in his hands trying to stop the spinning and the dizziness that tried to overwhelm him. He reached back with his hand to feel the wound and was surprised to find a knot that filled the palm of his hand. He gingerly touched it and examined it as best he could, despite the throbbing pain. He reached down for his hat and tried to put it on only to wince at the pain and dropped his hat beside his foot.

He remembered the last time he had a knot on his head. It was when he and his brother, Talon, were trying to break a new crop of two-year-old colts that were the product of mustang mares and his dad's Appaloosa stallion. One especially rank colt, a strawberry roan with determination in his eyes and freedom in his heart, matched wits and strength with Tyrell. After Talon snubbed the colt down and they saddled the nervous horse, Ty stepped aboard, Talon yanked the eye cover and let loose the snub, and the roan exploded. Ty was surprised at the spring-loaded legs that launched the hump-backed roan into near orbit while the stud-horse tucked his muzzle between his front legs, twisted in the middle and kicked at the clouds. When the front hooves plunged into the deep dust of the corral, they quickly came up as the rear legs stood firm and the roan scratched the blue sky with his front hooves while screaming his protests. Ty leaned as far forward as the pommel of the saddle would allow and felt the mane whip his face as he fought to keep from pulling the horse over backwards. In an instant, the roan switched ends and acted like a sunfish showing his belly to the clouds as he tried to unseat the cowboy from his deep seat between the high-backed cantle and the wide swells of the pommel. Ty had his boots deep in the stirrups and his spurs dug into the sides of the rank mount. Dust swelled around the contest of wills and the grunts of the roan that burst from the determined horse every time his hooves hit the ground were matched with the whoops of the spectators that lined the fence. The roan headed straight for the fence and Ty thought he was going to try to jump it or collide into it, but he was surprised when the horse stopped suddenly and he didn't. He saw the peeled log pass beneath him as he sailed over the horse's head and the top fence rail. He frantically waved arms and legs trying to control his fall but was met with failure as he turned end over end and landed almost flat of his back with his head hitting a rock and his backside planted in a cluster of Prickly pear cactus.

In spite of his discomfort, Ty chuckled at the memory of his mother picking out the many cactus spikes from his posterior while he moaned and complained about the roan, his head, and his determination to put that colt out of his misery with a .44. He looked over at the roan, now grazing on the grass on the creek bank and laughed to himself at the memory.

Ty struggled to his feet to see just how steady he was and quickly sat back down. He arched his neck and bent back to look at the sky that showed itself between the branches of the cottonwoods. The azure arch was devoid of clouds and the warm sunshine brought comfort to Ty as he waited for the troops from Fort Garland. He absent-mindedly picked up a stick and started drawing in the dusty soil at his feet and allowed himself to travel back along the trail of his past. He always liked his life on the ranch of his father. It was the first ranch to be established in the South West of Wyoming territory and Ty and his twin brother Talon relished every moment of their growing-up years. They learned ranching from Jackson Bubash and his daughter, Marylyn, the mother of Ty's wife Elizabeth. Their wilderness education had tutors from the Ute and the Arapaho, friends of the family that shared their knowledge of the wilderness, both people and animals. Other instructors of their youth included Reuben, the former slave and stevedore from the docks of St. Louis, their grandparents, Jeremiah and Laughing Waters, the shaman of the Arapaho, and of course the hardest learned lessons of personal explorations and mistakes. After the death of his wife and child, Ty left the ranch to escape the painful memories, but had long dreamed of having his own ranch and now with the Spanish gold hidden in his panniers back at the fort, he started to dream again.

Ty's reverie was interrupted by the return of Louie who reined up his big black in the clearing among the cottonwoods and greeted Ty with, "Ah, you are still sitting where I left you, whatsamatta, still too dizzy?"

"Just a bit, but it's not too bad," answered Ty as he watched his friend loosen the cinch on his mount and lay the reins over the black's neck to let him graze. Louie took a seat on a flat stone to the side of the fire circle that held a collection of black and grey cold reminders of past camps.

"I think the troops are coming. I saw a cloud of dust up the road a ways, 'bout where the road comes from the creek. Probably them," stated Louie as he stuck a stem of grass in his mouth. He cast a critical glance at Ty to measure his recuperation and grinned. "It would probably be best if you just pitched camp here and got you some sack time before you tried riding anywhere," suggested Louie.

Ty looked at the sky again and observed, "Well, I reckon it's gettin' a bit late for them soldier boys to launch an attack against them Apache. It usually takes them quite a spell to make up their minds about what they want to do anyway, could be dark when they do decide." Louie chuckled at his friend's remarks, then stood to walk to his horse and retrieve something from his saddle-bags. As he walked back to Ty he said, "Take off your shirt, I've got some Agave for your shoulder where the Apache arrow laid it open."

Louie had finished applying the syrupy liquid of the Agave to Ty's wound when they heard the approach of the troops. Louie walked from the trees and watched as the cavalry neared and waved them over. Both Ty and Louie were surprised to see General Carson and Captain Wilkins at the head of the long column of troopers. Lieutenants Barrett and McElmore were directly behind the General and Captain, followed by First Sergeant O'Hanlon and Sergeant Smith, and the rest of A Company of the 1st New Mexico Cavalry numbering just over 100 troopers followed in a long column of four abreast.

The general and captain stepped down from their mounts and Carson nodded to the Lieutenants, signaling them to dismount the troops. Carson walked to Louie and spotted Ty sitting in the shade on the big log and nodding at Louie, passed him by to join Ty on the log. The captain followed behind and found a seat on one of the several flat stones near the fire ring.

"So, Ty, tell me what happened," started the general foregoing any other greeting.

"Well, General, it all started when we ran into them traders not too far from here," started Ty and continued with his narrative of the events of the past couple of days. His concise summary held the General's attention and Ty concluded with, ". . . and Louie here's been playin' nursemaid since he saved me from that Apache warclub," as he motioned to the souvenir Louie had retrieved from the scene.

Kit looked at Louie and asked, "Did you get a look at the Rancheria?"

"Si, si, but I didn't get too close. From where I was I saw seventy, eighty lodges. Many women and children, but they all look ver' hungry. It is ver' dry up there and they have no crops left."

"Hummm, seventy or eighty, that's a big rancheria, I'm surprised. That would mean they have maybe a hundred warriors and now they've got rifles," he looked at Ty and asked, "How many rifles did they get?"

"Not sure General, they only got away with one wagon, but there could have been maybe ten cases of rifles and I don't know how much ammo. We did stop 'em from gettin' the other wagons, but I didn't hang around to ask them Johnny Rebs how many were in that wagon they did get," answered Ty.

Kit looked to Louie again and asked, "And you found the trail that leads to the top on the back side of that mesa?"

"Si, si, but there could be other trails, I didn't look any further," answered Louie.

"I know there's other trails, too many to cover all of 'em. I scouted this country back when I was fightin' the Mescalero and the Navajo." Carson stood, causing the Captain to jump to his feet as well, and turned to the Captain and ordered, "Captain, have the men bivouac along the creek bank here, post the guards and such. We'll wait till mornin' 'fore we take after them Apache." The general sat back down and looked at Ty and said, "Looks like you mighta stirred up a bit of a fracas for us. It'll be good trainin' fer some of these greenhorns."

To The Sangre de Cristo

Chapter Thirty-Two

Mesa

It was a restless night for Ty as he found it difficult to get comfortable with his head injury. As he would start to drop off to sleep, the dizziness would return and he would struggle to stay under his blankets as his temperature rose and sweat covered his upper body. He was relieved when long before first light, the First Sergeant started his rounds awakening the men. Ty rolled to his side, waited for the wooziness to pass then struggled to his feet. He staggered to the creek bank, leaned against the rough bark of a cottonwood and sucked in the clear air. The starlight twinkled off the smooth surface of the backwater and Ty fought to keep his feet. He knew this was going to be nothing short of a very challenging day.

Carson had given his instructions to his officers before they turned in the night before and they now busied themselves with their preparations for the coming campaign. No fires were allowed and the grumbling men chewed on jerky as they rigged their horses and were repeatedly admonished by the sergeants to "keep it quiet, ya wanna warn them Apache?" Ty snatched his saddle, blanket, and bridle and walked to the side of his roan to gear up for the day. General Carson stepped to his side and spoke to Ty and Louie in hushed tones, "Fellas, I'm gonna split you up today. Louie, I want you to guide the Captain and his troop around the back side of the mesa. You need to get them up top 'fore first light so he can close the back door. Ty, you'll scout for the rest of us as we head up thisaway," motioning with his head to the sandy draw that came from the flat-top, "'n we'll come at 'em straightaway. So, soon's you're ready, head on out." He looked at the men to see if they understood and as they nodded their heads, Kit turned back to his men to ensure their readiness.

As the thin line of grey showed the silhouette of the Sangre de Cristo range East of the mesa, Captain Wilkins, Lieutenant McElmore and Sergeant Smith were positioning the men of the 1st and 2nd platoons, A company, in a modified skirmish line with men about thirty yards apart, over the rocky hillocks and sandy knolls of the southern edge of San Pedro Mesa. The scattered clusters of Juniper and Pinion provided good cover but made it more difficult to maintain contact with the fifty troopers. Sergeant Smith had told each man what was expected and the need to maintain both silence and order, but the terrain did more to dictate their movements than the orders. Wilkins had expressly told Lieutenant McElmore that he would be held responsible if even one Apache escaped through their lines and he willingly accepted that responsibility. He was, after all, more experienced with Indians than the Captain who, Lieutenant Mac and the men thought, had gained his rank because of his father-in-law, Major General Lew Wallace. With a hand motion, the Captain started the disjointed skirmish line in the direction of the Apache rancheria.

Carson's contingent included the 3rd and 4th platoons of A company, with Lieutenant Barrett and First Sergeant O'Hanlon directing the movements. A separate squad, commanded by artillery officer, Lieutenant Pettis, handled the mountain howitzer cannon. The Apache village, or rancheria, was tucked into the thicker Juniper groves, giving them shelter and cover. Carson had instructed his officers that his signal to start the engagement would be when the howitzer was silenced, as he fully intended to make their presence known with the cannon.

After Ty had scouted the village before first light, he now reported back to the General. "I didn't see any activity. Looks like they're all still asleep, didn't even hear any dogs about. There was only a small herd of horses back East of the village, and unless they've got another herd I didn't see, either their warriors are gone or hidden out waitin' for us. Or else they just ain't got many horses."

The General nodded at Ty and answered, "If Captain Wilkins is in place, they didn't get out that way, and it's too wide open for them to have gotten past us, so they're probably over confident and sleepin' in. We'll wake 'em up." He looked toward the artillery officer standing by the howitzer and reined his horse in that direction. "Lieutenant Pettis, at my signal, I want you to throw a few shells around the edge of that village. No more than four, then we'll take over, understand?"

The eager lieutenant, standing at attention beside the howitzer, answered crisply, "Yessir, General sir! Four rounds around the village, yessir!"

The General pulled tight on the reins and backed his horse away from the cannon and reined him away from the small group of artillery men. He rejoined Ty and looked at the village of wickiup brush huts and scattered tipis that were now catching the dim morning grey light, then looking back to the waiting artillery men and raised his hand high over his head, dropped it briskly and was answered with the first explosion of the cannon. The first round was whining its way through the air as the men worked in a frenzy to reload the destruction bearing weapon. The sudden explosion of the cannonball thundered throughout the village and the ground shook with the impact. The resulting blast leveled two wickiups and scattered the debris across the camp. Screams of terrified Apache women and children were quickly muffled when the second round hit the opposite side of the camp with similar destruction. An old man staggered from his nearby lodge, blood streaming down his head as he looked in fear for an escape. The third and fourth rounds brought even more death, destruction and panic. Smoke and dust choked the panicked people as they ran in all directions, stumbling over the remnants of lodges and bodies. Women were screaming as they grabbed at crying children, old men were trying to pull others from lodges and debris, a half-naked toddler staggered with tears streaming down his face. He stumbled over the body of a woman and fell across her chest, thinking she was his mother. An old woman lifted her man to his feet and with his arm over her shoulder and her arm around his waist, they walked toward the center of the village where others were congregating.

When the howitzer fell silent, General Carson waved an arm for the line of cavalrymen to advance on the village. He had instructed his men to have rifles at the ready, but to not shoot unless fired upon. The crooked line of mounted men advanced at a walk and watched the villagers milling about but saw no one prepared to fire upon them. As they drew nearer, an old man, mounted on an equally old paint horse, started from the village toward the long line of cavalry. He held a long lance, decorated with feathers the entire length and with its carved flint point skyward, and a long white cloth attached, he slowly walked his horse toward the advancing soldiers. Carson lifted his arm to stop the advance of the troops, then gigged his horse forward.

The two leaders met and the Apache spoke first, "I am Fleches Rayada, Striped Arrows, leader of the Llaneros Jicarilla."

Carson responded, "I am General Carson, of Fort Garland, commander of this cavalry."

"Why have you attacked our village?" asked Striped Arrows, surprised to hear Carson speaking to him in the Apache tongue.

Carson chuckled and answered, "Your warriors attacked the village of San Luis and stole a wagon of supplies. You are supposed to be under a treaty and not be raiding."

"Your people broke the treaty, your leaders were to pay us and provide us with supplies and meat, but we have received nothing for many moons. Our people are hungry and we have no rifles to hunt the few buffalo for our village. We cannot let our women and children starve."

"Then return the rifles and send out the men that did the raid," directed Carson.

Striped Arrows looked at Carson and said, "I know of you from the time you fought the Mescalero and the Navajo. You said you would protect our people, but you forced them to walk to the reservation at Bosque Redondo and many died and many continue to die in that place. Now you attack our old men and women and children. What kind of man does this?"

"What I did with the Mescalero and the Navajo, I was ordered to do by General Carleton who is no longer in charge. Now I alone am in charge of these men. You say we attack your old men and women and children, where are your warriors?" asked Carson.

"All of our warriors are gone. They would not heed the council of the elders and chose to take the rifles to fight for the Tinde. They mean to bring our people meat and to fight any whites or blue coats that try to stop them."

"You mean there are no warriors in your village?" asked Carson.

"Only old men, women and children, and now many of them have crossed over because of your big guns."

Carson's shoulders slumped at this news and he looked past the old man at the village less than a hundred yards distant, and with a quick scan saw the destruction the howitzer had wrought. He looked back at the leader and said, "I will send my scout into your village to see if there are any warriors. If there are not, we will leave." He knew it would be useless to ask the chief when the warriors left or where they went, but he wanted to be sure there were none in the village. The men parted and Carson trotted his horse back to the line and waved Ty forward. As the scout came alongside, Carson instructed, "Ty, I want you to go into that village and look it over. That old chief said none of the warriors are there, that they've gone out on a hunt. You make sure there are none there." Ty nodded his head and put his heels to the ribs of the roan and started toward the camp.

The roan shuffled his hooves through the dust at the edge of the village. Ty looked at the destruction of the lodges, saw bodies and debris scattered and villagers trying to pull the remains of their families from the ruins. He watched as mothers clutched their children to their skirts and stared malevolently at the intruder. Children looked, turned away and cried as they sought escape from this terrible white man that they thought responsible for this carnage. Old men looked with snarled lips that told of hatred and disgust. Ty saw bodies lying next to wickiups with grieving women kneeling alongside. The wailing of the grief-stricken pierced the mind and heart of Ty as he walked his horse through the camp. Tears came unbidden and tumbled down his cheeks to drip from his chin and his stomach churned at the devastation and death and he fought to keep from puking. He gigged his horse, stood in his stirrups and turned away from the village to return to the General. He wiped his face, sniffled and blew snot to the side of his horse, straightened up and rode to the side of the General and reported, "General, there ain't anyone but old men, women, children and dead bodies in that village. Not a warrior to be found."

Carson dropped his head, put both hands on the pommel of his saddle, and looked at the distant village and considered what to do next. He looked at Ty and said, "Go find Captain Wilkins, tell him to go back the way he came, then at the bottom of the bluff to move out to the West. We'll meet him at the Southwest of this mesa."

Ty responded with a "Yessir," and reined his roan around to circumvent the village and find the Captain. As he rode he thought about what had just happened, *This ain't my idea of right. Even if the raiding party had been there, ain't no reason to kill women and children. Fightin's one thing, but slaughter, nope, ain't right.*

It was easy to find the detachment of Captain Wilkins and Ty soon delivered the General's message. When the Captain asked Ty what had been done, Ty gave a straightforward account of what he called a slaughter of women and children. The Captain was surprised to hear Ty's account and tried to defend the General but Ty just turned away and left the Captain standing with his mouth open and a confused look on his face.

To The Sangre de Cristo

Chapter Thirty-Three

Rio Grande

At the General's instruction, Ty and Louie started south on the track of the Apache warriors. It was an easy trail, with about one hundred angry young warriors in search of vengeance for the wrong doing from the lying government officials and the cries of hungry children ringing in their ears, they were unconcerned about the trail they were leaving. The wide flats south and west of the big mesa were watered by the shallow waters of Costilla Creek and had attracted many struggling Mexican families that tried to establish farms in the sandy and clay soil. Few had proven up on their plots of land, but the occasional adobe huts, occupied or empty, stood as silent monuments to their efforts.

"Ah, now we are getting into my country. My home at Taos Pueblo is just south of here and I spent my childhood exploring this whole area," Louie stated as he waved his arm in a wide arch to indicate the vast area of semi-desert that stretched before them. "I think I know where they go, in that direction," motioning with his outstretched arm to the southwest, "is the Rio Grande Gorge. It is a deep gorge or canyon the Rio Grande flows through way past Taos. The

207

Apache have a legend told by one of their ancients, Child of the Water, that tells of their creation story. If I remember right, Child of the Water tells about the first peoples, or Tinde, coming from this gorge and that the One Above turned the waters of the Rio Grande, one of the Tinde's sacred rivers, into the gorge to keep the Tinde from returning. It is a special place to their people and has many places for them to hide. Si, I think that is where they go," nodding his head.

The mid-morning sun shone from the clear blue sky and warmed the scouts as they walked their horses along the chewed-up trail. The hooves of their mounts stirred puffs of dust with every footfall and the occasional clatter of hooves on sandstone rock brought reminders of the desolate land. Ty looked about and marveled at the dry land that held clusters of cholla, prickly pear and barrel cactus, most starting to color the landscape with their blossoms. Some of the cholla held bright yellow blooms while others showed bright pink. The flowers of the Prickly Pear came from the dark red bulb and sprouted brilliant yellow. A long-eared jackrabbit stood on his hind legs and watched the passersby with little interest or fear. Ty lifted his eyes to look in the distance and noticed a thin tendril of smoke lifting skyward and unmoved by the windless desert. Ty reined up causing Louie to follow suit, and stood in his stirrups, shielding his eyes to see the source of smoke. Louie looked at Ty, then stared in the direction his friend was looking and said, "That does not look good my friend. That is too much smoke for a campfire or a cabin. I think it is much worse," as he motioned to the wide swath of tracks before them.

They kicked their horses to a canter as Ty said, "Keep an eye out, there might still be some hanging around." Within moments they drew near the remains of what had been a barn and home of a poor farmer. The small adobe dwelling was marked with black from the windows and a caved in roof. The door was burnt and hung cockeyed from one corner, and the stench of burning flesh assaulted the two scouts. Louie wrinkled his nose and Ty lifted his neckerchief to cover his nose and mouth. The smoke rose from the burned debris that had once been a barn. The body of a man, obviously the farmer, lay face down in the dirt with the tracks of many horses telling the story of the man being ridden down and trampled underfoot. The blood on the back of his head told of his scalping. Ty moved his horse to the low wall of the dwelling and looked inside to see a foot and naked leg protruding from under the caved in roof timbers. An empty cradle, partially burned, sat empty, but a splatter of blood on the wall caught Ty's attention and he dropped his eyes to the ground at the end of the cradle to see the naked body of what had been a toddler. Ty dropped his eyes and let out a long breath of disgust. Louie called from near the barn and Ty moved his mount to join his friend. Louie motioned to the pile of blackened timbers and saw the carcasses of two mules beside that of a young man that had the remnants of arrows protruding from his body. The blackened remains of his upper chest and head were under a large fire-blackened timber.

A short distance from the dwelling was the entrance to a root cellar, the door torn off and cast aside. Louie stepped down into the storage hole, and looked back at Ty, "Empty, it looks like there were many foodstuffs here, but now nothing."

"Alright, let's get a move on. If the General wants these folks buried or anything, he can see to it. We need to find them murderin' devils!" spat Ty as he looked at the destruction around him. Louie nodded in agreement and quickly mounted up to go with his friend.

As they followed the trail, Ty began to reflect. His youth on the ranch was a time of learning, growing, and exploring. Sure, there were troublesome times, confrontations with Ute and Cheyenne, grizzlies and wolves, but his memories on the ranch were pleasant. He smiled to himself when he thought of the growing-up years with his twin brother and the girl that became his wife. Those years, with the good and difficult times, made him the man he was and he thought of the difference between life on the ranch and this part of his life scouting for Carson. He shook his head at what he had witnessed just in this day and what might happen if they caught up with the raiders. *Maybe I should see about establishing my own ranch somewhere,* he thought as he looked around. *But not here, somewhere closer to the mountains where there's lots of grass for cattle and horses like we had in the Medicine Bow.* He stood in his stirrups and looked around at the nearest mountains which were the Sangre de Cristo ten to fifteen miles to the East and turning to his right he saw the jagged horizon almost fifty miles away that whispered of the San Juans. *Hmmm, maybe, I might have to do a little explorin' after this.*

Three more farms on the trail to the Rio Grande Gorge met the same fate as the first. Buildings burned, families massacred, and stores taken leaving nothing but smoke and ashes as witness to the destruction. With each new scene of atrocity, both Ty and Louie grew angrier and more determined to find the marauding Apache and put a stop to their madness. The last destroyed farm was near a cluster of cottonwood that told of a sometime spring and offered a good place for the scouts to wait for the troop. It was mid-afternoon and the horses and riders were tired and in need of rest and the men were hungry. Ty led his horse to the grove away from the adobe skeleton of the farmhouse followed closely by a quiet Louie. The usually talkative man had fallen silent with the last scene of murdered children still on his mind. They hobbled the horses and pulled their noon makings from their packs as Ty started a small campfire to make their coffee and fry up some pork belly. Louie produced a small wrapped bundle of tortillas he got from Juanita in San Luis and grinned at Ty's surprised response.

Just shy of two hours later, Ty spotted the tell-tale dust of the approaching troop. He stood and watched as Carson led the long column of dusty blue coats to the remains of the burned farm. He stood in his stirrups and looked around, spotted Ty at the edge of the cottonwood grove, turned to Captain Wilkins and gave orders to bury the bodies and break for their late noon meal. Kit walked his mount to the grove, nodded at Ty and said, "Guess you've been havin' it pretty easy followin' this trail," and looked at the shady grass by the spring and continued, "got room for 'nother'n?"

"Step down and share the shade," said Ty as he motioned toward the campfire. "We'll even share our coffee with you, if you've got a cup."

The general joined the scouts, seated himself on the grass and looked to Louie as he asked, "You know this country pretty well?"

"Si, si, I have been all over this country since I was a niño," answered Louie.

"So, I'm thinkin' they're headed for the Gorge, you?" asked Kit.

"Si, si, since we passed the mountain," said Louie, referring to Ute mountain that towered over the flats and rose to their Northwest, "I'm thinking they are going to follow the dry arroyo that leads into the gorge. The arroyo has the same black basalt but is dry now so it has the best trail into the gorge for many miles."

"I know the place. I scouted for Carleton here, and also led a contingent of cavalry against the Mescalero down into that gorge. If I remember right, that might be a good place to get them buggers," stated Carson, looking into his coffee, he thought about the area. His glassy-eyed stare told of deep thought as he considered the coming action.

The trickle of water that led from the spring was soon crowded with the troopers bringing their horses for a refreshing drink. They were all careful to keep the horses back from the flow of the stream, knowing it would be easy to muddy up the small stream and prevent many of the horses from getting their much-needed drink. The men came in small groups to the cottonwood oasis to fill their canteens and Carson instructed the officers and top sergeants to join him at the small campfire. When all were present, he began to lay out his plan for the anticipated conflict in the bottom of the Rio Grande gorge.

To The Sangre de Cristo

Chapter Thirty-Four

Skirmish

Ty, lying belly down on the point of rock overlooking the Rio Grande Gorge, strained to see the bottom of the wide and deep canyon. His eyes locked on the horses that stood hipshot on the grassy flat near the water's edge. It was near mid-night and he had only starlight and a little moon light, that the clouds let through intermittently, for him to not just find the Apache, but to identify their number and exact location. He had been watching for almost an hour and it had taken him that same amount of time to work his way to this point of observation. His horse was tethered in a cluster of pinion well back from his location and he knew it would take every bit of another hour to work his way back, unseen by any Jicarilla that had been placed on watch. It was well into the dark hours when he took up his lookout, but at least the dwindling cook fires had given him a good look at the many Apache below. Louie should be in position across the basaltic arroyo to locate any Apache that were standing watch at the only entrance to the gorge for many miles both North and South.

After General Carson had outlined his plan to his subordinates, the scouts had been dispatched to provide exact locations and numbers of the Apache. Carson was very familiar with the area and the probable site of the Apache camp and had laid out his plan of attack, but it depended on the report from the scouts. Although the dark of night worked to the advantage of the scouts' approach to their promontory lookouts, it hindered their sight of the camp well below in the blackness of the basalt canyon. But Ty was satisfied with what he saw and believed it would be the report that Carson sought, so he started crabbing his way back from the promontory and began his return. As he started to lift himself up, a subtle sound near the arroyo stopped him. As he froze in place, he let just his eyes move to survey the arroyo edge and listen for any movement. He knew the Jicarilla were masters of stealth, but with the years spent with the Ute Ty was just as skilled and his patience served him well. As he watched, a stocky Apache rose from beyond the edge of the arroyo as he walked to the top to search the night for any intruders. Ty watched as the man stood, partially hidden behind a scrub sage, and scanned the flats before him and combed the starlit night for life. Satisfied that nothing threatening was to be seen, the Apache lookout resumed his patrol of the arroyo and soon disappeared over the edge to return to his lookout. Ty let out a long-held breath and continued his crawl towards his tethered mount.

The troop, nearly three miles beyond, had a cold camp and were well obscured from view in the bottom of a wide gully at the base of a small bluff. Ty walked his horse toward the edge and was stopped by an observant guard that stepped in front of the roan with rifle at the ready. When challenged, Ty identified himself and moved past the guard, but asked him as he passed, "Has the other scout returned yet?"

"No sir, not yet, haven't seen any sign of him," answered the trooper with two stripes on his sleeve. Ty nodded his head in understanding and stepped down to lead his roan as he walked to where Carson waited. The general was seated on a rock, leaned back against the bank of the gully with his hat over his face trying to get a bit of sleep, when Ty approached.

Carson sat up and greeted Ty with a softly spoken, "Good to see you back, Ty. What'd you find?"

"Just as you thought, General," and was interrupted by Carson.

"I thought we had settled that General stuff, it's Kit," instructed the seasoned Indian fighter.

"Uh, right. Well, like you figgered, they're camped down by the river, just downstream of that white cap-rock wall. Looks like the whole bunch, but I couldn't get an accurate count cuz it was too dark, but I figger well over eighty of 'em." Their herd of horses was downstream of their camp on a purty good bunch of grass. But they've got lookouts in the arroyo, I 'bout got spotted, but he didn't see me and I didn't see any activity on the other side where Louie was scoutin'," reported Ty.

"Alright, well, I'm gonna get Captain Wilkins and his bunch started. Come along and give him any guidance you think necessary. I'll also have the rest of 'em rousted out and you'll be comin' along with me as we circle wide of that arroyo."

"Yessir, but don't you want to hear Louie's report? He scouted that North side and that's where the Captain's headed, ain't it?"

"Louie should be back before he takes off and he can guide the Captain where he needs to go," answered Carson as Ty reached in his pocket for some jerky and started chewing on it as the two men walked down the gully to find the Captain.

True to the General's prediction, Louie returned and joined the group that was busy preparing for the anticipated encounter. He had little to add to Ty's report except for more accurate details on the location of the several lookouts in the arroyo. The general instructed further on the particulars of his assignment, bid him good luck and he and Ty watched as the column of fours moved away.

At the first hint of grey in the East, the different divisions of A company were in place for the attack. Captain Wilkins men were afoot and approaching the edge of the wide arroyo that would lead them to the bottom of the gorge of the Rio Grande. He knew there would be Apache scouts waiting and the word would be passed to the rest of the warriors, but he hoped to have some element of surprise before the entire band rallied. The men had been instructed to be as quiet as possible and the Captain was pleased at their response. The scout, Louie, accompanied the Captain alongside the sergeant, and they were the first to step over the edge to work their way to the bottom of the arroyo and onto the trail that snaked its way through the scattered black basaltic boulders with the sandy bottom providing easier going. The jagged edges of the black lava rock would easily cut into even the thick soles of the troopers' boots but the trail with the sandy bottom, carried from the desert flats by years of storm run-off, aided in their attempt at stealth.

Captain Wilkins, an experienced cavalry man who fought well in the recent war, had little experience with Indian fighting and he incorrectly assumed their approach was unseen. The grey light of early morning did little to aid the troopers to see what lay before them. The arroyo, although about thirty yards wide at this point, was littered with boulders and jumbled rocks that gave the Apache good cover as they watched the approaching troopers. The Apache scouts had already sent word to their camp that the attack was coming and they now kept their positions, well hidden from the blue coats. The troopers did their best to be as stealthy as possible, thinking they were successful in their surprise attack, but the basaltic rock caused the men to group up at the bottom. The captain, busy with watching to the front, didn't realize the men were grouped so, until the attack.

The Apache watched and waited until the troopers were past them and on the downhill side of the arroyo, then at a silent signal, ten warriors stood and opened fire on the troopers. Surprised by this attack from the rear and uphill from them, the Captain was momentarily confused, but the sergeant shouted,

"Take cover behind the rocks!" and the men scattered searching for anything big enough to provide cover from the blistering fire of the Apache. The first fusillade had struck down three troopers and wounded several others, but all the living quickly ducked behind the many boulders and readied themselves to return fire. Without orders, the men quickly let loose with their own attack, which echoed throughout the arroyo and the resulting clamor blended with the war cries of the Apache and pierced the souls of the troopers. The first volley had brought blood to both the Captain and Louie, with Louie taking a bullet just above his hip and the Captain with a bullet caused trench through his scalp above his left ear.

The gunfire from the Apache had diminished but the arrows arched overhead seeking targets behind the large boulders. The Jicarilla were inexperienced with the Enfields and thought they were doing good to get off one shot, but the reloading was too cumbersome for them and after that first shot, the rifles fell to the side in favor of the bows and arrows. The attack now settled down to random exchanges of fire from both sides, but the Captain knew the rest of the Apache would probably be coming to the aid of their fellow warriors and that would catch the troopers in a deadly crossfire. He hoped the General was successful, and soon, with the second part of his plan that, if successful, would result in getting the Apache in the oft-used pincer movement.

As planned, the 2nd platoon of A company, had positioned themselves well back from the rim of the gorge and waited for the initial attack of the 1st platoon before they approached any closer. When the first gunfire sounded, the General stood and motioned for the men to follow. Ty trotted alongside the general to the sloping edge of the gorge where they would descend to the camp site below. The shoulder of hillside held a few pinion trees that clung tenaciously to the rocky hillside and gave some cover to the descending men. The general had given orders for the men to spread out and make the descent as quickly and silently as possible, he knew that the first report of

217

gunfire would send the Apache to the narrow trail around the basaltic point that was capped by the white rock, to the aid of their fellow warriors, at least that was what he was counting on as they slowly made their way down the steep shoulder of rocky hillside. The camp of the Apache was on the bottom of the hillside and scattered among the few grassy areas and less steep hillside. As they descended, Ty saw the last of the Apache moving to the trail between the two large up thrusts of basaltic stone that would take them to the black arroyo.

The rattle of rifle fire and the screams of the attacking Apache obscured the sound of the descent of the 2nd platoon. When they reached the gorge bottom and spread out to check for any stragglers of the Apache, the General led the way as they took to the trail to follow the Jicarilla that sought to catch Captain Wilkins in their crossfire. True to his plan, they were able to get to the bottom of the arroyo and spread out in a skirmish line as they started after the scattered Apache. Within moments they sighted their quarry and opened fire. The blistering barrage of rifle fire from behind them quickly demoralized the surprised Apache as many of them fell under the onslaught. The experienced troopers, outfitted with the big bore Spencers, kept up a continual barrage and the blood of the marauding Apache painted the basaltic rock. The scattered return fire from the few stolen Enfields did little to dissuade the troopers, and the Apache frantically sought cover behind the rocks only to be fired upon by the 1st platoon troopers entrenched further up the arroyo. The deafening rattle of rifle fire reverberated throughout the basaltic arroyo and the roar of battle silenced the screams of the now outnumbered and outgunned warriors.

General Carson gave a hand signal that was carried vocally by the loud-voiced sergeants and the rifles were silenced. As the echoes diminished and an uncharacteristic silence fell on the scene of battle, General Carson shouted to the Apache in their own language telling them to lay down their weapons and their lives would be spared. Carson waited a few moments for a response, and receiving none started to give an order to fire, but the sudden appearance of an Apache warrior standing on a boulder with arms uplifted stopped him. Carson stepped out from behind the boulder that had been his protection and looked at the man.

"I am White Stone Man of the Jicarilla. Does Carson swear that we can return to our people?" asked the leader of the Apache.

"Yes, if your warriors will lay down their rifles, I will allow you to keep your bows and arrows, and if you promise no more raids, I will allow you to return to your people," answered the General.

White Stone Man turned to his warriors, spoke to them sternly and watched as they began to stand with angry expressions painting their faces. White Stone Man spoke again, "We must get our horses," and motioned past the troopers now standing with rifles at the ready. Carson nodded his head and waved his arm to the trail that led to their encampment. As White Stone Man passed, Carson said, "My troopers will follow you to the mesa of your rancheria." He was answered with a grunt from the Apache as he passed.

Ty walked up the path at the bottom of the arroyo to meet his friend and was startled to see Louie sitting on a boulder holding a bloody bandage to his hip. Ty asked, "How bad is it?"

"Oh, it hurts like the devil and is bleeding plenty, but I don't think it is too bad," answered Louie, obviously straining to talk with the searing pain of his wound.

"Are you going to be able to ride?" asked Ty.

"Maybe, at least I hope so. If it wasn't so far, then it would be better," he answered.

Ty looked at Captain Wilkins who was sitting nearby and holding a bloody bandage to his head. Carson stepped to his side and asked the Captain, "Have you taken a tally on the casualties, Captain?"

"The sergeant is getting that count now, General. I know we lost at least three men in the initial attack, those blasted rocks caused the men to group up on the trail yonder and we were sitting ducks!" exclaimed the Captain with obvious disgust.

Sergeant Smith returned with his report and told of four fatalities and five wounded, two seriously in addition to the Captain and scout. Carson instructed the sergeant have a burial detail take care of the fatalities and the Lieutenant was given orders to prepare litters for the wounded. Without any sizable trees or other sources of wood nearby, they would have to use their rifles and blankets and carry the wounded by hand. The Lieutenant would accompany the wounded with a squad of troopers that would alternate carrying until they could find suitable saplings to make travois.

Ty asked Louie, "Isn't your home not too far from here?"

"Si, Si, Taos Pueblo is probably closer than returning to the Fort," answered Louie, hopefully.

Ty turned to the General and asked, "Sir, would it be alright if I take Louie to his family and let them patch him up. I could return to the fort afterwards if needed."

Carson looked at his scouts, then said to Ty, "I don't see why not. I would like you back at the fort by the time the Utes come callin' but we don't know when that'll be, so sure, take Louie to his family." The General grinned at Louie, bent to shake his hand and added, "And thanks Louie, you've done well. I'll look forward to your return."

Chapter Thirty-Five

Taos Pueblo

When they were out of earshot of the troopers, Louie grinned at his compatriot and said, "It is a bit further to Taos Pueblo than back to the fort, but the way we will travel is easy. If we push hard, we could make it by dark but it might be better to stop along the way."

Ty chuckled at Louie's subterfuge that had put them on the trail to his home and asked, "Are there any towns along the way that have good cantinas and maybe a hotel?"

"Si, si," laughed Louie, "there are two towns or villages but I only know of the hotel and cantina in San Antonio del Rio Colorado. It is not too far, I think."

It was nigh unto noon when they rode into the small settlement of San Antonio. The single street was a dusty but rutted road leading between an odd collection of adobe buildings with peeling white wash. The larger building bore a sign that read *Auguste Lacome, trader* and beside it was a smaller building that bore a smaller sign with a simple message *Cantina.* They tethered their mounts at the hitchrail and stepped up on the weathered boardwalk to enter the cantina. Greeted by the coolness, they paused to let their eyes adjust to the dark interior and were welcomed by a portly woman with greying hair, dark eyes, and a broad smile. "Buenos Dias señors, bienvenido," and motioned for them to have a seat.

Louie spoke to her in Spanish and ordered a table full of food, the like of which Ty hadn't seen in a long time. It excelled their last cantina meal in quantity and they were soon to find it rivaled it for quality as well. When the matron saw the bloody bandage at the hip of Louie she asked what had happened and was surprised to hear about the battle with the Apache. She suggested, "The wife of Señor Lacome," motioning to the trading post next door, "is a healer from the Comanche and she is very good. You should have her look at it for you."

Louie looked at Ty and at Ty's nod, he turned back to the woman and said he would, but right now was a time for eating. She smiled at his response, always glad to see hungry men enjoy her cooking, and went to the kitchen for refills for their coffee and tortillas. After their meal, Ty suggested they "get a move on" and see the healer so they could get back on their way. The Comanche woman quickly tended to the wound by cleaning it and applying an herbal poultice and instructed Louie to change the dressing often, giving him some of the herbal ointment in a small square of oilcloth.

Dusk caught them on the road and Louie said they were still more than a couple of hours from his home and suggested they camp for the night in the nearby junipers. Ty readily agreed since the previous night had been spent on their scout and he was anxious to reacquaint himself with his bedroll. A small fire was all that was needed for their coffee pot, since they chose to forego another meal what with still being stuffed from their over-indulgence in the cantina. Filling the pot from his canteen, Ty set it at the side of the flames and waited for it to heat and sat down on a flat rock and said to Louie, "So, Louie, tell me about your family."

Louie grinned broadly as he began to talk about his favorite subject. "My mother, her name is Walks in the

Willows, and she is a beautiful woman. The very best cook, that one. And my little sister, Flower of the Desert, is just as pretty, no prettier, than the most beautiful flower you will ever find in the desert," he smiled at the memory of his sister and looked at Ty as he continued. "She too, is a good cook. But she is very skilled with her hands as well. She can make the most beautiful designs with beads and quills, and when my Madre makes the clothes, my sister will decorate them. My Madre makes clothes from the trade cloths but the best ones she makes from buckskin," he paused as he recalled the handiwork of his family and looked at Ty. "You like to wear buckskins, you would appreciate what my mother and sister can do, beautiful!"

"And where do they live?" asked Ty.

"Oh, in the Taos Pueblo, of course. That's where my people live."

"But, what in? Are they adobe like the village we came through or like the wickiups of the Apache?"

"Oh, adobe of course, but not like what you have ever seen before. I cannot describe it to you, but you will be amazed. It is different than anything else you have ever seen," proclaimed a proud Louie.

"But what is it like?" queried Ty, now that his curiosity was raised.

"You will see, you will see. But you have to wait until tomorrow, I can tell you nothing more," grinned the mischievous Louie.

"That's a fine thing, you tell me about it, but you won't tell me about it!"

"Si, si, you will have to wait, amigo," chuckled Louie as he dropped the coffee into the pot to await its brewing. They soon turned in for the night and a much-anticipated rest before continuing their journey.

It was late morning and the trail had kept Ty's interest. The roadway originally paralleled the Rio Grande, but well back against the foothills, but now followed the contour of the terrain and cut across a wide swath of barren flats marked by many gullies that carried run-off away from the Sangre de Cristo's. The mountains in the distance still cradled deep ravines with snow and glaciers and Ty enjoyed looking at the towering granite peaks that rose high above the valley they traversed. They had passed several settlers attempts at farming and Ty could see the valley beyond that nestled at the foot of the Sangres held considerable greenery that told of more successful farms. Louie stopped and pointed, "There, closer up against the foothills in that cut, that is where my home, Taos Pueblo lies. We will be there soon, come on amigo, quite dragging your feet, I am anxious to see mi madre!" He dropped into his saddle and gigged his horse to a canter, making Ty spur his mount to catch up.

As he pulled alongside his friend he said, "I thought your wound was hurting too much to bounce along like that!"

"Si, si, but mi casa is near, we must hurry."

When the pueblo came into view, Ty reined his horse to a stop and he stood in his stirrups to stare at the structure before him. He dropped into the seat of his saddle and was mesmerized by the sight of the pueblo. Rectangular adobe structures, stacked five and six stories high with each level having fewer and even smaller structures. There were few doors and windows, but the roofs of the lower level structures provided the floors and terraces of those above. Ty had never seen anything resembling the impressive structure before him. He tore his eyes away and looked at Louie, who sat grinning and watching his friend. Ty pointed at the pueblo and asked, "This is your home?"

"Si, si, not the whole thing of course, but mi madre lives in one of those. Come, come, let us go and see," answered the grinning man as he gigged his horse toward the pueblo. Ty followed but continued looking at the strange building before him.

There were hitchrails along the front of the structure and many of the terraces held people, busy with some handiwork, that watched the arrival of the visitors. A shout from above caught the attention of Ty and Louie and they looked to see a young woman jumping and clapping as she hollered down, "Luis, Luis!" It was the sister of Louie shouting the greeting and expressing her joy and surprise at the return of her brother. A woman stood beside her and looked down at the visitors, then motioned for them to come up. Ty watched as Louie made his way to a nearby ladder and started the struggle of climbing up with his injured hip, looked back and motioned for Ty to follow.

The home of Louie and his family was on the second level and as soon as Louie stepped off the ladder, his sister jumped in his arms and hugged his neck, chattering all the while. His mother stood back, looked at her son and at Ty and waited for her turn to greet her son. As soon as Desert Flower released her brother, he reached out his arms to his mother who stopped and motioned at his wound, "You're wounded! What are you doing standing, come inside quickly and let me tend to that," she ordered. Louie grinned at her and said, "Later, momma, first give me a hug!" After she complied and leaned back to look at her son, she smiled and said, "I'm happy you're home. We've missed you." She turned to look at Ty, standing to the side, and said, "And who have you brought home with you?"

Louie looked at his mother and sister as they looked at Ty and grinned, "This is my friend, Tyrell Thompsett. He is the chief of scouts at the fort and my boss," declared Louie.

Walks in the Willows and Desert Flower said almost simultaneously, "Welcome Tyrell." Ty had removed his hat and nodded his head at their welcome and replied, "Thank you, m'am. Pleased to be here and to meet you folks. Louie has talked about you a lot and I feel as if I already know you."

Walks in the Willows said, "Come inside, I must tend to my son's wound and I'm sure you both are hungry. Flower, go get some food going, hurry now." The young woman nodded her head, smiled at her brother and let her gaze linger on Ty, causing him to blush a bit, and turned to hurry off to their home.

The home was accessed by climbing a ladder to the roof and descending another ladder through the square hole that was the entrance. Ty noticed a few of the homes had some form of doorway, but most were accessed like this one. When he followed the others, and dropped into the home, he was surprised at the well-lit home that gained its light from one thin window and the entrance hole overhead. The home had two rooms, one for cooking and storage and one for living and sleeping. Willows made her son lie on a sleeping pallet under the window and began her ministrations by removing the bandage. She sniffed at the poultice, nodded her head, and asked, "Who put this on you?"

"A Comanche healer, she was the wife of the trader at San Antonio del Rio Colorado," answered Louie.

Willows nodded her head in agreement and started cleaning the wound. She was pleased with the beginning stages of healing and reached for her parfleche that held her needed items for her work. When she finished and re-bandaged the wound, Desert Flower brought platters of food for the men which were happily received by both Ty and Louie. Ty was seated on a bench of sorts that appeared to be a part of the adobe wall and Louie sat up to lean against the wall beneath the window. Flower returned from the cooking room with two more platters of food, gave one to her mother who was seated next to her son, and carried the other to seat herself beside Ty. She smiled at her brother's friend and started with her meal.

During the meal, Flower would often look, somewhat shyly, at Ty and Ty would sneak looks at Flower, but little conversation passed between them. Louie carried on a one-sided conversation as he related all that he had done since he left the home and was finally finishing his monologue when Flower quietly asked Ty, "You have never seen a pueblo like this before have you?"

"No, and I find this place fascinating. I had no idea anything like this existed. How long did it take to build this?" he asked.

Flower giggled and answered, "I do not know, but I do know this has been here for over three hundred years."

Ty was flabbergasted and sputtered, "Three hundred years? You must be joshin' me."

She looked at Ty and smiled at his response, as Ty noticed Louie had stopped talking and both Louie and Willows were watching his response, both grinning. Willows spoke up and said, "Yes, Tyrell, this has been here at least that long. Maybe longer. Our ancestors for many generations built this pueblo and our people have had to fight for it many times."

Louie added, "Si, si, even my grandfather, Pablo Montoya and Tomasito, a leader of the Pueblo people, had to fight against the whites who wanted to make this a part of the United States. They were the ones who killed Charles Bent, the governor and then went to Sante Fe. But they had to come back and defend the pueblo. They were in the San Geronimo Mission when the troops blew it up with their cannon and killed them all. But since then, they have left us alone."

Flower asked Ty, "Would you like me to show you around our pueblo?"

Ty nodded and answered, "Yes, I'd like that very much."

Louie said, "Flower, why don't you and Ty take our horses around to the corrals and take off our gear, then give him the grand tour."

Flower smiled and nodded her head as she gathered up the platters and readied herself for the tour. Ty stood and asked Louie, "How long you plannin' on takin' to heal up, compadre?"

"Oh, I dunno, we'll have to see. Sometimes it takes a long time to heal from a wound like this, don't you agree?"

Ty grinned at his friend and answered with a "Ummmhummm."

Flower watched as Ty unsaddled the horses, placing the saddles and other gear on the top pole of the corral and Ty continually looked at the young woman. He finally asked her, "Just how old are you?"

"I have seen seventeen summers, and you?"

"A few more, but sometimes it seems like a lot more."

The tour became more of a get-acquainted stroll around the pueblo and into the nearby woods. The constant conversation told the life story of both and neither one wanted to return to the pueblo. They sat beside one another at the edge of a small spring-fed stream and shared thoughts and dreams and Ty began telling her about his dream to establish a ranch somewhere in the mountains, like the one he enjoyed in his youth. He told of his family and the life on the ranch and how he wanted to have a family and raise his children to enjoy that lifestyle. Flower listened, nodding her head in agreement and said, "But you need a wife for all that, don't you?" Her implication was obvious and Ty agreed, "Yes, and I never thought I'd even think about that since I lost Elizabeth," he had told Flower about his childhood sweetheart who became his wife and about the loss of her and their child, and continued, "But, I know life goes on and I'm certain she, Elizabeth, would want me to continue and build a life with another and children."

Flower smiled, pulled her knees to her chest and wrapped her arms around them, rested her chin on a knee and looked at Ty with wide eyes. He couldn't keep from looking at those big brown eyes and wondering if God was working things out in his life in a wondrous way. He leaned back on outstretched arms, crossed his legs and looked back at Flower and asked, "Why hasn't a beautiful woman like you taken a husband?"

She smiled at his question and countered with, "You think I'm beautiful?"

"Yes, of course, you're one of the most beautiful women I've even seen. You could have your pick of men anywhere."

B. N. Rundell

"Until now, I have never seen a man that I would "pick" as you put it."

Ty had noticed her "until now" and smiled at her response. The thought of her picking someone else brought a tang of jealousy to his heart and he wondered at that. *This is crazy, I just met this woman,* he thought.

Ty had planned on spending no more than a day with Louie before returning to the fort, but the one day turned into three and the time was not spent with Louie, but his sister, Desert Flower. But Ty knew he had commitments with Carson and must return to Fort Garland. On the morning of the fourth day, he stood by his horse, tethered at the hitchrail in front of the Pueblo and with his hands at the waist of Flower he looked into those big brown eyes, now with tears forming in the corners, and promised, "I'll be back. I've made a promise to Carson about the Utes and I must go to the Fort and help with the treaty. But I promise you, I'll be back. I just can't see myself without you."

Flower leaned her head against his chest, "I will wait for you, and as you said, I pick you." Ty smiled at her remark and pulled her close to him and they hugged one another, then she lifted her face to him and he kissed her as she clasped her hands behind his neck, holding his lips to hers. When the embrace ended, Ty looked longingly at this beautiful little woman and smiled. He gave her a quick hug, turned and mounted up. He dropped his hand to clasp hers and repeated, "I'll come back for you." He reined the big roan around and started for the fort.

To The Sangre de Cristo

Chapter Thirty-Six

Treaty

As the fort came into sight, Ty was surprised to see the many tipis clustered near the cottonwoods on the banks of the creek to the West of the fort. He quickly realized these were the Ute under Chief Ouray and had apparently been camped there for a while. He thought of his friend, Grey Wolf, and became anxious to visit with him again. He wondered about his woman, Walks Far, and hoped they were with the gathering of Ute. He reined his horse toward the encampment, choosing to visit with Grey Wolf before reporting in to the fort. When he walked his horse among the lodges, he was met with curious and stern expressions from both warriors and women, and when he asked a rather prominent looking warrior that looked somewhat familiar, "Is Grey Wolf with your village?" he saw the man register surprise that this white man spoke in the language of the people. The warrior looked at Ty and answered, "Why do you seek Grey Wolf?"

"He is my brother, we have been together since our childhood, and I would like to visit with him," explained Ty as he looked down on the man from atop his long-legged roan.

"His lodge is near the trees, there," and pointed at the cluster of tipis under the shade of the cottonwoods. Ty nodded his head and gigged his horse toward the indicated lodges and as he neared, he reined up and stepped down, leading his mount toward the lodge. Grey Wolf was sitting with the aid of a willow back rest and visiting with a couple of other warriors as they worked at shaping arrows. When Ty spoke, Grey Wolf looked up, smiled and jumped to his feet to greet his friend with a hug, slapping him on the back and chuckling.

"It is good to see you my brother, I wondered where you were when we arrived. The blue coat said you were with the others after the Apache but when they returned and you did not, I was worried about you."

"It is good to see you too, my brother," said Ty as he looked around, hoping to see Walks Far Woman but was disappointed by her absence, "are you alone?" he asked.

Wolf grinned at his friend, knowing what he was asking and replied, "No, my wife, Walks Far, is with me, but she is visiting her mother. Are you going to the fort now?"

"Yeah, I've got to report to Carson and see if I can help with the treaty stuff, you know how it is," replied Ty.

"Then you must return and take dinner with us, we will talk about all that has happened."

"I'd like that. I'll check in at the fort and see if I'm needed with Carson, then I'll be back about dusk, how's that?" asked Ty. He received a nod of approval from Wolf, then mounted his roan and moved out to report in at the fort. He stabled his horse, racked his saddle and blanket, and carrying his bedroll, saddle bags, and haversack, walked to his quarters on officer's row. He saw Ouray and three other leaders of the Ute including Tall Bear, exiting the general's office in his quarters and waited for them to leave before reporting to Carson.

Carson was pleased to see his scout, asked about Louie, and began to tell Ty all about the negotiations with the Ute. "They had the Treaty of Conejos from '63 but weren't 'bidin' by it. So, I've been negotiatin' with ol' Ouray and I think I 'bout got a deal done. I just gotta get the approval of Washington and get some signatures and it should be a done deal." Carson leaned back in his chair and clasped his hands behind his head as he looked at his scout. "Can you imagine payin' them Injuns $60,000.00 a year to keep the peace. 'Course, they gotta get outta the San Luis valley for the doin' of it, but it'll be worth it if we don't hafta go traipsin' after 'em all the time for doin' in some prospector or settler. Yessir, Ty, I think I'ma gettin' too old for this stuff. I just might hafta take my family and skedaddle after all this is done."

"I understand that, Kit. I'm thinkin' along the same lines myself. I think I'd like to head down to the San Juans, find a nice valley with lots of grass and start a ranch, kinda like my Pa did in the Medicine Bow. 'Course I might hafta get me wife to go along with it," he grinned as he looked at Carson's expression. Kit asked, "What'd you do, find yourself some little senorita when you took Louie home?"

Ty grinned and blushed, ducked his head and mumbled, "Think so, she sure is a pretty one, too."

Kit dropped his legs to the floor and leaned on the desk, "Well, speakin' from first-hand experience, my little Josefa has kept the home fires burnin' and given me some mighty fine children. Seven of 'em, by the way, and I'm mighty proud of every one of 'em, yessir."

Ty stood, extended his hand to shake with Carson, and said, "Well, if you won't be needin' me for a while, I'm goin' to visit my brother with the Ute."

"Your brother?" asked Carson with a confused look.

"Well, he's like my brother, we grew up together. His mother is a Yamparika Ute and his father helped my father on the ranch. So, we always called each other brother. He's with the Mouache at their camp yonder and I'm goin' to have dinner with 'em and chew the fat a mite."

"Alright Ty, but you'll check with me before you decide to do anything like leavin' won't you?"

"Of course, Kit, I'll not make any decisions without letting you know," answered Ty and turned to leave. Carson stood to bid him good-night, and Ty went to his quarters to clean up a little before visiting his friend.

Ty spent most of the following three days in the Ute camp with Grey Wolf and Walks Far Woman and shared his thoughts about starting a ranch in the San Juan area. "I've never been in that area, but from what I understand from Carson, there are some mighty pretty valleys that would make a good ranch. You know, Wolf, I'd like you and Walks Far to come with me, you know, like when your Pa helped mine and they started the ranch in the Medicine Bow. I also think it'd be good for us to go back to the ranch and see our folks sometime soon." Ty noticed the exchanged looks between Walks Far and Wolf and saw Wolf start to speak before Walks Far interrupted with, "I have told my husband we should go see his family. That would be a good thing."

Ty nodded his head and asked, "What about you, Walks Far, what do you think of the idea of going to the San Juans and starting a ranch?"

"I do not know about ranch, but wherever my husband goes, I will go too," she declared with a wide smile. "But what about you, Ty, you should have a woman to warm your blankets also."

Ty ducked his head and grinned at the remembrance of Desert Flower and answered, "Yup, you're right, Walks Far, and I'm workin' on that."

His declaration surprised Wolf who looked up at his friend and smiling said, "Oh, ho, tell me about this woman Ty, where is she?"

Ty began to explain about his recent meeting of Desert Flower and how they both spoke of being together and that she was the brother of his fellow scout, Louie, who was due to return any day.

"Are you going to go get her?" asked Wolf.

"Are you and Walks Far going to go with me to the San Juans?" countered Ty.

Wolf looked at Walks Far and back at Ty and slowly grinned, "It sounds mighty good, my friend, and it would be good to ride with you again."

"Then maybe the four of us oughta do some plannin' and decidin' don'tcha think?"

Wolf chuckled at his friend and replied, "And when did you ever do any plannin'? You usually just jump up an'take off and take things as they come."

With dusk dropping its mantle on the Western plains, Ty stood to leave. He had walked to the camp from the fort and now turned to go. Something caught his eye to the South of their camp and he looked to see two riders approaching the fort. The one looked a little familiar, but the fading light and distance hindered his recognition. He turned to bid his friends good night and started to the fort. By the time he reached his quarters, he saw the riders had stabled the horses and were now walking through the main gate, carrying gear over their shoulders. Ty noticed one was a woman, then looking at the other, recognized the familiar walk of his friend and fellow scout, Louie. He quickly looked back at his companion and realized it was Desert Flower. He sucked in a breath and tried to still his quickening heartbeat and started toward his friends. His grin split his face as he approached the duo and quickened his pace seeing Desert Flower drop her gear and start towards him at a run. They caught each other and wrapped their arms around one another as Ty laid a long firm kiss on her lips that she held with her arms clasped behind his neck. When they came up for air, Ty heard Louie say, "Well, Flower, I guess he is glad to see you."

She giggled and kissed Ty and said, "Don't ever leave me again!"

"Don't worry, I won't!" he replied, smiling down and looking into those beautiful dark brown eyes. "I've got plans for us."

About the Author

Born and raised in Colorado into a family of ranchers and cowboys, B.N. is the youngest of seven sons. Juggling bull riding, skiing, and high school, graduation was a launching pad for a hitch in the Army Paratroopers. After the army, he finished his college education in Springfield, MO, and together with his wife and growing family, entered the ministry as a Baptist preacher.

Together, B.N. and Dawn raised four girls that are now married and have made them proud grandparents. With many years as a successful pastor and educator, he retired from the ministry and followed in the footsteps of his entrepreneurial father and started a successful insurance agency, which is now in the hands of his trusted nephew. He has also been a successful audiobook narrator and has recorded many books for several award-winning authors. Now finally realizing his life-long dream, B.N. has turned his efforts to writing a variety of books, from children's picture books and young adult adventure books, to the historical fiction and western genres which are his first love

Discover more great titles by B. N. Rundell and Wolfpack Publishing at:
https://wolfpackpublishing.com/b-n-rundell/